THE CONJURING COWBOY

THE CONJURING COWBOY

MARTIN CONNOLLY

SNOWCHILD PRESS, IRELAND

Snowchild Press, Ireland

First Edition

ISBN-13: 978-1911100089
ISBN-10: 1911100084

Ashoog! JimBro! Yeehaw!

CONTENTS

CHAPTER ONE

'Just up that street,' said the old bloke with the duncher, after a moment of studying the flimsy newspaper cutting I'd shown him. He then pointed to a street I simply hadn't noticed before. I thanked him and checked for traffic both ways before crossing diagonally to get to the next stage in my journey. It wasn't a particularly big street, the one I was coming into now, just wide enough for a car and a half, with the occasional lay-by on one side or the other to easily accommodate the passing of two vehicular conveyances. None were here for the moment however, just a few other random bipeds like me, left and right: a twelve-year-old-looking boy tearing down the street in gleeful terror as a nine-year-old-looking boy chased after him with a stick - brothers, I presumed; a young man, wielding a light cane, possessed of a cheeriness that defused the import of his somewhat shabby appearance; a young woman taking her huge dog for a walk, straining as she held onto the lead, so maybe the other way round then, and a punkish-type late-teenager fellow, plugged into his Walkman and mouthing out the words of whatever song he was listening to. It was technically springtime, so there were those still wrapped up and those who were happy to dispense with the scarves and the mittens. I'd left my leather jacket open, but then I always did, and not wearing a scarf was a prerequisite just for the looks, no matter the breeze: leather jacket into scarf don't go. And no need for gloves, with both hands free to stuff in my pockets, carrying nothing, the mark of a man without business...

Without employment for sure. Most of the year now, I'd been wandering around the old town half the time, free time in abundance, and not wishing to stay cooped up forever inside, 'reading my life away', as an (employed) acquaintance put it -in typically clichéd fashion, I might add. Nowhere to go in particular, I'd be happy to visit the usual places: the library, the second-hand bookshops, the pub on Fridays if anyone was available, the cinema occasionally, the park, the hill overlooking the town —that was the best. Only a half hour up to the top, but what a sight to behold: the town below, with its toy buildings, and an enveloping green, as far as the eye could see... I could lie down on one of the benches, just long enough to accommodate my not very considerable length, and look up at the sky or the clouds as they passed, hearing only faintly the sounds of the cars and the buses far below, and the factories clanking away, and the feet of the people traipsing this way and that —or 'scuttling' to be Eliotian about it— blended into a rolling, almost musical, hum. What peace!

Not that I was living much in the way of an unpeaceful life. Since the government seemed content to dole out the dosh fortnightly, even for the rent on my studio apartment, I was certainly content to receive it. Yes, I assured them, 'I'm looking for work, I'm looking for work, of course,' looking all flustered and serious as I said so. In reality, I dreaded the prospect of being sat behind a nondescript desk in a nondescript office, totting up figures and trying to talk intelligently to people on the telephone. Wandering about the town, dipping into the odd book, and even attempting to pen my own literary masterpiece, seemed the noblest, finest and most productive way to lead one's life, for now at least. Precisely what I was contributing to society may have been up for debate, but having recently suffered the mental demands of tertiary education, I felt I had earned the right to do very little for a while. *Cast a Cold Eye On Work. On Purposeful, Productive Life, Horseman, Pass By!*

But where was I now? I'd never heard of Curtis Street, or been in this neck of the woods either. I'd been told to pass down this street 'just a smidge', as he'd put it in his very throaty Northern rasp, me wondering how many cigs he got through in a day, and so I kept the pins moving, ever hopeful. It really was quite a nondescript street: unappealing rear-ends of buildings on both sides. Brick upon brick upon brick either side, and all a dulled uniform brown. The few windows which gave onto the street were small and encased in metal grilles; each was also effectively opaque, darkened with age, and neglect. The buildings were all about three storeys high, with the occasional wall which travelled further up and appeared to end in a chimney. I paused momentarily, as people who have very little to do often do, leant back and looked up, following the dull brickwork up and up. I could just discern traces of smoke, or a dark mist, feeding its poison into the air. Oh, what wondrous delights be here, I mused at my most sardonic. Were it not for the slow passage of a tiny, distant passenger jet amid the gloom overhead, I could well have been dear ole William Blake.

Suddenly a bus, looking like something out of an old postcard, a charabanc, then, blustered past, catching me quite unawares. An enormous yellow contraption, with ribbed sides and dodgy-looking tires. I strained, somehow out of instinct, to have a glimpse in at the seated passengers, and seeing they were mostly middle- to older-aged women out for the day by the looks of it, cackling up a riot, smiles plastered all round, felt strangely satisfied, uplifted even. The noise of it was surpassed in its impact only by the clouds of oily smoke it left in its wake. Just then a dog broke free from somewhere and ran pelting after the clunking vehicle, barking just a tad madly for my taste. I noticed it was trailing a lead, and soon enough along came the owner after it, a middle-aged bloke, panting away, not likely given to sports of a weekday, hoping to retrieve his wild charge. The general commotion at least had the effect of adding some colour to the street. I ambled on.

Ambled onto a fork, it was becoming apparent, a left and a right, neither any more attractive or impressive than the other, more like side-streets the both of them; nevertheless, I knew this was just the point the duncher-man had informed me of so nicely. Street plaques, street plaques, I found myself chanting internally, oh, street plaques, street names, or any such relief, begging your pardon, I would like to find just where it is I'm supposed to be heading, if you don't mind... I almost took the first one that I saw, which read almost too conveniently, 'off-Curtis Street' in squirly curlicues, going for a bit of elegance, I thought. And yet, the other one was, maddeningly, but similarly curlicued, 'off-off-Curtis Street', and so I found myself consulting once again the keystone in this all, the flimsy bit of paper I had torn out of yesterday's rag. I now noticed, wondering how I'd missed that bit before, that it was indeed 'off-off-Curtis Street' that was printed in bold black on the increasingly yellowing white. So, 'off-off-Curtis Street' it would be! And so, *off-off* I strode.

If the last street had been a tad on the narrow side, this little off-shoot, or off-off-shoot, was definitely more like an alley. There might be room for one stout vehicular conveyance, a lorry rather than a bus, with not much else to spare either side, but then perhaps it was just for pedestrians. Talking of which, the sides of this street seemed to be all terraced housing, the pavements spotless, and leading off to the right in an inviting curve. The other arresting and attractive feature, I was only now beginning to notice, was that the street between those pavements was gleaming with cobblestones —even though 'gleaming' was just an expressive touch that encapsulated my initial surprise. What 'olde worlde' had I stumbled into here, I wondered to myself, feeling that whatever the end of my destination, the journey had satisfied something in me already. 'Very nineteenth century!' I exclaimed, if only to myself, feeling very explorer-like indeed. I took my first - slightly timorous- step onto my first cobbled stone since leaving university, which had boasted a whole campus covered in them.

It was pleasant to rest the sole of one shoe on the face of that first cobblestone and then, as I occasionally did at uni, pivot the whole of my body in a brief twist. Certainly, I knew it must look childish, but who was here to say so? I then hopped with the other foot onto the next best candidate stone and, looking thoroughly like a child enjoying hopscotch, advanced a few more dancing steps into 'off-off-Curtis' Street. Presently, as I lost interest in what was below my feet and found my attention drawn rather to the terraced houses either side, my gait returned to normal, well, normal for me: a kind of gliding, dandering stride, with a touch of swagger thrown in now and then for good luck. Well, however I did it, I proceeded down the quaint little street, on and on and on, following a right-leaning curve that never seemed to straighten out.

I soon decided, perhaps out of a sudden self-consciousness, to forgo the centre with its cobbles and instead walk on the left pavement. That, it occurred to me, rather late in the day, would be the slightly more normal thing to do after all. Three generous steps, but only three, brought me past each residence, each with its dry, dark brown brick, unrevealing curtained windows, generous window sills, positioned invitingly at elbow-level, and solid wooden doors. What I could make out, the few times I furtively looked inside the window space, was often enveloped in interior shadow, a lace-covered table here, a vase there, a dark impenetrable space there, nothing to give the impression of movement or activity. Variation between each was provided only by the always-matching thickly-painted colours of the window frame and sill and door: glossy dark greens, seemingly still-wet dark blues, the occasional daffodil yellow, and, by contrast, the odd black-as-a-coalmine-at-midnight black. All of which further intrigued me regarding the as-yet-unseen inhabitants.

I had come across the most ridiculous ad in the previous day's paper, and, being of a mind to be blown by the wind or by fancy, I thought I could do worse than to follow it up.

MAGICIAN WANTED

NO EXPERIENCE NEEDED

This was followed by location details, the intriguing 'P.P.P.', and then, 'General Store, P.E.C. Rhumboldt', who must be the owner. If I'd had any friends living nearby no doubt I'd have shown it to them, and laughed it all off in a moment, but after university, everyone had dispersed, usually to follow their careers, leaving me on my own. Then again, there was always a lot of daft stuff in the papers, so who would have cared? But this had been an actual Classified Ad in a mainstream paper, and must have cost money to place, and so, following the dictates of conscience, as an unemployed man, I had a duty to follow it up, ignoring the others, like: 'BOTTLING FACTORY VACANCY', 'DOG POUND ASSISTANT NEEDED', or 'ABATTOIR, HELPERS REQUIRED'. It had summoned memories of childhood. Firstly, the solo magician-cum-clown who'd visited our Primary School, with his sausage-like balloons being made into poodles and pyramids and such. I'd been called onto the stage and, despite repeated attempts, couldn't manage to blow up a single balloon -distressingly, I soon realized, to the delight of everyone watching. Then, the ones on TV, all dressed up to the nines and assisted by some bimbo in lace, sticking swords into boxes, pulling rabbits from hats, releasing doves out of white-gloved hands. It always struck me as daft until one day when I saw this bloke pass a china cup through a table. It was all done quite slowly for the viewers, with no breaks in the camera-work, very impressive, but his hands had hidden the actual passage. Then, someone else –oh, what idleness in front of the box!– or maybe it was the same *wunderkind*, allowed a guest to slice open a grapefruit, apparently chosen at random from a stack he'd prepared, which, to the amazement of all there -not to mention those like me, glued to the screen- contained the other half of a previously torn playing card, complete with the guest's signature on it. *Shazam!* Stuff like that had made an impression, at least to the degree that a wandering ne'er-do-well with nothing better to do and time aplenty to waste would follow an ad as ridiculous as the one I had in my pocket now.

The houses on both sides of this slender street were, if anything, getting smaller, it seemed. Now it seemed to take only two and a half steps, not three, from boundary to boundary of these fortresses against the world of woe. Not only that, although I couldn't be sure, the sides of the street itself seemed to be gathering closer. But was the passage *actually* becoming narrower, or was it just me, wandering myself into a daze, perhaps affected by, as I was beginning to think, dehydration, or just general fatigue? It did seem to be becoming a rather hot spring day, after all. Surely there was a shop somewhere here, for the worker drones to get milk and bread and fags. How else could they live? I trundled on. Momentum is an obstinate beast.

I hadn't seen it, perhaps because of the curve, but now I was almost upon *another* side-street! If I can just make it there, I told myself, I can take a look in and if it's nothing but more of this monotonous fractal pattern of windows and doors, I can just head back out toward civilization... I fished out from my jeans pocket the paper ad and studied it once more. I saw a very curious thing: it now appeared to say 'off-off-off Curtis Street'. That couldn't be true, I told myself reasonably. I blinked, shook my head and then returned to the thesis that my senses were becoming dulled, and that perhaps I'd followed this wild goose chase quite enough. Very probably it was time to back out of this maze, as I was beginning to think it to be, and return to the world I was acquainted with. If it was dehydration, a good solution to present problems would be a trip to Monahan's Bar, a slow draught of some lager cold enough to knock sense back into my head. The owner was a decent scud, too, always up for a chat. The more I thought about it, the better I could see the row of brass taps shining lustrously in the mid-afternoon sun, ready to dispense wonders of a liquid kind to all and sundry. It was a very attractive proposition, to just give up, re-trace my steps and succumb to the call of the taps. And yet, to have come so far, only to turn back now seemed a trifle premature, as though I was still being blown by the breeze... Completing the journey would counter that. Despite how silly the whole idea now struck me as, a retreat at this point would just make a mockery of my efforts, and add to my recent nagging suspicion that my life was seriously devoid of purpose. Purpose, I lectured myself, was relative, bound up with the tiny detail of *this* pressure and *that*: sometimes the overall pattern was not immediately apparent, but, by taking care of the small stuff, that pattern would emerge. In this spirit, then, a few steps into this off-off-off passageway were hardly amiss.

The cobblestones had given way to a plainer surface, not tarmacadam, but rather something closer to a hard dirt road. It struck me as strange that it should be so, but this whole enterprise was getting weirder and weirder with every step. On left and right sides of this little street, and in sharp contrast to the bland terraced housing of before, there was a variety of individual, independent buildings: some seemed to be residences, some looked more like shops, and the rest, purpose unknown. Most by far were wooden, but there was the occasional one made of brick. Still nineteenth century, but different in character and atmosphere to the previous terraced all-identical residences. Gone was the industrial, replaced with something more individual, more inviting. Was that a photographic shop over on the right? I suddenly found myself asking. If it was, it seemed very old: the sign above the door read 'Kodak Ltd.' and was done in tin, albeit in good condition. Very retro, I thought. I succumbed to curiosity and crossed over to have a little peep in through the window.

The first thing that caught my attention was the stark black box occupying centre stage in the display. As the accompanying plaque explained, it was, quite simply, 'The Kodak Camera'. You couldn't argue with that. Obviously from Yesteryear, I wondered if this wasn't the first Kodak ever… Just a rectangular box with a hole at the front, facing me. 'You push the button,' the info read, 'we do the rest.' On either side were assorted oddments: trays and chemicals and brushes, jars, ancient-looking photographic plates, and large sheets of 'Photographic Paper' (so the label said), and even candles. The other sizeable object of note wasn't a camera at all, but a lantern of sorts, with a round base and a square body: the 'No.2 Kodak Darkroom Lamp'. Must be an improvement on the No.1, I mused flippantly. Still, I wondered how it might be employed: you didn't put film in there, did you? And was that bulbous thing at the top some kind of button? And if you pushed it, what happened? Anyway, why would someone sell something like this now? it then struck me to ask. Of course, I concluded, antiques had never gone out of fashion. What was more attractive than some item from the past to adorn a mantelpiece, and provide a conversational focus for guests to a house?

Personally, I'd never had much of an interest in antiques, and always found the interior of shops selling them to be a bit musty, but I was willing to concede that some people loved them, indeed spent their whole life collecting them, discussing them, researching the historical context of each item, or what could be learned about the technology of the time... Perhaps this was an area devoted to such pursuits. That, I realized, would explain why I'd never been here. (These antiques were in pretty good nick, though...)

I crossed back to the pavement I'd been on. To my immediate left, the wooden exteriors of the buildings were punctuated by windows, which unfortunately were all so far closed; the general lace curtains-enclosed dark within dissuaded me from casually peering in. Still, very fetching, I thought. And yet, there was still no-one else but myself to be...fetched, or impressed, by my intriguing environs. It must have been at least ten minutes, maybe more, since I'd seen a soul. It was the middle of the day, near enough, so likely most were away –the worker drones– slaving over hot coals, with hammers pummelling white hot iron, as sparks flew in every direction. Yet, it did feel unnerving in some way. Whatever was going on, my attention was now drawn to what appeared to be another sign, maybe also made of tin, which stood out from the wall on the side I was walking along. It seemed to be a little more elaborate than the Kodak one, with cut-out shapes dangling beneath. That, I decided, might just be the place I'd been searching for all this time.

Curiously, just as I was arriving at this yearned-for spot, I saw my first humans: two children, a boy and a girl. They had just exited from what I assumed was a free-standing, but rather narrow, wooden house on the opposite side of the street. What attracted my attention was their garb, all wools –and pretty formal with it–, and their play, which involved running after a large hoop with sticks to keep it rolling. If they hadn't arrived in some sort of time-machine from the nineteenth century then I believed I was simply hallucinating. Whichever was true, I was well and truly flabbergasted. Apparently, however, I was as curious a sight to them as they were to me, for, upon noticing me, they both stopped precipitously, an action which resulted in the hoop carrying on of its own accord …and directly towards me! Instinctively, I put my hand out and stopped the wooden hoop, so that now all action had become frozen, indeed like a 'Kodak moment' in 3D. Within those few milliseconds of what I assumed was a mutual astonishment, my eyes feasted on their elaborate clothing of woolen layers and caps and buttons and lapels carefully creased, looking all pristine and new. The girl's garment was of particular note: from her neck-collar the checked material seemed to sprout two further, and much larger, collars, which were caught in a kind of cascade, radiating outwards and down. Before I could stop myself, I gave utterance to my astonishment: 'Your clothes…'

'That's what we call a "double-breasted gretchen", if I'm not mistaken,' said a deep-sounding voice behind me. 'Very popular nowadays,' it continued. Half-terrorized and half-fascinated, I turned to see a large man, taller than me for sure, with a shock of fair hair, wearing a plain apron over a minimally-striped collar shirt, and sporting a moustache the size of a large cigar. 'The boy's in knickerbockers, of course.' 'Of course,' I found myself replying, and re-saying, 'of course.' I threw a querulous look at this new presence at my back. 'You'll be giving them back their hoop, mister, if you don't want them hollerin',' he then confided, keeping his tone a little low, so as not to be heard by the children. 'Of course,' I replied, realizing as soon as I said so that I was repeating myself. And, so, turning back to the kids, I wheeled the hoop back in their direction; the girl caught it and, to my amazement, curtsied. The boy touched his cloth cap and gave the slightest of nods, and they both resumed their vigorous play, as though nothing at all had occurred. I turned back to the figure behind me, only to note he had now disappeared, or rather, was in the process of doing so. In fact, he turned around in the doorway of what I was now beginning to realize was his shop –*that* shop, the 'General Store', the shop I'd been looking for all this time, the end of my bizarre search. He was holding the door open for me, a generous expanse of frosted glass within a richly grained wood frame. 'You'd best be coming inside, if you're of a mind to,' he called out. And to which I answered, before I could stop myself: 'Of course,' feeling desperately and embarrassingly vocabulary-challenged as I did so.

Just as I did step inside, I scanned the words etched into the glass of the door:

POLY'S POTS & PANS
GENERAL STORE

Poly's Pots & Pans... That would account for the P.P.P., I realized in a moment of staggering deduction. It was certainly well named, because the first thing I noticed upon entering this establishment was the remarkable array of pots, pans, kettles, skillets and other metal containers and implements forming a kind of grotto-like frame for the lead-in walkway to the shop proper. Said pots and pans and kettles etc. were either placed decorously upon the floor, left and right of the passage in, regaling the tops of cut tree-stumps (of stepped sizes), chairs, stools, small tables or, most noticeably, hanging left and right on the walls and from the low arch above the entrance and walk-in to the counter. However they were positioned, they grabbed my attention for sure, something to displace the thought I'd had of the shining taps in Monahan's. I hardly noted that the man to whom I had just been showing off my impressive linguistic skills had now ambled round to the end of the counter and was appearing to make ready to welcome a customer, which, 'of course', could only be me. I ended my eye-feasting and decided it would be impolite not to approach and say a decent hello.

'Nice place you have here,' I proffered. 'Very kind of ya,' came the reply, confirming what I had noted from the start but not focused on: American accent, and more than vaguely Southern with it. 'New round these parts?' he, who was very probably named 'Poly', then asked. There was a confidence in his diction, even a slight swagger to his accompanying body language that struck me as very reassuring, and indeed had done so from the start. Here I was in an unknown part of the town, confronted with a rather unusual situation, both from out in the streets and lanes I had wandered down, and from inside this 'shop', yet, this gentleman emanated an at-ease-ness which assuaged all my potential misgivings or feelings of disorientation. There was, it struck me, a logic to all this, and perhaps I just needed to fill in a few blind-spots and then everything would be hunky-dory. 'Well, I suppose you could say that, yes…' I replied, although something told me his question might equally apply to himself. After a moment of indecision, and potential awkwardness for me, not quite knowing what to say next, I realized that the best way to explain my presence would be to show him the newspaper ad. It was still in my hand, now quite crumpled, and, to my dismay, somewhat moist from the sweatiness of having resided in the grip of my palm. Realizing this, I wasn't sure that I wanted to actually pass it over to him, so, instead, following in one smooth action after saying 'yes', I looked down and read out the sparse main message: 'MAGICIAN WANTED. NO EXPERIENCE NEEDED'. Upon doing so, I felt profoundly silly, and wondered what sort of a reaction my words would bring, feeling that perhaps, after all, I shouldn't have strayed beyond 'of course' as an utterance.

'Let me see that!' Poly, as I imagined must be his name, suddenly exclaimed, and not, it seemed, without a trace of annoyance. In one swift action, he leaned over the counter and ostentatiously grabbed the apparently offensive strip of paper out of my hands, bringing it up to his eyes to study for himself. Rather than expend any great attention on it, however, his examination lasted only a second or two, as he, again ostentatiously, even over-dramatically, threw it away behind him somewhere and bellowed gruffly: 'HA!' These sudden actions left me perplexed and wondering whether it might be better just to leave, after a few polite words of excuse. He was obviously mad.

Yet, as quickly as he had broken his composure, he resumed his control, placing his hands squarely upon the counter between us and saying, in tones of the most perfect shop host: 'Sir, you have come to the right place. I am at your command. The name's "Poly" [rhyming with 'holy', I noted]. Well...' he appeared to correct himself, '"*Paul E. Clarence Rhumboldt, Esquire*" to the bank manager, but [rising to a flamboyant twang] good ole "Poly" to my friends and customers. Nice to make your acquaintance!' He then extended his left hand, which connected to a half-bare forearm, one of two, of course, conspicuous with abundant fair hair. In extending my own, I felt he had me beat on sheer bulk: the girth round his bare arm was greater than that round my jacket-clad forearm. Indeed, Mr Paul E. Clarence Rhumboldt, Esq. was quite a physical presence, not intimidating in any way, but taller than me (who isn't?) and with a girth to match. A tad 'roly-poly' in fact! (He must have been told that one a few times...) It was unfair to describe uptop as 'a shock of fair hair': it just possessed a volume I wasn't used to, contrasting with my own meagre fare, and it was more light brown (touch of red?) than fair. His round wire-rimmed glasses displayed his eyes like they were two jewels, shining with animation. His nose was the cheerily bulbous centre of a face that emanated kindliness and warmth, and his upper-lip-obscuring moustache seemed to have been wrought from beaten copper wire. Must be about fifty, if he's a day, I mused. Meanwhile, his hand almost crushed mine in the finest down-home and folksy traditions of the American West.

The American West! That was it! If anything, this place had all the markings of a Wild West Frontier shop, if a very high class one. It was a strange revelation to be having as we locked palms and bonded for what seemed like an age. My logic rebelled precisely as my body language was drawing me deep into acceptance of whatever it was I had gotten myself into. As the handshake endured, something reminded me that handshakes had long been a sign not merely of greeting but also of mutual agreement in business. If we were shaking on a deal, then precisely what was it I was letting myself in for?

Like magic, a word which seemed somehow essential to understanding all this, the shaking stopped, Poly retracted his hand like a whippet out of the cage, and his demeanour altered: not in any negative manner, just a sudden reversion to the shopkeeper-customer relationship after the headiness of bonding. An American thing, I suspected. 'Have a mosey round,' he suggested in all shopkeeper-like friendliness. So much for getting an answer to what the ad was all about... Well, that was kind of a relief, I felt and, anyway, the shop itself was like a surrounding presence, demanding my attention in bucketloads. So, after my 'Thanks, I will', I had me a good ole 'mosey round'.

And what a place it was, what an establishment of riches! Dissatisfied with my earlier cursory and truncated inspection, I returned to the pots, stepping back a few paces. It was indeed like a grotto. To the left and right, I now noticed, hung the difficult-to-classify pieces, curious shapes in gleaming aluminum, or was it tin? Cake cutters of every shape, and cake-rings, churns, and skillets, canisters for condiments both large and small, for hotel scullery or kitchen. Shakers, jelly moulds, and tinware buckets here and there, some the size of a large mug, others big enough to cover your head. Scoops and sieves and colanders and spatulas and pans of every shape and size. The pots and pans and kettles took pride of place, hanging from the ceiling like trophies from some war fought against an army of tinmen. Many of the pans were iron and flat and black. A few were deep, and one was smoothly concave, almost semi-circular and black. 'That be a wok,' called Poly following the aim of my eye. 'Chinese, for frying rice and anything that's chopped.' I acknowledged the info with a nod and a smile. Iron saucers, skillets with a range of shapes hewn into them: stars and circles and ovals and squares and rectangles, for pastries? Fudge? Brownies? Madeleines? What went into the stomachs of Wild West Frontier people after meals? I wondered. Nickel-ware and implements of steel also hung down. There were kitchen utensils attached to the wall, radiating outwards from the archway all the way up to the wall-shelves, boxes of knives and spoons and forks and other items whose function was beyond me, leading the eye to adjacent shelves, high above the counter area, bearing canisters and jars in two tiers. Opaque clay canisters sat on the upper tier, with the names of herbs daubed on each: *Basil, Thyme, Rosemary, Dill, Caraway, Cilantro, Black Mustard, Lemongrass, Orris Root, Paprika, Nutmeg* and *Fennel*. On the lower, oversized transparent glass jars housed a startling variety of teas: *Oolong, Formosa, Darjeeling* and *Pu-erh, Yellow* and *Earl Grey, Golden Monkey, Butter (Butter tea?), Rose Hip, Labrador...* The grains and textures of the tea inside (the occasional flower, too!) just visible if I squinted.

I could hardly take it all in. More awaited me directly below the counter area. I scanned all the goods from left to right, slowly, half-aware that Poly was likely enjoying all the attention his array of goodies was receiving. Basket upon basket of bread cobs, loaves, scones, stacks of biscuits, Jam and Butter (as the dainty square porcelain containers declared in black lettering), streams of beef jerky hanging down, strings of garlic bulbs and peppers, red and green and yellow, and everything in overflowing abundance. Next to all that, stacked tins of Powdered Milk and Mustard, and giant sacks of vegetables, 'Potatoes' and 'Yams' and 'Rice' and all kinds of 'Beans', stencilled on each, lounging together like pals after a few drinks. Acting like a stopper for these, a huge barrel filled with red and green apples stood guard at the end of the counter. Now that I'd moved to the right of the wooden-topped counter, I could see into a connecting chamber reaching round the back. My eyes sought out Poly's for permission to proceed in that direction and he reciprocated with an exaggerated look of tacit approval, eyebrows flaring up in concert with a very firm nod of the head. Poly had a way about him, I sensed, that wouldn't go amiss on the stage.

So, I tripped on through to the back, briefly bathed in the yellow-tinted sunlight of the store's main window, with its legend 'SNAP & STOP S'YLOP', as I could read it, adjusting for the reverse-effect of the lettering. I was thoroughly intrigued by every tiny detail my eyes caught sight of, and in a state of quite fevered expectation. This was propitious as the backroom, I soon noticed, a modestly-sized area of wooden cabinets and display cases, seemed to be dedicated to the feminine side of things. I wouldn't normally be entranced by soap and toiletries but it was hard not to be impressed by the orderly arrangement to my immediate left: row upon row of paper-wrapped soap bars on delicately stitched linen draped over an open display cabinet. According to the printed sign strategically placed behind the exhibits, 'JAS. S. KIRK' was the producer of such novelties as 'Club Bath Soap', 'Cocoa-Nut Oil Soap', and 'No.178 Glycerine Soap'. (Wasn't that dangerous? I asked myself, or was it only when 'Nitro' was added?) Most were oval in shape, but a few were stolidly rectangular, square, or properly cube-like, some with labels, like 'Carbolic Toilet Soap' and 'Jim Hun, No.188', which seemed designed to take the fun out of bath-time. Each was quite large, too, and somehow, perhaps because of their general solidity and their obviously well-thought-out applicability to clearly defined ends, they put me in mind of internal organs. My eyes skimmed over the lot and I brought my nose down for a quick snoop, a kind of an olfactory fly-by. *Elder Flower! Columbian Transparent! Cocoa Ball! Maezawa Lavender! Glen Honey! Palestine Lily!* Yet, the soaps refused to properly divulge their scents, leaving me with a kind of serious yearning to buy one and just dowse it in hot water until clouds of scented suds came billowing out.

Glassware! In abundance! Just over there! My senses were ganging up on me, like salesmen gone mad with the desire to entice and attract the eye of the helpless-to-our-wiles customer. A vista unfolded on the adjacent cabinet of myriad bowls and jugs and tumblers and what-not in cut-glass; each with a different function, possessing its own special shape and own special design, crinkly-edged and gleaming translucent shapes for every occasion. I began to move toward these but an unexpected glint from somewhere else caught my eye and I was drawn irredeemably over to a glass-topped display cabinet on the other side of the room, in which its items were on show at a 45-degree angle, to catch the sun, no doubt, through the latticed window on the right-side. I had to move closer in order to see what all the fuss was about, but diamonds are diamonds, garnets are garnets, and sapphires are sapphires, and none will be satisfied with anything less than serious attention. Gold has its wiles, too, and silver no less so, especially when wrought, as it was here, into the tiniest of exquisite shapes, both abstract and recognizable: stars and roses and the odd goddess-like visage in miniature, staring off into the -horizontal- middle distance. And yet, jewelry usually tires me for being just that, inordinately selfish in clamoring for attention. So, my initial bedazzlement soon shrank to a daze, brought on either by sensory overload, or the fatigue that comes from gazing into a world that could never be mine.

As I retreated and turned to the entrance I'd come through, I couldn't but dally a moment on the last display, which seemed themed with the first, as in related to things of the skin, a collection of white and off-white opaque bottles and jars, of various sizes, the labels all very prettily decorated with elaborate flourishes, the occasional image, say, of a fountain or flowers, and legends done in the most organic of fonts: 'The Queen Mary Eau de Quinine. Tonique', or 'Aqua de Florida', 'Rose Water', 'Florentine Orris', whatever that was, and, curiously, 'Queen Mary Pure Alcohol', which, I decided right there and then, must be the best. Something inveigled me to read the sign which accompanied all these items: *The Queen Mary Toilet Goods are made in our own laboratory, from the purest ingredients, by practical perfumers, and are fully equal in quality to similar goods usually sold at higher prices.* I was glad to hear that: one more incentive to make me want to reach out, pluck one and take it to the counter, my mind conjuring the delicious moment of initial contact between 'Extract Peau de Espagne' and the not-very-feminine back of my hand. Or... now as my eye roved further, just to the right, onto things dental, I wondered just what the taste was of 'Dr Sheffield's Crème Dentifrice', or precisely what would happen if I applied 'Brown's Camphorated Saponaceous Dentifrice for the Teeth' onto *my* teeth? At one dollar seventy-five cents, you'd just want to know before buying. Or that Face Cream, perhaps I needed that too, a touch of 'Tappan's Rosebud Combination', for my 'Complexion', of course.

I left the room as though floating on a cloud of cleanliness, with a heightened awareness of bodily needs, combined with a sense of the need for fine sensibilities and a practiced refinement as part of one's daily approach to the rough and tumble of daily life. I had briefly connected with my feminine side, so there was something serendipitous and balance-restoring about my then noticing, way over on the far side of the main store space, past the archway, and past where Poly had remained, scribbling something into an open notebook, what could only be -I realized with boyish glee- a wall-full of guns. How had I missed that? 'Guns!' I exclaimed rather loudly, as though wishing to announce that the man in me had survived intact. Rifles mostly, shotguns, pinioned to the wall with brackets. 'Winchesters!' I announced, now that I'd hurried over (making a bit of sound as I did, upon the wood panelled floor) and was drinking their image in in hearty draughts, scanning the little information cards accompanying all. 'Repeating rifles!' I further enthused. 'And six shooters, too!' Indeed, I now noted, there were plenty of those little power tools on show.

I'd glance at the description written on cards below each and then look longingly at each piece itself, like the breathtakingly alluring 'Colt Single Action Army .45' with its eagle-engraved ivory handle, smooth polished cylinder and long, shining barrel. Or the elaborate 'L.D. Nimschke Colt .44 caliber rimfire open top revolver', with curlicue engravings so plentiful on its handle and barrel I imagined whoever held it would be too distracted just looking at it to ever get round to pulling the trigger. In contrast, adjacent, a black 'Smith & Wesson, 3 single-action revolver', shorn of such décor, looked like an effective instrument of death & destruction, or was that law & order? Cute, and not-so-cute, snub-nosed little Derringers punctuated the flow, looking like babies among men. My gaze then returned to the rifles, and long-barreled guns. A smooth nut-brown wood-stock 'Remington-Hepburn' rifle, with, I now noticed, a 'pistol grip' for single-hand use: 'Ingenious!' I exclaimed to myself. Then, 'Spencers' and 'Henrys' and, starkly, because it was given a kind of special thin metal bordering on the wall, the 'Sharps .50 Caliber Buffalo Rifle, 1876.' (How many glorious beasts had it felled?) This latter piece had me checking the dates and kick-started me processing the details of each description in a manner more conducive to rational thought.

I then moved onto the Winchesters, the ones which had originally caught my attention. In my need to process the information, I found myself reading out loud, if *sotto voce*, the details before me, poring over the fine print on each, as in one particularly fine Winchester: 'Model 1894, 38-55 caliber, 26-inch octagon barrel, weight 7 3/4 pounds, $24.44'. Upon taking this in, I felt suddenly compelled to call out to the man at the centre of all this, in need of corroboration. So, I turned round and called out to Mr Paul E. Clarence Whatever-the-hell his last name was, still standing behind his counter, scribbling away: 'Twenty four dollars forty four cents? For a Winchester Repeating rifle? Is this for real?' As I spoke these words, it then suddenly dawned on me in one earth-shattering, ground-breaking, filibustering (filibustering? -a word I've never understood) moment, how stupid I had been: Of course, this could only be... *a museum. Not a shop!*

'You think I'm over-charging there, fella?' was Poly's response, delivered with a tentativeness that seemed almost out of character. His face and even his general body language, now that he had extricated himself from the counter area and was ambling over to where I was, seemed to show a measure of concern. 'Not at all!' I replied, eager to assuage him, 'not at all!' Then, having decided that my assessment was correct, continued: 'I'm just admiring the... *authenticity* of the place.' Unfortunately, this response appeared to make Poly's face contort even further, as he grappled with the concept I'd just thrown him: '... Auth..en..ticity? Mister, *whatever* do you mean to imply?' Then things went like this:

Me: It all looks so real!
Poly: Why wouldn't it?
M: [nervous laugh]... because...

P: Because what? Spit it out there, fella.

M: ... [increasing uncomfortableness, manifested in a certain unnecessary shifting of leg and feet, the mind working feverishly until it had found an answer to the conundrum of all this]... because I thought it was a shop! But in fact it's a museum!

P: [silence, querulous look]

M: [silence in return, a mimicked querulous look, the moment lasting almost beyond the bounds of social excruciation, with more minute but noticeable micro-shifting of legs, followed by a concomitant, and extremely otiose, movement of upper limbs, and a sudden re-realization that this man, Poly, did indeed possess quite a large physical presence: he loomed]

P: Feller, I think you need a drink.

M: [feeling massive relief] I think you are right.

So, Poly lead me to an area I hadn't even seen, tucked in behind the wall behind the counter. It was a smaller room, and largely shorn of the kind of items dotted all over in the main 'business area', and there was a smallish wooden table, quite rough-and-ready, but attractive with it, surrounded by a few wooden chairs, each with its own cushion placed on the seat. He simply, but politely, indicated one of the chairs and I sat, taking in the surrounding walls a little more casually than I had heretofore. Pictures in frames, clumsy oil paintings, a few notices of what looked like store regulations, all very Wild West, ornate script, mostly too small to read, though, brown ink, all very nice. Lanterns hanging, too, here and there. A shelf, I now noticed, lined with bottles of booze, just over the right-side area of the table. Poly reached up and grabbed one of the bottles, then produced, magically it seemed, as I didn't notice him getting them, two shot glasses, plunking all down on the table in tandem with the arrival of his own generous posterior on the cushion-laid chair opposite me. 'This is good stuff,' he explained very casually, 'top dollar for this hooch. Only the best.' He uncorked the bottle and tipped it into the glasses, like oversized thimbles, and pushed one over to me. 'Sláinte,' he said. 'Sláinte,' I replied, only momentarily surprised (because aren't all Americans Irish?) that he knew the Irish word for 'Health' said before drinking. We both knocked them back in one go.

Good stuff and strong, indeed. Before I could raise my head to initiate some chat —I was going to compliment him on the libation— Poly cut me short with a look and a hand gesture that clearly meant 'Wait!', as he poured again and indicated the need for synchronous downing. I saw little chance of dissuading him so I played right along and tipped the glass back. This one was stronger-tasting for some reason, or maybe I'd had a few milliseconds longer to navigate its taste. I grabbed the bottle and read the worn label: 'COWBOY JACK'S' and on the next line: 'RUSTY WATER DISTILLERY', and, below the image of Cowboy Jack himself, astride a brown horse and decked out in all the gear, the legend 'WHISKEY', and on the bottom line: 'TIME HONORED TRADITION' with 'Since 1849' in a horizontal oval inset before 'TRADITION'. 'They certainly like their upper-case letters,' I commented, thinking that very clever. 'Gotta catch the eye, by hook or by crook,' shot back Mr Rhumboldt, who now seemed well at his ease, and open for talk.

'Your ad caught *my* eye… And the goods you have here, man, it's just amazing…' I hadn't yet broached the topic of precisely what it, this place, was, feeling that maybe I should wait until we could just dance around a little first. 'Oh, you know, a man's gotta make a livin'…' was his answer, and before I could use that for anything meaningful, Poly assumed a new tone, contemplative and confidential-like. 'Been in the family, generation after generation, my Great Granddaddy… no, lemme see, that'd be my *Great*-Great Granddaddy, he come from Ireland, would you believe…'

he said with a broad smile, 'a little place in the North West, so we all heard... Dongaul, or was it Dongaulen... or something like that...' 'Donegal,' I suggested, hiding, however, my confusion, my doubt that anyone from Donegal would ever be called Rhumboldt... 'Whatever...' he resumed, '... well, they was all poor and, so the story goes, in the famine, down to the last cousin near enough, and saw crossing to Americay as the last chance the family had of continuing...' As he told all this, his head was inclined, as though studying the grain of the wood on the table, and his hand reached up smoothly and slowly to remove the cork from the bottle, dragging it back toward his side of the table. He poured this time in slo-mo, as it had become secondary to the talk, reaching over and filling my glass, too, without the hurry that had characterized the first two shots. I accepted the glass and the idea that now was a time for slow sipping, not chugging. 'Yessiree,' he continued, '...and, through sheer dint of his efforts, battling against all the odds, well, he became a Mercantiler & Victualer, a man respected in his community.' This called for a sip and a half, synchronized, as we were honouring the past, the good and the dead. I wondered when I could get into the conversation, or if it would wind its way round to where I was concerned, and what it all meant.

'Rhumboldt,' I pronounced slowly, 'Rhumboldt...' rolling my head to one side, and casting my eyes down. My tactic was to hope that he'd mind-read my desire to address the geographical conundrum his name posed. Yet he simply looked at me as though waiting to catch the end of my utterance. 'Rhumboldt...' I intoned now, like some kind of prayer. 'Paul E. Clarence *Rhumboldt*, Esquire, that's right! To my bank manager, anyways!' he said so forthrightly I felt awful to ask, and so I danced around it: '...What part of Donegal would that be then? That you're from... your family, that is... the Rhumboldts... and all...' 'Ah! You're confused!' shot back Poly, thankfully realizing where I was headed. 'Don't sound none too Irish, do it?' he 'joshed', as I imagined he might put it (feeling some kind of need to slip in an Americanism whenever I could), slapping the tabletop with as merry a whack as he could muster. 'Forgive me, forgive me! Granddaddy converted to a pure-hearted Baptist because of his partner-to-be, and took her name, thinking it might sound a mite better than "Maguire", the old family's name… to mix in and all, with the Baptist folk.' I was delighted and showed it. I raised my glass in a gesture of, well, I wasn't quite sure what —solidarity? absolution?— but however I meant it, I was surprised to see it summon a frown from my interlocutor: it was obvious we had a lot of ground to cover before we'd ever see quite eye to eye. What was it now? I worried, feeling I'd made a serious cultural *faux pas*. 'Granddaddy wouldn't be too happy to have someone drink to him, liquor that is…' spoke Poly in a tone that might be classified as 'deadly serious'. He looked into my eyes with a stare one might use when fighting a bull. I didn't know what to say; furthermore, my arm had frozen where it was, glass (containing alcohol, liquor) held high still. 'Being a Baptist and all!' shouted out Poly with a sudden explosion of mirth: all at my expense, of course. What a relief! Poly had made a joke! What a desperately curious character he was! Poly raised his glass up to the same height as mine, still suspended in air, and we clinked glasses so hard they nearly broke. And then we supped what was left in each. 'You had me there, Poly, you really had me there!' I said and joined in the fun and the -by now- raucous laughter.

It took us a while to resume normalcy of some kind, but when we did, I felt I had no choice but to plunge head first into the deep, seeing as we'd now broken the ice a crack or two. 'So,' I ventured, as innocent a smile on my face as I could manage, feeding out my question careful word by careful word: 'this… is… a… *shop*, you were saying?' ''Tis surely,' came the reply, Poly looking up, eyes staring through me for all they were worth. 'And, fella…' the look from his eyes narrowed perceptibly, mysteriously, too. Was this to be another moment beyond all expectation? Usually it doesn't take so long to figure out how someone communicates. But with the figure sat before me, as large, vivacious and engaging as he was unreadable, I had no idea what was coming next. Another joke, perhaps, or something just simply American and beyond my cultural acquaintance, or something *sui generis*, a 'Polyism', perhaps? It seemed the latter category fit best, for now Poly, drawing out the moment for all it was worth, dropped a bombshell from nowhere: '…*It's all yours now, boy!*' In a flash, before rational thought could ever hope to unravel the madness of his utterance, Poly flung out his massive left hand, gripping my leather-jacketed forearm, almost shouting: '*All yours from now on, Mister Honey!*'

Thankfully, and I say 'thankfully' because I had no idea what else might break the eeriness of that moment when he grabbed my arm; the very next moment he tipped his head back and roared with laughter. Despite its cause being completely unknown and unknowable to me, his laughing was irresistibly infectious. And so, probably helped along by the whiskey, I was soon tipping my own head right back and roaring along with him, as laughing has a way of enveloping all, and burying commonsense. Between the burbles of delight this obviously brought to my interlocutor, the occasional phrase slipped out too: 'Yours for the taking!' and 'You'll never go hungry again!', 'Lordy, Lordy, what a day, what a day!' and, finally, delivered with perfect weight on every word, 'God bless the child that has it all!' he whooped.

'*Billie Holiday!*' I shouted on hearing this. Shouted, no less. If I had understood nothing else, I at least recognized that. 'That's Billie Holiday you're quoting! Billie Holiday, right?' This brought laughing matters to an abrupt end when Poly brought his head back, recovered himself and asked: 'Billy Holiday?' Then, speaking really slowly, he continued, 'Don't know no Billy Holiday!' He appeared somewhat irritated at having his moment of hilarity stymied by my sudden question. 'Billy the Kid, perhaps?' he threw back. 'Doc Holliday, you mean?' So, I tried to explain. 'No, no... Billie Holiday... you know, Thirties and Forties jazz singer, black, great voice, had a hard life, was a prostitute once...' Upon this latter key-word being uttered, the expression on Poly's face went from confused to something closer to upset, as though I'd said something I shouldn't have, stepped over the line, so to speak. 'Mister,' he blurted out, 'don't know what you're talkin' about there... don't know what you're trying to say there, fella! *I don't know no prostitutes!*' His tone matched his facial expression, which was hurt, bordering on annoyance. This of course horrified me, and yet, I wanted to clarify. 'No, no... I mean... I mean... that was just something that happened to her once... she was a mother and a good person, just down on her luck... but, Poly, what a voice, she was the Mother of Jazz!' Poly wasn't having that either. 'Mother of *what? Jazz?* And what's that in the name of the Lord and for crying out loud?' he asked. His apparent lack of enlightenment on the subject had me at a loss, but I was determined to teach. 'You know... Jazz!' I imagined that simply saying the word in a very up-beat tone of voice might help. Or louder: 'JAZZ!' No reaction. I persevered. 'New Orleans and all that... Louis Armstrong... and trumpets... and swingers and stuff...' That was my crystallization of the near-century of a rich and multi-faceted cultural phenomenon, begun in America, but now part of a world-wide cultural fabric: *...trumpets and swingers and stuff...* Confronted with the increasingly quizzical look on the face of the man before me, I ploughed on, determined to make myself clear. A little history lesson was in order, I suspected: 'BLUES! You have to know the Blues!' But the face told me 'no'. *Black people's music!* I virtually screamed. 'In the cotton fields, "Call-and-

Response", singing while toiling away...' No reaction. 'In the cotton fields...' No luck, it was having no effect, and indeed, Poly's face was becoming even more twisted with confusion and growing bafflement edging into downright distaste for the fanciful words emanating from my mouth.

So, I started singing, and not without stumbling, improvising completely off the top of my head, in my best lilting Blues voice: 'Woke up this morning.... at a quarter past three.... Ain't got no baby, she did... gone...' I hurriedly tried to think what rhymed with 'gone' but gave up, and chanced: '...walked out on me...' To my enormous relief, my performance appeared to be having success: the lines on Poly's face began to smooth out and it was even possible to discern the lineaments of an incipient smile. (Never has rhyme –the 'three' with the 'me'– meant so much to me!) As I went on, now just wordlessly humming, frankly unable to make things up on the spot, Poly reached instinctively for the bottle and the glasses and poured us both measures, his eyes never straying from me all the time. 'OK. That was the Blues. And it's essential to know that before we get into the other stuff. Now for some Jazz,' I announced. After a brief moment of arrangement in my mind, and a stiff sup of the booze, I then shot up from the chair, cupped my left hand round my mouth in a cone shape and blared out a sound that I thought must sound like a trumpet: 'Doo 'n doo doo DOOOOO!' Somehow my mind was drawing a blank in terms of choosing any actual song, but I made do with some scat-like bebop swinging trumpet-style groove which I imagined summoned the spirit of Mr Armstrong and others. Maybe it was the whiskey but I was certainly enjoying myself and, thankfully, so too was Poly, who, despite the odd quizzical line on his face, appeared to enjoy what he saw and heard. After a few more moments of a performance that made up for in energy what it lacked in content, I sat down with a final trumpeting flourish and we finished our drinks and even poured two more. 'Bravo!' shouted Poly before we did. 'Bravo!' And he clapped generously into the bargain.

They were having their effect, these little shot glasses brimming with fierce nectar. Our chat had become freer, and whatever social awkwardness we, or perhaps only I, had experienced up till now was evaporating rapidly, becoming as evanescent as the liquid in the bottle. And, talking of bottles, I didn't see Poly reach round for a second, he just sort of conjured it out of nowhere, for, there, making company for the old one, stood the new, and a new brand, too. 'This is a bottle of Rye,' explained Poly, and he showed me the label emblazoned with: 'RYE'. Only that, until your eyes wandered all the way to the bottom of the label where it read in small printed upper-case: 'STILL. 100% PROOF'. No image, no other details. 'This one looks dangerous,' I ventured. Poly, who appeared to be still quite sober, at least compared to the way I was feeling, shot me back another of those expressive looks of his, this time meaning: 'You think? Mebbe so…' Then, he did a curious thing —a flick of the wrist you might call it, or a sudden half-violent shake of the hand, his right, and a flicking out of the fingers. He cursed: 'Darn it!' I could tell that 'Darn it!' was a 'cuss' (again, my vocabulary was wandering) to him, and had not come out easy, me being a customer after all… Before I could wonder again the wherefore of it all, he did it again, the flicking action with his right, fingers splaying back, just above the surface of the table. And as he did so, this time it was me who cursed. 'Jesus!' I let out, shrieked out, more like, in tandem with an impulsive and robust kick back of my chair, the four points of the legs making a sudden ugly sound over the surface of the wood floor. Another bottle had appeared! From nowhere!

'Now, *this* you can't complain about, Mister! "Slug Sixty Malt"!' announced Poly, with obvious pride. To which I replied, suddenly feeling strange: 'I think I might stop, actually, Poly, if you don't mind. I'm seeing things. I think I really am…' I then indulged the old impulse one has at such times, like when you think you're hallucinating, or you're going to keel over, and drew the palm of my hand over my eyes, as though to wipe off the filter that had made me see what could not be seen or believed. I pushed myself back with the chair even further, but more deliberately now, so that I could have some free space directly before me, to hang my head down. It was a gesture that brought exclamations of worry from my partner in booze. After a few moments of a back-and-forth where Poly offered to help and I declared I was fine, I thought it best to just ask for some water, as surely, of all the liquids on the planet Earth, that was the one I was most in need of right now. 'Done!' said his voice, as my face buried deeper and deeper into the comforting black of my right palm, the left hand massaging my head, the next best thing to do in the absence of a medical doctor or a qualified nurse. Yet, something was wrong even so. With Poly's vocalized 'Done!' there was an accompanying thud, along with a few other smaller thuds on the tabletop, that didn't quite add up, didn't seem quite right. In my blindness, in which, it's said, the other senses come into their own, I could know it wasn't the sudden slap of a hand, or even an elbow. So I looked up, and, in doing so, felt sudden great shock: there, beside the three bottles of booze (one two-thirds empty), now stood a bulbous glass jar, filled to the neck with cold water! Condensation all around the glass, and within, bobbing, little blocklets of ice. Two new tumblers had materialized also. How could that be? Vocalized: 'How could that be?' directed at Poly, in a tone which was new to our interactions, containing more than a grain of terror. The effect was amplified by the matching look on my face. Poly, I could almost swear, had not moved an inch.

Not one to be dragged into answering when he didn't really want to, Poly, however, proceeded to pour out more than a swigger of the transparent stuff into one of the newly-arrived tumblers, which he then held out to me: 'Get this into ye,' he said. Seeing little wrong with the logic, I broke out of my shock, and gratefully accepted the glass chalice before me, knocking back its contents in one voracious go. I asked for another, then another, one more, and then one last one, 'Just for luck,' I declared, my humour returning, to the delight of my fellow. 'You'll get used to it,' then said Poly, almost tiredly resuming the norm of our interaction, fully believing rapport had been re-established. 'It's just a bit of oul fluff, to be sure.' This statement was delivered with what might be termed a mock-Irish accent, no doubt capitalizing on earlier mention of his ancestors.

'Fluff?' I enquired, after I'd returned the glass to the table top, and lost the debate concerning whether to pursue the issue at hand. 'Yeah, fluff...' replied Poly. 'You can do it yourself.' And before I could know it, he was out of his seat, and, to my surprise and even a modicum of alarm, had soon got round behind me, grabbing for my right arm. 'Easy, man,' he spoke, in tones that were designed to put me at ease. 'Show me your wrist... that's right, let me grip it, just once...' I felt like a soft-toy or a puppet, so completely unaware of what was happening that I just let it happen, somehow believing it could hardly be bad; that, or I was just resigned to the general unexpectedness of everything by this stage. 'And, hey, presto!' he said with a certain *éclat*. He had taken hold of my wrist and now shook it once, till the fingers splayed out as his had done earlier. And yet, nothing particularly otherworldly had occurred. Poly seemed confused, and released me from his grip. But, alas, it was only a fleeting moment of conspicuous pensiveness.

'Got it!' he then declared: 'What do you want?' He bent his head round to my face so that we were eyeball to eyeball. 'Another bottle... no, maybe not... a pan, or a pot? Or a kettle? Some tea, or some spices?' To each inquiry, I would shake my head, very slightly, but enough to be answer, indicating 'no' each time to whatever it was he was asking. 'A skillet? A new jacket, perhaps? ...Something better than *that*?' he blurted, glancing down at my shoulders with a look on his face, which he then replaced with a slightly embarrassed smile, thinking he'd maybe been too blunt. 'A cigar? Do you smoke? Likely you will... Or maybe some lotion? For your hair?' He was getting desperate now, asking me repeatedly what did I want, what did I want, what did I want, 'Oh Jimmy-Jack Cracker! What *do* you want?' and in the midst of this veritable chant to materialism, I suddenly realized what it was that I wanted, because I'd fallen in love with it the first time I saw it, and so shouted out loud, with an enthusiasm every bit as manic as his: 'A Winchester Repeating Rifle, 1894!' Deadlock having been broken, Poly beamed, grabbed my wrist again, shook it up and down vigorously just once, but with such force I was shocked, and yet something was happening, something inside: like electricity, it began in my shoulder, and then sparked its way down through my arm, shooting down through to my extended right hand, and then... there! yes, right there, right before my widening eyes suddenly appeared a long solid metal object from out of the space at the end of my arm! And it was growing longer, at great speed, developing a fine contoured nut-brown wood body, shooting forward, the butt and metal brace speeding away from me and ahead at full steam, into the water jug, the whiskey, the glasses... It smashed right through them all, breaking the jug and sending the remains to the left, its ice-cube-filled water exploding all over the table, the whiskey bottles toppling like bowling pins, the tumblers scattering like transparent dice. Chaos in motion, as the object ploughed through and landed with violence roughly and heavily onto the sorry surface of the shard-covered, wet table.

I stood up like a man shocked with eight hundred volts, pushing Poly back and sending my chair backward onto the floor with a crash. A sharp shrieking sound, in the key of F sharp, emanated from my lips. Before I could know it, however, fright collapsing into a feeling quite like nothing I'd ever experienced before took hold of me, and a smile broke upon my lips. 'You did it!' shouted Poly, 'You did it, you did it, you did!' To which I replied, in kind, 'Yes! I did it! I did it! I did!' For one insane moment, the two of us started shouting and clapping and laughing like kids. *What had just happened?* my rational mind wondered, but every other faculty within me knew only too well... I had conjured something out of nothing. *I had summoned forth a solid object out of thin air!* Poly and I then stopped what we were doing, advanced gingerly toward the table top, and stared down at the beautiful slender thing gleaming before us with its lovely sculptured walnut wood and its lustrous, dully glinting metal. It looked strangely peaceful.

Neither of us wanted to move just yet.

CHAPTER TWO

So, that's how, and where, all the madness started. It wasn't clear to me the next day how things would turn out; indeed, I didn't want to think about it at all. I wanted to imagine it was all just an alcohol-assisted hallucination, and so not taking it seriously seemed to be the best course of action. Magic, however, can't be just ignored; if you have it, it's going to manifest itself whether you want it to or not, a point I wasn't well apprised of at the time... The events of the previous day were hazy at best. There was a nagging thought (unhappily accompanied by a nagging hangover) that I'd signed up for something without knowing precisely what. We'd toured the vast interiors (there were many more rooms, both upstairs and down) and seen a wealth of wondrous and curious items, but now for the life of me I couldn't quite recall why. This was in part because of my tendency to coo and caw and generally fall all over myself upon seeing some outstanding piece, be it a particularly exquisite gilded German-made fob-watch or a pair of multicoloured and elaborately stitched Texan cowboy boots. And I couldn't really get it how ole Poly knew nothing of jazz or the Blues, and other things, too, but I could never somehow work up the courage to pursue that line of inquiry. Each time it struck me as rude to ask too much. I had persisted in the role of customer throughout it all. Perhaps Poly had gone into it deep, the ole nineteenth century thing, and blocked out the world as it was. There are some beings like that in every town, digging out an existence in complete diametric opposition to the one before them. Considering the state of the present world, I reflected, that was hardly an unreasonable stance to take. Poly'd managed to accumulate a vast store of goods belonging to a different, long-gone world, and there he'd installed himself in it, oblivious to the here and now. I had to admit it was impressive, and it sure had been fun, wandering around, gawking into every nook and cranny, getting the tour, and generally just dropping my jaw at every perfect piece. That, and the other little thing to consider, even if I did my best not to, that I'd been given the 'gift' of conjuring up objects out of thin air. Oh, that old thing...

Curiously, we hadn't returned to that topic in any great depth subsequent to me conjuring up the Winchester. Again and again, it felt like once Poly had said his piece on any particular topic, thereafter it was pretty much closed for discussion. That, or I'm just a wimp when it comes to finding out what's what. I suffer from this tendency when listening to older people, or people deemed to be important in some fashion, to listen with apparent great attentiveness and respect, my head inclined like a dog at the table. And, like a dog at the table waiting for scraps, I tend not to bark, or to question or say things like 'I'm sorry, could you explain that part again' or 'You said what?' or 'You must be stark-raving mad!' either. Even really difficult things get past me: I squirm in my misunderstandings and only with great personal discomfort do I ever manage to throw a feeble hook out, just hoping it will catch. I must have gotten that from my parents, who were both old school. So, I'd somehow just accepted, hook, line and sinker, that (a) the shop was now mine for the taking (no idea what the hell that meant in all seriousness) (b) I could conjure up whatever the hell I wanted anytime from inside Poly's Pots & Pans (no idea in hell how) and (c) when Poly said 'I'll be seeing ya!' and I responded just as cheerily, I had no idea on the planet as to when I was supposed to journey back and take up my supposed position, and what was to become of Poly if I did. The blind-spots in this whole affair, those attributable to the drink and those to my pathetic approach to communication, were innumerable, and coupled with my hangover, and a serious desire to blank it all out, I was happy to just roll over in bed in my little studio apartment and dream of walking on some exotic beach picking up shells or of flying through vast stretches of interstellar space at warp factor ten.

In similar fashion, the energy required to narrate what happened next in any great detail would require a profligacy of time, speech and effort far beyond me, not to mention the attention of anyone unfortunate enough to have to read this far. The very thought of going into all the ins-and-outs of what happened next just makes my lids feel like the leaden-doors of a steam train's boiler-furnace. Doing so would take up too much time and make my story into this meandering mess of silly incident upon even sillier incident, which, of course, in many ways, is what it is. So, rather than provide an extended blow-by-blow narrative on what did happen next, I mean immediately subsequent to the foregoing account at P.P.P., and what led to what, the whys and the wherefores, and all that, I think a half-decent summary, a not-very journalistic pressé, if you like, of immediately subsequent events should suffice. It's all a bit speeded up, but it does actually go somewhere and where is the interesting part. Furthermore, it's all a bit of haze, to be perfectly honest, because it was nothing if not bonkers.

So, pull up your breeches, and hold on to your hat!

****

Charity? Jeez… That I would become a 'charity worker' (not quite accurate but it'll do) was not something I would have anticipated at that stage in my life, as (a) not being particularly disposed to helping my fellow man *for nothing*, and (b) being in possession of a bizarre and magical super-power. But then, concerning the latter, I suppose it's a bit like being some massive celebrity: why not convert a little of that star power into helping the disadvantaged? Well, yes, and no, I never thought I was a celebrity, and certainly didn't act like one. Indeed, you'd be hard pressed to find a more furtive philanthropic creature in your life. Furthermore, they hardly make it a very easy process. You can never just do charity at the drop of a hat and think everyone's going to pat you on the back. No, apparently you have to fill in forms, be interviewed, undergo medical checks because you're dealing in food to be distributed to the public, and, oh, sign 'an insurance waiver', in the eventuality that I 'cause death or injury to persons unknown'. What a lot of something unpleasant underfoot on a hot summer's day! But, after getting noticed doling out loaves to a bunch of homeless people who'd been queueing up forever to get into McCrory's Soup Kitchen which had now just closed its doors, I suddenly became a very hot item.

I was so hot, in fact, I was sweating. It was another warm spring day and I'd been touched by the plight of the poor sods who'd been turned away. It all happened very quickly, as I acted on an instinctual desire to help one poor fellow who looked almost on the edge of tears. 'Here you go, mate!' I said in my best cheery manner. Apart from a heart-felt 'Thankee, kind sir!', he didn't comment upon the sudden appearance of this crusty nut-brown beauty, but, thinking back about the way he'd gingerly accepted it, as though it was somehow a little out-of-the-ordinary to be receiving something like this, it struck me later that he was probably wondering more about why I hadn't wrapped it up. A few others did actually vocalize that sentiment, and, curiously, never about the apparent magic behind it all, and at such moments, I'd go into this automatic bow-and-scrape routine, saying 'Terribly sorry about that' and 'Beggin' your pardon' and the like. I produced cob after cob, loaf after loaf, or slightly less munificently, scone after scone, like a basketball -or tennis- trainer passing them into the expectant hands of the lined-up hopefuls. Mostly I'd get 'Very nice of ye' and 'Thank ye kindly', for the best part of an hour, feeling strangely wowed, but also a tad exhausted, by the whole experience.

Indeed, it was from this experience I learnt that my gift could be draining -the conjuring of any solid object out of thin air involved the passage of what seemed like electrical impulses via the length of my arm, or arms, starting in the shoulder. I usually also accompanied the conjuring thing with a touch of bodily movement, not unlike a subtle but noticeable dance move, a minute undulating of the arms. That can get tiring after a while. I also learnt that the gift was finite. Rather, I was *reminded* of this by the precipitous staunching of the flow, and the old bloke opposite me no doubt wondering precisely what it was I was doing spasmodically, but subtly, undulating my arms, with no bread in any shape, manner or form coming down the pipeline. Poly had told me, but I'd forgotten (until I remembered): 'Only one day's stock for one day. It gets replenished on the morrow.'

After an initial glow, when the charity people

'discovered' me, and inveigled me to join their ranks, telling me what a 'huge contribution' I would make 'to society' (egad, not just our town), it soon struck me, as I said already, that it could never be just as easy as sitting down and doling out goodies -not for a person of my particular talents. So, I scarpered when I saw the chance, having figured out a better way, which I would think of as 'guerilla charity'. With one of the few assistants who seemed less concerned about regulations and more concerned about just helping others, we cooked up a wee scheme. I met her surreptitiously, both of us in disguise -me, because I didn't want the publicity ruining my life, and she because she was acting against the code of her employers- and we set up little 'Flash Charity Giveaways' to crowds of the needy who had mysteriously gathered all at once in the same place. In fact, my helper/handler, Edie, had 'done all the footwork' and 'put out the word' and told everyone to keep 'hush hush', as she was as eager as I was to keep it 'under wraps'. She loved her little set phrases, for sure.

Well, to cut a long story short, another stock saying - which makes me wonder if I'll ever be able to say anything original either, memories of being vocab-challenged not long before- while it sounded just dandy, in reality it was all a bit manky. (There's a nice Irish word for ye!) Imagine having to turn up in a field, when it's drizzling, emerge from a hastily put-up tent, plant your backside on the stool provided and then just spend an hour doling out loaves and other kinds of food, apples, beef-jerky and canisters of nuts, and all the time wearing a stupid mask! As for that, it was a cobbled-together affair if ever there was one: a white handkerchief, large enough to be tied by the corners and then covering most of the face, the occasional pull-down over the nose, to breathe in air that didn't smell of my own flesh. A long-rimmed blue sports cap up top, and not even my own mother would know who it was, unless the standard leather jacket and not very well preserved jeans gave me away -not to mention the ancient faded-brown near-shapeless shoes that were so awful that anyone seeing them once would never forget. Yes, I was quite the superhero, wearing quite the splendid costume, to boot!

'How could I go on like this?' something inside me asked. Fields. Parks. Outside the run-down Mulcreevy's Sporting Ground on days when no event was taking place. Down side-streets that played host exclusively to stray cats, vermin and dustbins. 'THE LOAVES AND THE FISHES ALL OVER AGAIN' was a headline in the paper. I was being compared to that bloke who'd lived two thousand years ago and had made such an impression with his own magic tricks. Yet, naggingly, the thought persisted, *was that really me?* I'd read some of the stories they wrote and, well, the person they wrote about didn't sound like me at all. Yes, they got the glorious superficialities right, but all attempts at an in-depth portrait of the 'man and his motivations' were just plain wrong. I had been 'inveigled' and that was it: I was no more philanthropic than the next man, and no lover of hardship either. The reality was that I had no idea what I was doing, being led by the handkerchief-covered nose by a charity maniac who genuinely only thought about other people -well, all except me! I was thanked profusely and even hugged on occasion, by herself and the odd recipient, most of whom I would rather not even want to look at, never mind embrace, not wishing to come across a bit harsh, but you had to be there... And this was happening day after day after day. I would do my thing, then escape -I had to literally run away. Only then was I allowed to return to my ubiquitous wandering, disguise-free, and still at a loose end. The best place, as I mentioned before, was the little hill above the town, which I clambered up most days, unless it was raining or windy or just miserable. The peace up there was now even more precious than it had been before. Now I was having a taste of life *with responsibilities*, a life in which people needed me to do things, to be some place, and to accomplish some task. It hardly mattered what it was, and so the idea that I could do magic gradually began to lose its sheen. Was this why Paul E. Clarence Rhumboldt had passed onto me that bit of 'oul fluff'? Indeed, was it 'just a bit of oul fluff', not some new, and quite incredible, astounding, laws-of-physics-defying phenomenon?

This all explains why I threw in the towel on the oul philanthropy bit, hard luck to the folks with their caps in hand and the well-meaning lady with her finger on the button of the movements of the disadvantaged of our town. It just wasn't me. What was I wasn't sure yet, but shivering in the cold and handing out food just wasn't in my bones, especially after having undergone an experience like that when I had produced the Winchester rifle. To go back to that particular moment, that moment when, and I quote, 'a feeling quite like nothing I'd ever experienced before took hold of me', I had never properly processed what that feeling had been. And yet deep down I knew precisely what it was. Very simply put, I had satisfied an urge, that urge which starts with seeing some object, some item which attracts for some reason. Liking it came next, enjoying its surface qualities, or its promise, and then a feeling of wanting it began. Soon enough, this would increase to desiring it strongly, and then, finally -and in my case, magically-, getting it, having the goddamned thing in my possession, even if it did have to first crash-land onto a table and smash everything there to bits. It had made quite a splash, yes, but sure that only added to its glamour. Yes, I had experienced the thrill of Consumerism! Albeit in a slightly different form from the one most people get to feel, those gently pushing a big trolley round a muzak-piped supermarket, or those with their index finger idly pointing out desirable items in a catalogue. Consumerism: the 'often derogatory', according to my trusty, dog-eared dictionary, 'preoccupation of society with the acquisition of consumer goods.' Of course, mine was an extreme form of the seeing-wanting-getting-having thing. When I analyzed all that jumping up and down and clapping hands with Poly, it was analogous to winning the lottery, that ultimate breaking-of-the-laws-of-economics moment, when you transform from having zilch in your pockets to suddenly becoming this personage of seemingly infinite riches, visions of cocktails by the pool as you adjust your Ray-Ban sunglasses and wonder what you'll do with all the free time and the dosh. Who wouldn't act like an idiot in such a situation? And, furthermore, no-one could tax me on a Winchester. So why, I asked myself coldly, helped by the fact that I was in an actual cold field when I asked it, *why* am I giving it all away? Is that why I became a magician? The answer to that was a pretty emphatic NO. And so, I quietly slipped away, out of the tent, after having exhausted that day's stock, and after having mysteriously taken overly long to say farewell to the well-meaning charity lady. I didn't have the heart to 'spit it out'. I left the ole charity scene, and walked into the distance, and into the blur of an uncertain future.

Actually, I knew where I was going, but I wasn't sure how to get there: Curtis Street, or off-off-off Curtis Street. If I could just find that bloke with the duncher... I'm not very good with directions, as any astute observer could tell, and my first attempt to re-find said street, and thereby get back to P.P.P. General Store, ended in failure. I walked myself in circles, seeing dull brown brickwork everywhere and yet none which yielded any little side-streets leading to other little side-streets, and not a cobblestone in sight. The second time I tried, it was raining, and that really complicated things, as I hate to bring an umbrella anywhere and I can only walk down a street so far holding a newspaper which is becoming increasingly sodden over my head, eyes straining for landmarks and turns I might have taken. I could have given up, but obstinacy is written into my genes, and wandering into my *jeans*. After the longest and most meandering journey one day, it was with extreme disappointment that, when I eventually did find Poly's store, it was closed. Locked. And, to my great dismay, there was a little sign, written in somewhat rough lettering, hung on the door handle, which read: 'Gone fishin'.

I took it badly, entertaining no thoughts of a search of nearby rivers, lakes or any potentially promising bodies of water teeming with fish. I took it badly in the sense of not knowing now what to do with my powers, back to square one in terms of having a handle on my purpose in life, direction, meaning, all that rubbish. I wandered back slowly to where I had come from, back to the town proper, and into a bar, the first one I came to, as an anonymous customer seeking some form of solace, be it liquid or otherwise, otherwise being the hope of bumping into someone and at least salvaging a half-decent conversation out of the day. The barman seemed like a decent enough bloke, but he had his hands full with serving others and doing the odd bit of tidying up and wiping glasses etc.. I sat at the counter, sipping a large pint of black, occasionally using the tip of my pinky finger to draw lines in the foamy head. Once this action was noticed, however, I caught myself on, and pretended to be intent on something a tad more intelligent, injecting seriousness into my vacant but wandering stare. There was a newspaper near to hand. I overcame initial reluctance to have a look at it, feeling aggrieved at what a situation I had gotten myself into by finding the Classified Ad in the paper the other day, and picked it up.

The usual end-of-the-world headlines screamed at me: war-torn countries, atrocities, government crackdowns, grisly murders, shootings by crazed individuals, political dysfunction (nothing new round here), 'rampant terrorism', martial law, disease and famine, plague and, almost, locusts by the millions darkening the land and leaving no green leaf unchewed, or something disgusting along those lines. My eyes preferred to rest upon the margins of the pages, where the commercial advertisements dwelt. That's interesting, I thought, forgetting my earlier distaste. Ads for luxurious new cars, ads for headache tablets that would put a smile on anyone's face, ads for tea-bags that didn't have nasty metal staples holding the tea in (if I may paraphrase), ads for biscuits which had been 'approved by a panel of experts', ads for a new housing estate in which early-bird buyers would get to design their own porches, ads for a fitness supplement guaranteeing huge biceps after only a month of use provided you followed the accompanying -no doubt punishing- daily work-out, ads for shampoo which was simply better than any other brand because it was 'shinier', ads for tropical fish, from the rainforests of Brazil no less, the possession of which would ensure a dreamy feeling of being 'at one with nature', ads for window-cleaning services, 'most reasonable rates anywhere', undercutting all rival firms, ads for under-arm deodorant for business types, slim and easily slipped into a briefcase, ads for boots, made in Mexico and by a firm established in 1891... At this one I stopped and stared. These were Cowboy Boots, and boy, did they look desirable, or what? Sculptured, tall, elaborately stitched, shining with history, association to long ago when...

My examination ended with a rambunctious pat on the back. It was an old school pal of mine (Brian Something-beginning-with G), now working for some -oh wonder of wonders- insurance company, and he was all set to wile away the time, chatting and drinking alongside me. I was glad about that, even though I wasn't dying about his timing. A session was just what I needed, and yet, a part of me realized, it might just make everything blurry, including the parts that needed answers, and I didn't really want to get into *my* recent activities. Yet, relief is relief, and this was precisely what I had hoped for, if not what I had bargained for. This refers to the fact that, a few pints on, and after I'd realized there was a reason we hadn't met for ages, I began to seriously dwell upon that ad for cowboy boots, anything to add a little spice to what was becoming the standard chat on the depressing state of the world and the unexpected joys of employment, neither of which topics I found particularly enthralling. Not thinking much about how I would introduce it into the conversation, or where I would take it, I made it clear, to my pal and to the barman, that I was looking for the newspaper I'd seen on the counter just an hour or so previous, the one I had perused so lovingly. The latter directed me to a chap, dudded out in biker gear, complete with bearded jowls, sat apparently by himself at a table just behind where we were perched. Dutch courage swung my legs off the stool and had me ambling over, asking to have a 'wee look for a minute' at the item in question.

He spoke English, but an early 16th century variety, employing a word with apparent Germanic origins, which, anyway, signified a negative response. I compromised by explaining that my perusal would just last 'a wee second', bringing my hands together in a form suggesting prayer, hoping that reverence, and a desire to see the laws of physics challenged (I mean what can a body really do in only a second?) within the confines of a pub, might work. He wouldn't budge. 'I just want to have a look at the ad for cowboy boots, on page 16,' I announced, quite reasonably. This incurred in him a coordinated network of small bodily movements and facial gestures, devoid of vocalized sound, that seemed to further impress upon me the need to desist from my request. Yet, something in me kept me at it: 'Cowboy boots!' I pronounced, emphatically. 'Cowboy boots!' Accompanying the second of these utterances was a sudden raising of my arms in the direction of the biker, with the appalling consequence, given my recent tendency to summon solid objects out of thin air, that two long, elegant, and elaborately stitched, brown leather cowboy boots shot out of the space from the end of my ten out-stretched fingers and flew, heels-first and rudely, towards the face of the seated, leather-jacketed, beard-jowled, clearly-not-very-happy punter before me. 'Cowboy Boots!' I confirmed, as the (probably wooden) heels of both made blunt contact with his face, and then fell inelegantly down, making havoc with his drinks on the table, spilling liquid all over him, 'I just wanted to see the ad for Cowboy Boots!'

Chaos ensued. I won't go into the details too much, as this is only a summary, but, feeling discretion the better part of valour, I did a Falstaff and hightailed it out of there, hoping that my earlier recourse to prayer might come to my aid this time in order to save my skin. In fact, when it came down to it, it was my legs which were more useful: as the air filled with indecent imprecations, I was well aware of being pursued 'hot-foot', as they say. But I was the fleeter and fairly kicked up the dust, even if there wasn't much actual dust to kick up on a pavement. I was sorry I hadn't time to take farewell of my school friend, and to have left him hanging, but consoled myself with the fact that this would provide him with good material for a chat with his mates/colleagues for some time to come. More important was the fact, dawning on me now like the New Year's first sun does on its uninvited disciples, that the episode had opened a portal to me, a door out of the dark and into a realm that might accommodate my new-found magical powers. It wasn't just, I could see now, as I ran down the street like a Valkyrie, that I had merely wanted to *see* those cowboy boots in all their glory: I'd wanted to *wear* them, too. And another thing: I didn't enjoy being 'run out of town', to coin a phrase from the Old West. With these two considerations rattling around inside my head, not to mention the effect the alcohol was having on my fine sensibilities, as I fled down the street (and into an alleyway), I began to entertain the notion of a new me. *A NEW ME!* And, in that state of embattled self-discovery, I stopped dead.

I looked around. No-one was following me. Indeed, no-one was there at all, perhaps because it was the darkest, smallest, most unattractive alleyway I could find in my panic. It seemed the perfect place to do what I felt I now should: cast off the old and step into the new. Within minutes, my transformation was complete, and I left the alleyway. Subsequent visitors there would be confused by the sight of discarded clothes: a fully functional leather-jacket, albeit one which had seen better years; a nondescript off-white collar shirt (which the charity lady had insisted on); and, finally, a pair of the most astonishingly unattractive soft and near-shapeless leather shoes. That was only one pile, however. In another, less visible, because it seemed like someone had tried to stuff them behind a huge rubbish container and so were well out of the light petering in from the main street, a veritable hoard of… large-brimmed hats, waistcoats in a variety of styles, embroidered shirts, and… forming a little mountain all by themselves, layer upon layer of cowboy boots! If you examined them closely you could discern that each pair were of a different size.

A report from the Daily Gazette for the evening of the next day fills in what happened next better than I could, in its article entitled: 'Incident at Pub Astonishes Patrons'.

'Police were called to Phelan's Bar on the outskirts of the town at about 8pm, evening of April 3rd, in response to a disturbance involving a man dressed up in clothes resembling those of a Wild West cowboy and brandishing pistols, according to numerous reports. By the time the police had arrived, the man in question had already left, destination unknown; two officers fled in pursuit, in the direction signaled by passers-by, while two remained to question those inside the pub who'd had direct contact with the man. Apparently, the person in question, who is still being sought by police, had had an altercation with one of the customers at about 7.30pm, and had fled the bar, it seems, in order to 'avoid conflict', as one of the patrons put it. While

things seemed to have quietened down after that, it seems the man who had fled then made a surprise return about twenty minutes later, this time wearing very different clothing. The proprietor, Mr Barney Phelan, was quoted as follows: 'the fella must have gone to some fancy-dress outfitters somewhere, because when he returned he was wearing this black Texan-style cowboy hat, some kind of flowery denim shirt, a smart black waist-coat, jeans, and these cracking big cowboy boots.' These details were corroborated by a number of witnesses. Furthermore, the man was wearing a large belt, stocked, it was reported, with a number of rounds of ammunition, and, on either side, holsters, both holding what everyone said looked like authentic or very good replica 'Wild West six-shooters'. Initial reaction, it was also reported, was general hilarity, as most stopped what they were doing and stared at the man. It was only when the man, after standing for about a minute, looking around him, drew out both pistols and held them up in the air that the laughing stopped. It was then noticed that his attempts to pull the trigger on both weapons seemed to fail. Most concluded that the pistols were not real, or if they were, had no bullets in them, and so, the laughing started again. It was at this point that one of the customers, Mr Kevin McDonnell, stood up and began to rush the man. It was apparently an attempt to finish the evening's business, as it was Mr McDonnell who had been in the earlier altercation with the man who had now returned wearing cowboy gear. Despite the call by the owner for order, it seemed that things would now take a turn for the worse. It was at this point when, according to reports from all there, the most astonishing event of the evening took place. Quickly replacing his guns in his holsters, the 'cowboy', as we may call him, then thrust out his two arms sharply at the on-coming Mr McDonnell, shouting the word 'Beans!' very clearly and, as was reported by some, 'at the top of his voice'. Subsequently, 'seemingly from nowhere', which encapsulates how most remember the moment, the 'cowboy' suddenly produced a huge cloth sack, 'half the size of a grown man' according to Mr Phelan (colourfully terming the development 'fantaaastic!'), and which was later shown to contain dried kidney beans, between his hands and then threw it with some force at his would-be attacker. This resulted in the stymying of Mr

McDonnell's intentions and a brusque end to the drama. The 'cowboy' then clapped his hands together in a sideways movement seemingly indicating the successful completion of a difficult job, turned around and left, walking, not running. Mr McDonnell was apparently unhurt, but had been literally floored by the experience, and watched in silence and some confusion, as the 'cowboy' left the scene. The proprietor commented that he was glad he [referring to Mr McDonnell] hadn't decided to further pursue the matter in hand. In a further twist, Mr McDonnell produced a pair of expensive-looking cowboy boots, and, in a sworn affidavit to the police, stated that the man who had returned wearing cowboy gear had earlier thrown these at him, too. He rebutted the suggestion by the officer in charge that he had been 'in cahoots' with the 'cowboy'. 'Not at all, officer, I've never seen him before in me loife,' Mr McDonnell is reported to have said. The police are asking anyone who was at the bar and may have noticed anything else which may be of use in their investigation, to come forward. They noted that the time when people dress up is usually much later in the year, and, intriguingly, no shops selling fancy costume-wear were in the vicinity, or if they had would have been closed at such an hour. The investigation into this curious incident continues.'

Such detailed focus on this incident might seem to go beyond the boundaries of a summary, but it is key to understanding subsequent events. In the space of a few hours, not to mention a few pints, I had gone from ragged philanthropist to self-centred materialist, if materialist with a difference: I *materialized* items out of thin air. Note that prior to actually conjuring anything, the impulse to see, get and have had already taken root. It was likely not just an accident that my eyes had swallowed up the image of those elaborately stitched leather boots in the newspaper I'd found on the bar counter, their after-image preying upon my febrile consciousness, now released from the hell of endless giving. It was clearly because what had really preyed on my mind had been the until-now-repressed experience of Poly's Pots & Pans. Was it just a bunch of items at my fingertips, or was it rather a whole world, and with that world, a new way of living? Such articulations, such approach to reasoning, were always just beyond the realm of the conscious decision-making process, yet, something floated there just before my closed eyes, and it wasn't just a concatenation of leather, nails and wood to keep the toes dry in a storm. Rather, it was the possibility of a new me. *A NEW ME!*

That possible 'new me' was a potentially dangerous chap, I soon realized. Going into a bar with weapons, even if they weren't loaded yet, and even if I'd only done so to put the fear of God into my rival, was quite a step. And yet, I decided, I liked it. It had been a blast, as they say, even if I had conjured up actually unloaded guns. The duds (meaning the clothes, not the lack of bullets) had helped! Indeed, they were themselves key to seeing how any transformation might take place, because if you're going to be a new self, you have to look new, too. Not that I had worked any of this out as yet... Indeed, reason had little to do with it, or commonsense, which likely dictated keeping my head low for a while. Instead, that very night, I ambled into a different bar in a completely different part of town, fully decked out in my cowboy gear, and still sporting the two pistols, if safely holstered and latched this time. Of course, it being a different part of town, and no-one imagining in a month of Sundays I'd be wearing actual guns on either side of my denims, after a few stares and politely repressed guffaws, I could take a seat at the bar and resume the evening's entertainment. Just to make things sweet with the barman, I conjured up, when no-one was properly looking, a few bottles of unopened, wax-sealed bottles of whiskey. Slug-Sixty Malt, if I remember correctly, and two with hand-inked signs on their otherwise bare labels, which read 'Rub 'o the Brush'. These looked particularly authentic and attractive, and the barman was just happy to receive them as gifts, after, that is, taking a little sample of each to be sure of their contents. I was in friendly country.

Things started slowly, but word soon -after a week or so of occasional visits by my good self- got round that there was 'this character' who, 'if you asked nicely', would 'produce' some choice items 'out of thin air, ha ha...', and he'd give them to you 'for nuthin', if you just left him alone after that. Strangely, the police didn't seem to hear about this, which was well for me. Well, the police in our town were more like the Keystone Cops, and five years on one case was average by all accounts. Anyway, I could breathe easy and I did, enjoying my new role. Decked out in my gear, I'd be happy to oblige most requests, and took it (a) as a way of showing off, (b) the price of being seen as a little different, a mark of specialness, and (c) a funny way to punctuate the evening. The punters hardly knew what to ask for; they'd just say 'anything you like, Mister' and be contented with a copper kettle or a honey jar. Maybe they were more captivated by the magic of it all, which I allowed them to peek, if with a bit of sleight of hand thrown in, just so as not to freak them out entirely. I was a bit of an attraction, and the barman thought of me as a good talisman, a way of ensuring a full crowd most nights. By week three, though, it was becoming a bit ridiculous, not to say *extremely annoying*, with, at one point, two punters arguing with each other about 'whose turn' it was to go up and ask, even though they'd come the night previous and been regaled with some nice cut glassware and a lasso. When I heard them muttering away at my back, I turned round from where I was sitting at the bar, and kind of slid off the stool I had been plunked on for a few idle hours, making sure the heels of my Texas cowboy boots made hard contact with the floor. I then just stared at the offending pair. They appeared to note that my attitude was not especially cheery, indeed, they appeared to note that my demeanour had transformed, slightly but perceptibly, from cheery to obviously less than, and that made them stop still, eyes on me. 'Fellas,' I said, in as drawl-like a manner as I could muster, '...Fellas...' and then, again with a minimum of ostentation, I straightened up my body a tad, positioned my legs squarely into full-support-mode, in a gesture which screamed 'Confrontation!' I dropped my arms down slowly by my sides, elbows slightly bent, my fingers flexing, as though limbering up, until my hands were in a position that could be described as hovering over respective gun handles, stuck into my -they suddenly noticed with some dismay-now unlatched holsters. I let the moment stretch out a minute, my eyes on their eyes, their eyes on my eyes, and occasionally, on my still flexing, floating, hovering fingers, and then said: 'Fellas, just go on home now.' They were two statues by this point: they had somehow processed the possibility that the little replica guns I carried by my sides all this time were not in fact replicas at all, but the real thing, capable of delivering metal bullets through the air at high velocity. Maybe it had been something about the way I had addressed them just now, maybe it had been the posture, maybe a combination. A follow-up sudden shout did the trick: 'GIT!' Within a second of this utterance hitting their ears, they had turned round and made for the door with a speed that was unbecoming. At which point, I again took to my stool. I was never bothered for trinkets again.

What a life it became! And, disturbingly, what a person I was turning into! This 'new me' was taking me to a place I would never have thought remotely possible. It sometimes took me up my treasured hill, but then on past it, to an area of open countryside not much frequented by anyone, and had me do shooting practice. There were always farmers somewhere on the outskirts of our town, so anyone hearing my shots might well have thought it was them, keeping their flocks safe. But, no. It was me, the new me, and I'd materialize jars, and stick them on cut-tree stumps (sorry, Poly, for nicking the display props for the ole pots & pans) which I'd also conjure up, pace back a short distance, and then do a quick draw. Part of it derived from watching the odd video at the library: they didn't have a huge collection, but every scene with guns, and shoot-outs, I'd watch intently, and even rewind and watch again. (I liked *My Darling Clementine*, but *The Hour of the Gun* really got me going, as did *The Left-Handed Gun* -I found myself identifying with Garner's increasingly nasty Wyatt Earp and Newman's wild & wicked Billy the Kid... *Winchester '73* also got my vote!) I had to build up to this shooting lark, of course, but I had a virtually endless variety of targets to shoot at, with no-one telling me I had to go back to the office and fill out reports or type up inventories or meet clients and be polite to them, or any of that rubbish. I was free! I was free to conjure up weapons and fire them all day if I wished. I just didn't see that doing so would have an unseen effect. I didn't see how it would change me.

Not exactly 'trigger-happy', I was 'gun-happy', feeling empowered by what I wore on either side of my body in holsters. I was careful not to let the authorities get wind of things, and always wore a huge raincoat to cover my gear after target practice, but I kind of liked the feeling that I was courting confrontation. It didn't help any that I was sousing myself stupid every night. Mornings were either slept through, or crawled through. One morning in particular illustrates just how far I had gone. I woke up feeling extremely drowsy, still half-drunk, to be honest, but aware, even as I stared upwards at the ceiling that some other presence was occupying the dim-lit room. Peripheral vision informed me there were large figures standing at some remove, standing but not moving, yet, in the shadows, around me... For as long as I could, I remained motionless, vaguely aware that my next move might be my last: intruders had surrounded me. This was the thing I hadn't seen coming with the guns: the paranoia. Someone, I hurriedly surmised, had taken umbrage at my strutting and was hoping to take me down a peg (*oh, for an original phrase!* I lamented). Or, they were just thieves, ready to fleece me of every last exquisite item I could conjure up for them. Diamonds and pearls, to be sold off through the black market. They might even hold me in captivity, where I'd be their golden goose, under pain of a beating unless I complied...

They wouldn't just attack outright, I guessed (my mind concatenated scenarios), there would have to be some vocal interchange, the old verbal to-and-fro to establish what was happening, why, and precisely where the victim would go, the victim being me. Whatever it was they were doing there, their very presence was already an intrusion, an act of violence. They'd soon make their move, be upon me, fists raining down, maybe sticks, iron bars...

I closed my eyes briefly, and concentrated on summoning up two Colt .45s, one for each hand. I'd have to remember this time to insist they were loaded -somehow I could tailor things if I thought about it- and I'd have to be quick. Very. They certainly had the drop on me, as I believe the expression goes. I'd also -thinking at the speed of light now- have to make sure the damn conjured guns didn't do like they might and fly forward out of the space at the end of my hand, disastrously beyond my reach: as well as probably being curtains for me it would look goddamned silly, too. It was a technique I had been working on of late, however, up on the hill: 'summon & grab', I called it, one ultra-fast smooth movement, that I had almost, if not completely, mastered. All that training would certainly have to work now.

A voice within piped up: 'It might not be fists, or sticks, or even iron bars, to contend with...' My fears began to grow exponentially as I lay there, feeling more and more vulnerable, and so fists evolved via sticks and hard iron bars into bullets, the threat of the gun. More than a few 'cowboys' in this part of the world, after all...

I steeled myself, still unmoving, still apparently helpless, but, silently, counting down from ten. Nine, eight, seven. The adrenalin had started pumping before the count, and in the stillness of the morning air, I could feel the blood course through the veiny pathways of my recumbent form. Six, five, four. I was a tiger, statue-like but focused all on one idea, the rather complex operation of a sudden kill, all compassion gone, machine-like now. THREE. I saw the image of my body go forward. TWO. And the guns materializing in each grabbing hand. Fire shooting out. Blood shooting out. ONE. Lights! Action! Shoot! In one fell movement my upper torso rose, arms stretched wide but directed down to where I had sensed my attackers must be, hands greedily but expertly grasping onto the magically-appearing pistols. I saw no less than six -six!- giant forms spaced at regular points all around my bed-area, closer than I had realized, six meaning that even if I managed to shoot three or four with some pretty handy gunplay, I still likely wouldn't survive. But, I'd go down fighting, which, in my gee-ed up vortex of maddening emotional rush, I felt was perfectly OK with me, a millisecond expended on the idea that life was goddamned meaningless anyway. *Blast! Blast! Blast!* That was three, and I'd taken them by complete surprise, and so, *Blast! Blast! Blast!* again. I shot the others pointblank too. What a cacophony then ensued! Instead of groans or screams issuing from the huge forms, rather it was something more like the breaking of glass, the splintering of wood, the inglorious notes of what sounded like long-pent-up springs and coils being released precipitously. And yet, they, my intruders, my potential attackers, did not fall. Still they remained upright, and it was only when the dust settled, and I had, in a growing fright of my own, wondering upon the possibly supernatural horror of what all this might mean, that I had thrown open one of the curtains behind me, Colts still in hand, wisps of smoke rising from their barrels, and turned back again to take it all in.

Light poured in, illuminating the beautiful woodgrain of six very large grandfather clocks, each marked in their upper regions by an obvious ruin of splintered glass, rudely exposed broken wood, and the odd spring caught in a frieze, jumping out in perpetual 3D. I collapsed back on the bed, infinitely relieved to be able to still do so, but nursing the worry that something not entirely wholesome had entered my consciousness. *What if they'd been people?*

In my dreams, as I had done here and not realized it, I would summon up all manner of stuff from Poly's Pots & Pans. I'd then find myself having to navigate through a room chock full of tins of baking powder, barrels of coffee beans, giants cuts of cheese, sharp utensils in bizarre shapes, pots of every size, loaded and unloaded rifles, soap bars, cut glass vases, jewelry in and out of jewel boxes, lengths of hemp, strings of garlic, sheets of leather, cut for boots, ready-made cowboy boots, mountains of hats, rivers of bottles, some broken and spilling their contents over everything, releasing alcoholic vapours into the air, bundles of cigars over here, piles of little chubby Derringers over there... Knives. Gunbelts. Boxes of bullets. Gunpowder stacks. Matches! It was dangerous to dream. But how could I stop? How could I live like this?

Easy. Just sell stuff. Make a mint, and live like a king. Of course it wasn't me who had this bright idea but a girl I'd pegged as a gold-digger from the get-go. With a moniker like 'Ruby' I had to be asking myself from the start if this girl was serious or not. The answer was 'not', certainly about some topics, among them: life, how to earn a steady wage, being responsible, buckling down and getting up every morning at 6, settling down in any form, and, finally, and most elusively vague, love. Of course love comes in many forms, or can be calibrated on a range from almost innocuous interest to downright love-or-death obsession, unless it's just plain fake. Ruby's position on the range was never clear to me until the essentially-wary-of-each-other stage was through. That took some time, but she was the only person to whom I'd now dispense much in the way of Wild West goodies, not counting the barman, with his easily-met mercantile needs. The first chat went something like this:

R: [taking the stool next to mine, at the bar counter] Who do I have to sleep with to get a drink round here?

Me: [taking a glance at the utterer of these words] Moi.

R: You the barman, then?

M: No, but I could provide you with a whole bottle if…

R: It was just an expression!

M: It was just a joke!

R: Well, wearing an outfit like that I'd hardly expect to hear something serious.

M: 'Something serious'.

R: OK, you got me.

M: Just like that?

R: I meant you… What the…? [Ruby mimed exaggerated frustration] Where'd you learn to speak French so well?

M: Moi? Well, I have a gift.

R: [Coyly] For me?

M: A bottle of… Mmmm… I'm wondering what you drink…

R: [Now eyeing me intently, even somewhat mysteriously] Something spiritual…

M: You said it. [with a flick of the right wrist, I conjured up a bottle of 'PURE SPIRIT RYE', otherwise unmarked, which clanked onto the counter] Voilà!

R: Jesus Christ!

M: Not quite, and, well, he only did wine…

R: You really do have a gift after all!

This was the kind of conjuring I enjoyed. It was flattering to my ego, which of course had 'developed', to put it mildly, in recent times. With Ruby, I began to see how I could channel all my cowboy swagger into something fun, without the benefit of sloshing myself into insensibility. I did think, once she realized the power at my fingertips, that she was a kind of gold-digger, but I wasn't especially worried. I had the power to summon up whatever I wanted, to exhaust a whole day's stock of any of the goods from P.P.P., and not have a care in the world about it, whether used or wasted. But, as illustrated previously, I had little time for spongers and hangers-on. Ruby was also beautiful. This made things different.

Ruby had bobbed auburn hair, a face that would launch a thousand ships, was not taller than me (a relief, after we got off our stools!) and, *pièce de résistance*, had voluminous ruby-red lips. The lass also possessed a perfect hour-glass figure, which I did my best not be caught sizing up. She was everything I had ever thought of as the perfect woman/girl. And, we hit it off, as perhaps the unofficial transcript above suggests we might. Neither of us spoke proper French, but we managed to communicate in broken everything else. I eventually got round to gently, banteringly, berating her for her opening words, which I suggested 'gave the impression of a loose woman'. I should have been prepared for her response: 'Loose woman? *Moi?*' I wasn't prepared either for her way of dealing with the particularity of my situation. 'My friend claims she is able to have physical messages imprinted onto the shells of chicken eggs. Her husband's a farmer... The world's a weird place.' We talked about it a little. 'You mean she can imagine some message and then that would appear on the shell of the chicken egg? Like what kind of message?' Ruby looked down, as though attempting to recall the precise details, and then, her head coming up abruptly: 'You know, I never thought to ask her!' After a pause of about five seconds (could have been longer) in which we just looked at each other, or our eyes locked together, and our bodies remained completely motionless, safely on respective stools, we suddenly exploded in mutual hilarity, hands out from both her and me, pawing the air between us, as though in mime of what we might get up to if we were ever closer.

The peculiarity of my chosen exterior persona was both a plus and a minus: looking like a cowboy in a small town like this where no one looked like a cowboy was somehow attractive to her, and yet it was also a barrier, because it suggested our worlds were different. I put her right with a quick summary of events, telling her, and feeling so relieved to be able to do so, that I was more sinned against than sinning, and that I had never thought or hoped for any of this, and was still just wondering what the hell the point of it all was, and precisely where I was headed. 'Precisely', what a horrible word, and yet one I was seemingly addicted to: I had no idea where I might be 'precisely' headed, or even remotely, vaguely, mistily, general-directionally. Ruby, thankfully, cottoned on to the nub: I was adrift on a sea the like of which no one had ever encountered before. It extended as far as the eye could see in all directions, and... it didn't even have a name, unless it was called The Poly Ocean, or Oceanus Polyanus, or The PPP Sea, we mused, staring into our respective glasses, enjoying the capricious nature of our talk. I'd punctuate that with the odd manifestation of some item I deemed to be attractive to her. The first was a 'snood', a kind of ancient hair-net. 'Not really my taste,' she said gently, 'but I've never tried one on, to be honest.' 'It's from a poem,' I flubbed, not quite sure why I'd suddenly conjured that up. 'I've never seen one before, myself.' 'Well, then, how could you just... "get" it...?' That, I had to admit, was mysterious even to me. It was usually an image I concentrated on. Here, I had thought of a word, and Voilà! it had appeared. I kept things simple after that, and there's nothing much simpler than a real, honest to goodness, down home, large as life, 'trinket'. Well, OK, a trinket in the shape of a pewter bracelet, with little twirls, looking like the fronds of some plant left to grow itself stupid for a decade or two, carved into the surface. It clattered onto the counter. A moment's silence. Ruby reached out her right hand, picked it up gingerly, and examined it, with a look someway between wonder and befuddlement, holding it beside her wrist as though to imagine wearing it. 'Not really my taste,' she concluded, again, in gentle tones. I took a sup of my beer, ordered another, and then closed my eyes and thought real hard. Silver, I thought. Silver. Who could resist the allure of silver? Flick of the wrist: out shot a number of large silver coins, some spilling down into the barman's area, some crashing against the side of Ruby's glass. 'Silver! There you go!' Ruby, wide-eyed, and looking suddenly brilliantly illuminated, exclaimed: 'Now that's more like it!' reaching over and giving my shoulder a generous slap. I knew from that moment that I had gotten myself into dangerous territory, but the smile on her flashing red lips made it perfectly OK with me. OK that what made her happy was good old fashioned materialism.

So, there was a period of true gold (or silver) digging, where she'd come into the bar, we'd have our little chat about anything under the sun, I'd summon up whatever took her fancy, and then she'd leave, sometimes loaded down with the goodies: from the second time, she brought her own sturdy and capacious bag… I knew I was being fleeced, but she was always very nice about it, and there was always the prospect that it might lead to something. After some time I wondered, however, if I could go on like this, and thought about just calling it a day. She was only interested in what goodies came out from my fingertips, after all. I was wrong. At the end of the third week of 'Ruby and me', at the latest hour on a Saturday night, things were about to change. I was sat, solitary and somewhat morosely staring into the array of bottles behind the bar, wondering if I was drunk enough to go home. Just as I was coming to accept that 'Ruby and me' was defunct, I was suddenly treated to another of those precipitous and generous slaps on the shoulder. It was with great relief to see that it was in fact Ruby doing the slapping, not the old friend from grammar school I'd met up with all those weeks ago in a different watering hole. Yet, I soon allowed my natural smile to succumb to a facial expression more in keeping with my now decidedly negative view of this auburn bombshell. 'Hey, don't look like that! You could kill me with a look like that!' she exclaimed, sitting herself down on the adjacent stool -which, I only now noticed, was strangely always vacant, as though no-one was ever interested in getting too close to me. And before I could say anything, she slapped her hand down again, but this time onto the counter space between us. Only when I looked carefully could I see paper under her palm. It was Ruby's turn to say 'Voilà!', following that up with, 'You're not the only one who can conjure something out of nothing!' Retracting her palm, I slowly -trying not to show too much enthusiasm- reached out and turned over the thin crinkly paper. It was some kind of receipt or invoice or something like that. I studied the only detail that mattered and then put it into words: 'Five thousand four hundred and fifty one pounds?' I then stared at her, eyes expressing something like horror, the horror of thinking this was what she needed from me. 'Now, don't you look at me like that, Mr Conjuring Cowboy. That is what *I made* from all that junk you conjured up.' 'Junk?' I asked, feeling a little hurt. 'Junk. Goods. Sellable goods. Desirable items, you name it. You're wasting your time, Buster!' My confusion was reaching breaking point, I had no idea of how to answer, but the word 'made' was nagging at me. Ruby fixed me with a stare I'll never forget, shorn of all bubbliness, as though this had now become serious business, and said, with molasses-slow deliberateness (to either imprint the idea or just to put me into a trance): 'Open... a... shop... Open... a... shop...' *Open a shop?* my mind repeated dully. *Open a shop?* By the look on Ruby's face, one that was transforming back into its usual radiant self, it was clear, even before it was clear to me, that something was happening inside that dull chamber between my ears. 'Open a shop?' I repeated. 'Open a shop?' 'Yes, dammit!' Ruby jumped in: 'Open a goddamned shop, why don't you?' There and then began the next stage in the course of my magical career. We would… open a shop!

Actually, we didn't just open a shop but also… a relationship. Unlike before, when it was time for me to call it a night there and we'd break up, many hours after this, for the first time, Ruby accompanied me. We were both fairly gone, it being nearly four in the morning, so it wasn't entirely surprising when chit turned to chat, push turned to shove, and touch turned to hold, and hold turned to hug. How that then turned into a tussle I can't quite remember, but tussle we did, back and forth, through the various lanes and back streets that lined the way back to my place. It was a veritable fight, indeed, where lips and the undersides of fingers rather than clenched fists became the tools of our mutual attacks. Plenty of grabbing lapels and throwing one another back onto walls and shop-shutters or whatever was there, too. I gave as good as I got. I acquitted myself well. We only quietened down close to my apartment block, erring on the side of caution, taking every precaution to avoid raising the attention of any sleeping souls inside, most especially my landlady, who was, nevertheless, fairly accustomed to hearing some pretty strange things emanate from my room, including small caliber gunshots (the incident with the grandfather clocks had happened in another place and had resulted in immediate expulsion, and the bribing of the landlord -with diamonds and gold- not to tell the police). This was all sadly complicated by the needless dropping of my keys into a drain, which, only through some heavy lifting and probing about in the depths, put a dampener on things. After a tiptoed entry to 'my place', however, and some pretty rigorous washing of hands, insisted upon (!) by Ruby, I could look forward to a tryst with the girl of my dreams. Pity she was conked out when I'd finished, enjoying her own dreams of God knows what, sweety mice and wee buns for all I knew. I slept on the sofa, feeling sadly saintly, but, also, strangely happily exhausted.

A physical shop was out of the question: 'I'd become a clone of Poly...' Eventually Ruby saw my point of view, and the danger it would attract. The mob boys would be round within a week of opening, looking for their 'cut'. Then there was the problem of how to stop pilfering, shoplifting. Could we really be ready to get into all that? It ain't like the old days, I argued, when people could be trusted to wander into a commercial establishment, take a polite look around, perhaps pass the time with the shop owner on topics unrelated to the goods, or for those with a little knowledge, entering into an exchange on the particular quality of the items on show, buy something, or not, and then leave. No, these days the shop owner needed to be 'vigilant'. None of this 'Howdy!' greeting stuff (the extent to which I was relying on Americanisms of late was shocking) was needed anymore either. Indeed, according to some schools of thought, I lectured on, it was better not to 'engage your customer' in any way until there was 'the strong possibility of a purchase'. People these days wanted to be 'left alone', and 'not hassled as soon as they entered'. And yet the shopkeeper had to keep his or her beady eye on them the whole time. Owning a shop now required a healthy meanness, in order to ensure relief from theft and general bad behaviour. I wasn't really into that. I didn't know where I had suddenly dredged up all these ideas from: they just came out naturally, but convincingly enough. Anyway, the idea of a mail-order shop seemed mighty attractive to the both of us. Or maybe just to Ruby.

I don't like to spoil people's enjoyment of a good yarn, but I could see this going the same way as the charity kick, if in a slightly different direction: down, down, and then take a left turn and go down a little more. (And, anyway, this was supposed to be just a summary of events, right?) There was no reason for it not to work, of course: the number of people interested in Old West goods, whether or not they believed them to be genuine, was staggering. Just using a simple P.O. Box, Ruby set up a system that worked like a dream. After getting out the publicity, orders came flooding in: for cowboy boots, hats, denims, spurs, lasso rope, flashily-stitched long-sleeved shirts, and other innocuous items. We hadn't advertised guns, though, and that was where the real money lay. 'I can go as far as Bowie knives,' I told Ruby, 'but, count me out with the ole death-dealers on a wide scale. Anyway, you need licenses... No, I'm pretty sure it's against the law, that's it.' 'But,' argued Ruby, 'if we advertise for buyers in specialized magazines, antique-hunters would buy just about everything you got. They're not crazies...' In the early days, we would wrangle over issues like this a lot; the best part was it usually led to a physical wrangle. We couldn't forget we were now a fully-functioning couple! Every morning, now that we had moved into an apartment which accommodated couples, with no questions asked, the sun came in through the curtains bathing us in a radiance that matched our mutual feelings of joy in each other and our general bodily entanglement, blah blah blah. And by the time we had finished breakfast, it was now a blinding glare that matched the sense that this was all a bit too much too soon, and what the hell were we doing anyway? 'How can you just conjure stuff up out of thin air?' asked Ruby one time, a few weeks into the enterprise, as though she had never thought about that before. 'You got me there, Rubes. You got me there,' responded her similarly befuddled co-conspirator. And, again like an afterthought, Rubes said, in a voice so small it almost wasn't there, and so, I thought, didn't warrant an answer: '"Buster." I'm always calling you

"Buster"… Is that your real name or what?'

The routine was annoying. Collect the orders from the P.O. Box. Bring them back, open them, look at them in their tens, or hundreds even. Then, carefully putting aside the cheques and bank orders inside, I'd set about conjuring up each piece, which Ruby would then wrap in diligently prepared wrapping paper, and then address on diligently prepared seals. Conjuring seemed to be the easy part; certainly, I didn't envy Ruby with all that office-like efficiency, but it was also tiring, and beyond tiring, it was soul-destroying. Yes, soul-destroying because it seemed, again like the charity thing, a very strange thing to be doing with the amazing gift I had been given. And yet Ruby seemed delighted with things, and so I didn't want to break her vision of this being a meaningful, worthwhile and lucrative enterprise. Of course, it could be classified as 'lucrative', but as for 'meaningful' and 'worthwhile', well, I was beginning to have my doubts. And when there are unspoken doubts within a close relationship the possibility of things ending in tears goes up, another gem of wisdom I'd acquired from God knows where. It started with me having short whiskey or bourbon breaks between the conjuring, even in the afternoon. It was my way of dealing with the workload, I'd say, but it was actually my way of retreating from the responsibility of communicating what I wanted to say. Yet, booze had always been a part of our communications from the start, so it didn't seem to be a problem for Ruby, until things got out of hand.

When I drank too much, like when I dreamed too much, I'd sometimes conjure up all manner of 'junk', even if some of that 'junk' was high class goods. But when your living space starts to fill up with goods, whether they cost a dollar or one hundred a piece, you're still going to flip out now and again. This began to happen now and again, and then more and more frequently, until, a few weeks into our crazy money-making madness, it was just becoming nuts. The ole pots and pans came back with a vengeance. One time, after Ruby had come back from the post office, she had trouble opening the door. 'Let me in, what's going on? Let me in!' She was convinced I was blocking the door deliberately, but that wasn't so. It was rather that my gift had, quite literally, gotten out of hand, and spilled masses upon masses of goods all over the place. There were layers upon layers upon layers of some of the greatest items ever produced by the Wild West built up to a height over my head when standing. The smell of leather was almost over-powering, and whatever sounds happened to be made, especially the sound of raised voices, would be resonated and echoed by all the tin and pewter containers everywhere. Then, with a sudden crash or two, the pungent smell of whiskey, released from freshly broken bottles, would pervade the room, making it difficult for me to draw breath. Meanwhile, I was steadily becoming half-unconscious somewhere in one of the corners, half-insensible, and becoming more and more immobile as, madly, I continued to produce item after item after item from my -by now reddening- fingertips. Yes, that's what happened when I really got into my game: the tingling sensation was accompanied by an actual reddening, even a slight inflammation, of the ole magic fingertips. I was the victim of a gift that wouldn't stop giving and wouldn't stop zapping the goddamned lifeblood out of me! Midas, with a twist.

This particular drama was resolved by massive exterior assistance in the form of members of the local fire station using all manner of long-handled hooks and ropes, and battery-operated cutting gear, to remove the door, dis-encumber the doorway, and then, as fast as they could, the room, until they could make a path toward me. I was by that stage no longer half but completely insensible and so everything I know about the rescue comes second-hand. Insensible, but, they told me later, singing. 'What was I singing?' I later asked a nurse at the local hospital, apparently more intent upon that than on any other considerations. She had no idea, nor had she any idea why I had to be extricated from an apartment room with electric saws, hooks and ropes. Ruby, on the pretext of giving me a comforting kiss, had earlier drawn close to me, just as I was coming round, and insisted -*sotto voce*- that we say we were artists, and had planned to create an 'installation' based upon the Old West, and we hadn't realized quite how many items we had amassed. That we had 'stacked them up' but they 'had fallen down', causing the chaos. She had looked pretty concerned, and so I went along with her story, even though, when she told me it, I had little idea of why we had to make anything up. Of course I was still half-blitzed. It took a few minutes for me to begin to recall the incident, and then, like a bell ringing in the distance which you didn't realize was a bell ringing in the distance, but then gradually do, I recalled the whole wider situation in which I had now been embroiled in for the best part of two months… As I did so, recall, that is, I also had to face a few members of the rescue team who had called to ask if I was OK, and one or two policemen, who were beginning to get round to asking me what had been the cause of all this, and, 'incidentally, why are you dressed up in a cowboy costume?' Very cleverly, I stared them out, with the look of man who has been through a great ordeal and can only just look out at the world with idiot-staring eyes, doing my best to look like a little lamb. The best policy was not to say a bloody word. Thankfully it worked, and they all left.

I did my best to be 'normal' and get back into the swing of things, for Ruby's sake, or just for the joy of seeing her smile, but it was never on the cards. One night, in my dreaming state, I had suddenly, unbeknownst to myself, flung my arms out, probably because I thought I was being chased by a bear or something much worse, and had released a brace of very sharp knives, very probably in fast succession. This, or the fact that we had both over-imbibed the night before, explains why neither of us had woken up at that time. Rather, we awoke the next morning peering into the dim light all around us and wondering why there seemed to be mysterious 'things' sticking out of the walls surrounding our bed area. What were they, and how had they come to be there? Ruby, upon closer inspection, and no doubt in the throes of something like shock, screamed with realization: 'Knives! You threw knives all around you as you slept!' At this point she screamed even more intensely and went into a bout of hysterics, rushing out of the bedroom and escaping into the bathroom. This woke me up. It woke me up to the fact that I was getting dangerous, a fact Ruby had no trouble comprehending. But, once she calmed down, she was very nice about it. 'OK,' she told me straight after we'd had a chat. 'I'll move out, but I still like you.' That seemed fair, especially when she told me we were still on as a couple, and this was just a stop-gap measure until I got things sorted out. We continued with the business for a few weeks more, and I was on a strict ration of only non-alcoholic drinks. I accepted everything, feeling only relief I hadn't completely messed things up between us. Yet, I knew the 'until I got things sorted out' part was integral to any real future. Somehow, however, we never really found the time to discuss such matters in any depth, until one day, a Sunday, which, both of us being Christian-reared, but never probing beyond that, we kept work-free. It would be an unexpectedly important chat.

We'd come up to my 'sanctuary' of old, the top of the hill, where we often now came together. To get away from it all, to stretch our legs, to take in the view, to grab a little piece of heaven and other clichéd phrases that summon up the purpose and the joy of getting up there. I'd been thinking about my singing, and had done a bit of checking before I left the hospital those few weeks back. Apparently, it had been some old Blues song, or possibly jazz, but no-one could be really sure. 'So, Rubes,' I said, after we'd enjoyed a relaxing few minutes on our respective benches, listening to the distant hum and occasional clanking of the town below, 'what kind of a person doesn't know the Blues?' Because there was no immediate answer forthcoming I moved swiftly onto the next, related, conundrum: 'What sort of a person's never heard of jazz?' Of course, I was thinking about the one and only Paul Clarence Rhumboldt Esquire, seller of pots, pans and various sundries.

Ruby: Are you sure about that? That he didn't know that music.

Me: Yeah, as sure as I am about any of this. It was like he thought I was crazy.

R: Really? [with a sly smile]

M: Really. [noticing the smile] OK. But, you know, I wanted to get back to that and check why he was like that, but for some reason we couldn't, or didn't... go back to that topic, that is. The rest of our time together was spent 'moseying around' the shop, which, I can tell you, was really huge... cavernous...

R: Well, maybe... maybe... [Ruby hesitated, as though to say what she was going to say would be of little use, or just plain silly] ...maybe he had actually never *heard* such kind of music...

M: Well, of course, but why? Hit me with another 'maybe', baby...

R: ...because he was a real nineteenth century person? And it hadn't been invented yet?

M: [stunned silence]

R: [questioning silence]

M: [continued stunned silence]

R: [the-tightening-of-eyebrows kind of silence]

M: [the-calm-before-the-storm kind of silence]

R: ...you know what I mean?

M: Know what you mean? Know what you mean? You better believe I know what you mean! Of course, I know what you mean! [I had jumped up from the bench and was now hopping excitedly from foot to foot, until, with as much force as I could possibly throw into the action, I brought my two palms together in one enormous CLAP!] I'm so stupid!

R: [polite silence]

M: I'm so stupid! So stupid! I'm so stupid... and so happy!

R: [uncomfortable silence]

M: If I had a dollar for every stupid thing I'd ever done in my life, or even just recently, I'd be the richest man in this town.

R: Darlin', you probably are the richest man in this town!

M: You see, I told you I was stupid!

Right there and then, it was the beginning of the end. Ruby was surprised when I became suddenly quiet after this and sat down beside her on her bench, holding her hand in mine. I told her I couldn't do the business anymore. I told her I wasn't given this gift in order to help the world through charity, and that I wasn't given this gift in order to help myself become the richest man in town either. In fact, I told her it wasn't a gift at all. It was a curse. It was a curse, and I was destined to be destroyed by it. 'Look at our life,' I intoned, 'how could anyone live like this. Before you know it, I could be dead, if not through doing all this drinking, then through releasing some deadly weapon from my fingertips and killing some unfortunate innocent soul... like you, Rubes. Then, I'd die from the remorse... or the misery of a prison term would seriously curtail my longevity.' I inclined my head and bent forward, so that my head leant upon her chest. She reciprocated by putting her arms around me and then holding me ever tighter. I began to sob, but, I then realized, I still wanted to speak. Emotionally, I was building up to some transformational moment. Somewhat awkwardly, I opened my mouth and began to say what I felt was, or should have been received as, a momentous statement, and yet Ruby, no doubt feeling suddenly maternal, now began to stroke my hair (I wasn't wearing cowboy gear or hat) and to tell me 'it's alright, it's alright' in a soothing manner. I felt like a child, locked into an embrace I couldn't easily break out of. This was doubly frustrating because I liked being soothed in this way (who wouldn't?) and yet was growing impatient that my 'momentous' words had not been heard. Plus, it was getting quite warm down there, and my face was actually beginning to sweat. I could take no more: precipitously I arched back and broke free of maternal incarceration, now running a free hand over my face to smooth out the moisture on my cheeks and, furtively, inside my nose. With more than a touch of the amateur dramatics, I declared: 'I *have* to go back! I *have* to find Poly! I *have* to return his goddamned magic gift!'

I'd finally figured it all out. It was a simple application of memory and reason: the street with its strange olde worlde buildings, the children wearing hundred-plus-year-old fashion, playing with a hoop, and Poly, straight out of a Frontier town, unaware of the Blues revolution and of Jazz. He was probably unaware of just about everything that had ever occurred in the twentieth century, with his various goods 'selling' at nineteenth century prices, and the take-it-or-leave-it unforced insistence that this was a shop not a museum. These had all meant only one thing, which I saw now as incontestable: somehow Mr Paul E. Clarence Rhumboldt existed, with his store, and its environs, in the *real* nineteenth century, not in the twentieth. I had stepped over the threshold into his time, and place -America!- when I went in search of the person who had put out that ad in the paper. *How could that be?* Oh, what a question! Well, considering the bizarre nature of the gift given to me, to be able to materialize goods from that store out of my fingertips with a simple flick of the wrist, accepting that a nineteenth century American universe existed adjacent to the twentieth century Irish one I'd been brought up in wasn't such a hard cookie to swallow. In fact it was so crazy, it made perfect sense. I blurted all this out to my interlocutor and waited to see what she would say.

Now it was Ruby's turn to become serious. She also got up from her bench, but slowly, her eyes possessing a faraway look, which, after a moment or two, became an actual faraway look out into the scenery stretched out down below. I was aware that she must be mulling it all over, but when I looked, it seemed clear she was looking out not casually but rather intently, out there into the distance, to the left. 'Rubes,' I said, becoming all soft, as though a prelude to some comforting words of my own, or even incipient hugging. 'Rubes…' 'Shush!' shushed Rubes. I was a little confused, and confused further by her seeming insistence on scanning the horizon. After a moment, I chanced: 'Ruby, what are you looking at?' 'Where did you say Poly's shop was?' she interrogated me. 'Poly's shop? Near some place called Curtis Street…' I stammered. 'Yes, I know that, but… where's that?' she snapped. This had me scratching my head. After a moment, accompanied by a very wide and therefore vague gesture out over the landscape: 'Way… over there…' 'No, dummy, *where* over there?' exclaimed Ruby roughly, indicating the wide sweep of land before us. 'Where "Way out there"?' I'd never thought of thinking such a thing before, but (subsuming the 'dummy' reference as meant affectionately), after a quick mental calculation, never my strong-point, and consulting a nearby plaque on which were engraved directions to famous landmarks, I came back to where Ruby was standing and said, pointing westward: 'Mmm… in *that* general direction.'

So, we looked *in that general direction*. We looked and we looked and we looked. I looked intently out in that general direction because Ruby was looking very intently in that general direction, and continued looking until our eyes became used to looking out into the haze and became used to studying the distance, so that, after a long few moments, it became familiar territory, an area beyond the limits of the town. 'What are we looking for?' I asked Ruby gingerly, but she would not answer. So, I continued to look, in parallel to the auburn-haired girl at my side. After a few minutes, she finally asked: 'Don't you think that looks a bit strange? The brown part.' I had to concur that, in comparison with the usual green beyond the boundaries of the town, brown seemed a little odd (Emerald Isle and all that...). 'It's such a big expanse...' 'Yes,' I agreed, 'now that you mention it. It does seem rather ex..pan..sive...' 'Conjure up some sort of telescope, can you do that?' 'I can try.' So, I did. I thought about it real hard, even closed my eyes and clenched the fingers of one hand, as though that might help, and, Hey Presto! a nineteenth century telescope, or 'Nautical Spyglass' as the still-attached tag announced, appeared out of nowhere. Ruby caught it as it flew out, and saved it from flying down the hill. After fiddling about with it, twisting the smooth leather-covered main cylinder and then learning that you had to slide out the other brass tubes and twist once again to tighten, Ruby then raised the small end to her eye. After a moment or two of fixing the focus, not without the odd grumble seeping out, she scanned long and deep, as though on the verge of discovery. With a shriek of delight, she passed it to me, and I did exactly as she'd done, no more and no less. And then I saw it too.

Out, way out in the distance westward, beyond the limit of the town, beyond the general area where Poly's store had to be, down on the brown plain, I could just make out what it was Ruby had been watching: a cloud of dust growing like a line just above the surface of the dun-coloured earth. Its cause? Its cause was a furious flurry of legs under a bulbous long body, the shape complicated further still by the presence of a perpendicular two-legged body rising in the middle, a be-hatted figure, elbows working like pistons, the whole shape powering away as though one: horse and rider as one. To the left and the right, dotted here, there and everywhere, cacti the size of small houses, the odd scattered skeleton, too, of some long-dead giant beasts, and even, yes, even an abandoned covered wagon, as though maundering about further off, its torn canvas being blown about by the wind. A barren and dusty land we had found, unforgiving and bone-dry, but rich with it, too. Rich beyond dreams.

We had struck gold.

CHAPTER THREE

I had done a little supplementary reading in the library, attempting to fill out the grey areas of my knowledge, which were many and huge. The phrase 'Gone fishing' rarely had anything to do with fishing, I read. It was a term that went back a hundred years or so, and it was hung on shopkeepers' doors or windows to indicate that business was off for the day, and/or no-one was there to help with enquiries. Only later had it come to mean things like 'completely unaware of one's surroundings', 'daydreaming', 'mentally vacant' etc.. The first could definitely apply to Poly, in his nineteenth century store, unaware that the twentieth century existed a few minutes' walk away, and the second and third to me, as just a general way of being. Indeed, considering my inability to join up the dots, 'mentally vacant' pretty much hit the bullseye, too. If the whole of my recent history felt like a dream to me, now bordering on nightmare, it was one I now needed to wake up from. Ruby and I had talked about this and the need to 'put things right', but neither of us could really define what that meant, beyond returning my 'gift', or 'curse', and getting back to 'normality'. I felt this would be the best thing to do, but still retained a worry that 'normality' might be just as unpleasant an option. Ruby, never a great lover of normality herself, had, however, by this time, begun to believe it was the only thing that might save me, and us, and that even if it meant a life of complete boredom, it would be 'better than waking up with a Bowie knife sticking out of your head'. She was actually referring to her own head, of course, it being more likely for that to happen than for it to happen to myself (if you think about the physics of it...). It was a sobering image, and a sobering time. I had no idea what I would find 'out there', wandering around in 'Wild West World', but I knew I had to find Poly, and had to see how I could bring all this madness to an end. And, I knew I had to do it by myself. So, with all the sobriety I could muster, and not a little liking for the ole drama thing, I held Ruby in my arms and did my big farewell scene. I argued that it was better for me to go alone because it was better to preserve the conditions upon which I had first met Poly, but actually I didn't want her to come because of some presentiment of danger, which I wasn't going to share. This was all crystallized into the old mainstay in situations like this: 'A man's gotta do what a man's gotta do'.

So, off I went. I wore civvies, again because I thought I needed to keep to the way I had looked when meeting Poly first, and also because wearing cowboy gear as I traversed the town, including a ride on the No.7 bus, would bring unwanted attention, possibly even from the police, who, I suspected, must be still on the look for my Wild West persona. As for those civvies, some ancient impulse had led me to recover the old ones I'd ditched that night of my first transformation. I didn't like to throw stuff away, and I tended to wear clothes until they were threadbare, a trait I attribute to my father's education on the need to appreciate what you've got, especially when you don't have much, or something along those lines. As I turned into the little street off the long curving street of terraced housing, I began to wonder what lay ahead, and also to mull over recent momentous events in my life. At the back of it all lurked the questions 'Why?' and 'Why me?', but, being as yet unanswerable, remained in the shadows as my mind dealt with other niggling points. When I had entered that pub, kitted out as a cowboy, what was I doing attempting to shoot in the air with my pistols? Didn't I know bullets could have actually flown out, crashed through the ceiling and shot someone upstairs? Had I thought about that at that time? Looking back on that moment, it was a blessing the guns were empty. Had drink alone been the factor influencing me, or was it something more sinister, an absence of reason, or even care for others, playing up the role of the Western gunman? Look at my behaviour, I now reflected, in the other bar, sliding off the stool and facing the two spongers, hands floating over the gun handles. Had I really been about to unholster my 'irons' and shoot up the floorboards, make them dance a bit, or worse? Where had that sudden impulse come from, I wondered? Then, with the grandfather clocks! I had been murder-bound there for sure... Nothing under the sun would have made me behave any differently, I knew it. I'd felt the ole Darwinian survival instinct rise in my blood (apologies to Wallace!), with no space for delicacies like compassion, or doubt, to upset the outcome. Thank God they just been constructions of wood, glass and metal! Had they been men, even 'bad' ones, how could I have lived after that? I wasn't thinking about prison, I was thinking about living with the idea that I could have killed other human beings, and killed them in cold-blood, unerring in my actions, like a machine.

Come to think of it, without having killed anyone -yet- I could now see what I suspected Ruby could see only too well: this power, and this new-found persona, had transformed me from a human operating as most humans do, with compassion and care for their fellow man (stated as an optimist, of course), to this man with a hole in his heart, a gap, a broken window through which flowed a different strain of air, the cold, frigid air of survival-at-all-costs. From this perspective, the world looked a little bit different, and people looked a little less important. Death stood a little bit closer to everyone and everything, and time flattened out. It was less like walking up an incline, from the past to the future, where the effort required to advance is happily accepted, and more like a road pleasantly flat and untiring. There were tree stumps along the road now and again, where you could sit down for a while and just look at the dust and shrubs or wait for the occasional magical appearance of a fox or a raccoon, no need to hurry (into the future) and no need to worry (about the past). Life was just now. You could see every grain of that dust, appreciate every glint off the sheen of the raccoon's coat. And if someone got in your way, well, if they were of a tiresome nature, and wanted to give you some grief, well, you could just pull out your gun, and plug them to death. No! No! No! Was I to become such a man? Such were my thoughts as I spied the protruding tin sign that announced Poly's Pots & Pans.

As expected, the little roughly-written note declaring 'Gone Fishin' was still hanging obediently from the door handle, of the door which was firmly closed. Once again, I found myself impressed by the look of this portal into that rarefied world, with its elegant etched-out lettering and its elegant wood frame. There was nothing too fine for ole Poly, I concluded, memories of the store's interior floating back all too vividly, now that they were so near and yet so far. I tried the handle once more, but it was solidly unbudgeable. I crabwalked to the right and peered in through the lines in the lettering on the main window, past which I had walked on my way to the room with all the soaps and lotions, straining my eyes in the process, seeing nothing but black. So, I knocked on the window glass, and when that didn't work, I knocked on the door glass, and then on the door frame, hoping to satisfy myself I was making enough noise to waken the dead. No dead appearing, or living either, I checked at the boundaries of the store on each side, but there was no give, as it was a piece with its neighbouring buildings. Alas, said the man with a sigh, alas. Yet, now I had given my best to the task at hand, there was something that niggled: that hand-written sign. Poly wrote in a beautiful hand; I could see that in all of the little information cards he had penned all over the shop. Fine copperplate, not like this scrawl. Shopkeepers are proud buzzards at the best of times, obsessively cleaning the floor, even, or especially, the space right outside, where customers would linger, wondering if they'd come in or not. A bit of dirt here and there could turn someone away, especially someone with money. So even a little sign such as this did its part, saying 'I'm terribly sorry, ladies and gentlemen, we're closed at the moment, but will be back soon.' This excuse for a note, however, said something more like: 'Out. Hard bloody luck!' *Ipso facto*, I thought, Poly couldn't have written this note!

This was a 'lead', as they call them, a way forward, if only a step. You can tell a lot about a person from their handwriting, and that was what I was doing now. My feeble attempt at graphology, however, gave rise to a vision no doubt far from the truth of the matter: a rough beast of a man had executed this, or a little'un, but a rough being anyway, maybe carrying a gun. Or, as my muse expanded, I suspected the person who wrote this was only part of the picture, that there was a veritable party of thugs. The writer had scrawled this as an afterthought, upon the group's hurried advice, to stop people from prying too hard. Poly, arrested by thugs, outlaws (!), and then dragged away! Was that where my vision was leading me? Or was it just the product of an over-worked imagination with little to go on but thin air. Of course, thin air was something I was very familiar with… Well, I had come to explore, to see what I could see, and if this particular spot was to be a dead-end, then it was no place to stop, as, for the moment, it was no place to shop. I had to boldly, fully, step over the threshold of this nineteenth century world, well past Poly's shop, and out into the… Wild, Wild West? Very probably, if our eyes hadn't been deceiving us, ole Ruby and I, up there on the hill peering into the distance through that lovely brass spyglass. Horse and rider and wagon and glorious dust everywhere. Even the odd giant tumbleweed rolling this way and that in the wind. Cacti here and there, standing like guardians, with nothing to guard. What a sight it had been! And then, after the hollering had died down, our eager but inevitably empty speculations started on how it could be that our worlds dwelt in parallel…

But now I had to move on. So, I did, taking life in my stride, adding a slight bounce to my step as I went. It was the confidence of a man who knows nothing and therefore fears little. Gradually, the street began to alter as I made further progress, and I took all these changes in with a growing sense of wonderment. The surface of the street, a kind of compacted dirt track, began to grow dustier and dirtier the longer I walked, the occasional debris scattered here and there. Sometimes, to my surprise -and unexpected delight-, piles of something looking remarkably like the droppings of a large animal, too. The façades of buildings on both sides began to acquire ever more variation in their surface appearance, and the boldness of their construction. No longer did the side of the street I was walking on follow a smooth uniform line: now some buildings were sticking out, pillared porches appearing here and there, platforms now becoming a feature, until, after a few minutes' progress, it seemed to have become standard to have a raised wooden walkway outside each building. I was walking on a boardwalk when before it had been a stone pavement. There would be, however, side-streets opening up on this side and the one opposite, and I'd step off the boards and shuffle through the dirt to get to the next block of buildings. Side-streets! Aplenty! This was becoming a long journey, and a big town.

With the now very noticeable widening of the street, my sense of space blossomed out, and up. Suddenly the cloud-punctuated blue sky attracted the eye as never before: it was expansive, a deep crystal blue, and simply beautiful! Looking up one time, however, I got an eyeful of that giant burning orb in space, precipitously popping out of a coven of bright-white clouds. The glare momentarily blinded me, so, as I brought my gaze down to street-level, at first I was sure the shapes now moving throughout the vista were spots on my retina... And yet, they continued to move... and coalesce into more solid shapes just up ahead, shapes looking suspiciously human at that. After rubbing my eyes and passing -and even lightly slapping- both palms over my face, I stood stock still and stared. There were humans indeed! And horses, and wagons, and dogs! *Oh my!*

A be-hatted and very elegant-looking gentleman, in what appeared to be his Sunday best, a natty pin-striped suit, strolled not a few yards from me, crossing the street. He was aided in his gait by a walking stick, which, however, he handled with a kind of panache, suggesting a younger rather than an older man (hint of déjà vu there...). Not wishing to be seen to be staring I just caught sight of his mustachioed face and then looked away. He hadn't noticed me. Now my gaze fell upon a lady, stood on the other side of the street, the rear of her dress billowing out in great style. She then opened a kind of umbrella or small parasol, even though she was under the porch of a building. I wondered why she needed such as she was already wearing a kind of hat, or some arrangement with a bow. Her shoulders, or rather the cloth enclosing them, I then noted, ballooned out and up, and seemed a very strange fashion indeed. Then noticing a few stacked boxes or trunks behind where she stood, I guessed she must be waiting for the... stagecoach! The realization hit me with force: I was in an Old West town, experiencing the nineteenth century up close and personal! Was I? Or was this some *grande illusion* I was suffering from? Before I could think more on that, my eye caught the movements of another lady, less elegant, and decidedly more rotund, ambling down the opposite side of the street from where I was, carrying a basket covered with cloth. What was inside, I suddenly wondered. Something home-cooked? Cakes or some bread? I was so close now I almost felt like stepping over and asking her straight, or seeing if my olfactory sense might answer my query instead. She didn't look at me. Nor, come to think of it, did the gentleman with the walking stick. Was I just dreaming I was here? Was I invisible? Yet, not only my eyes, but my nose told me no. Intermittent wafts of horsedung, and worse, seemed to gently insist I was here, too. As did the backdrop of sound: heels thudding wood, the odd snatch of talk, the whinny of horses (yes, there were horses further away, tied to posts on either side of the street), the barking of dogs, the faint tinkling of a piano, precipitous bursts of laughter coming in on the breeze...

I was beginning to think I must indeed be invisible. That I didn't exist for them, only *they* existed for *me*. This curious idea took hold for a moment and allowed me to be so bold as to close my eyes, to stand stock-still, and to drink in the aural, olfactory concatenation of it all. Yet, as one often supposes might happen when you do close your eyes for any length of time outside the safe confines of your own bed, some surprise is inevitable: mine was to be tapped on the shoulder from behind! Within the half second it took for me to register that, I recalled being alerted in such a way at least twice before: in a distant bar somewhere back there by an old school acquaintance and then once by a girl with rubicund lips... 'Mister!' said the voice of a boy, in bright, cheery tones. I turned to see, to my great surprise, the boy I'd bumped into all those weeks ago, the boy with the hoop, the boy with the 'knickerbockers'. Up this close, I could see that what I had thought then of his somewhat brownish complexion was due to his vast collection of freckles, a feature which I now ungraciously thought of as somewhat cartoonish. 'Howdy, again!' he pronounced, as though he was meeting an old friend. I Howdy-ied back, and then felt slightly dismayed I didn't get quite the reaction I wanted. How could I ever hope to fit in in a place, a universe, like this? I soon found out: 'You still look funny, Mister! Hope you don't mind my saying like...' and he vaguely pointed in my direction, up and down. I did think it forward, but I was like a guest in someone's house, able to put up with a few insults if I had to, even from a whippersnapper like this, not wishing to mess with fluctuations in the time-space continuum and all that. 'Be Inconspicuous' was my motto. Then it hit me: *my clothes!* Quick, think of something. 'My sister's a bit of a seamstress... She makes all these designs... I'm her latest experiment...' None of these statements appeared to make any impact on the boy, who then said: 'Your clothes is funny, Mister, that's all! See ya around!' And he left. As he walked off, I suppressed a chortle, thinking his own sartorial sense had its failings, the old 'knickerbockers', braces and long socks decidedly not my cup of tea.

What the encounter had achieved was to wake me up to the need to do a quick change, before my appearance began to draw any more unwelcome attention. It was easy enough done, but I couldn't just have stuff pop out of my fingernails in front of all these townspeople. I'd either be arrested or shot on sight as the manifestation of some being from Hell. Looking round, I thought it best to retreat into one of the side-streets I'd passed by and look for a crook or a cranny in which to do my thing and thereby take one huge step toward joining the rest of the crew in this nineteenth century Wild West town. Well, it was certainly nineteenth century, but, I reflected briefly, as I made my way back, was it really so 'wild' after all? So far, the individuals I'd spied appeared really rather slick and nothing if not respectable, even the whippersnapper, with his braces and freckled, but well washed, face. Seems like quite a high class sort of place, rather, I noted with a faint sense of disappointment, as though I had been hoping to see a gun-fight or two already. I passed by a stoutish man with a waistcoat and a balding pate, and, as we almost collided, took note of his kind expression of 'Sorry there, fella' as further proof that this was a nice town, and that being so, I could likely get in and out with a modicum of trouble, get a sample of life in the Old West, if not the Wild, and get back to 'reality'. If I found Poly, that is.

I entered the first side-street I saw on the left, and ambled down it a few paces, eyeing its potential as a place for my transformation. It was definitely a side-street, in that it had no shop-fronts, but there were a few windows punctuating the brown wooden slat-work that made up the sides of the buildings, some fully curtained, some not. I'd have to take my chances that no-one peeked out just as I was conjuring up my gear. After ambling on a little further, I made use of a short fence and sat against it, glad it could take my weight without sagging. I'd chosen a spot beyond any ground-floor windows, and, blessedly, next to a large barrel, perfect for obscuring my doings, in one direction - street-wise- at least. I sat for a few minutes, like a man just relaxin', taking the weight off his feet, all the time making sure that this place was what I hoped it might be, unworthy of anyone's attention. I'd look around now and again, pass my fingers through my hair, do a few yawns, and generally assure myself the coast was clear, until, concentrating on what it was I wanted, I shook out my fingers, pointing down toward the dirt ground. Out came, first things first, a pair of long cowboy boots, light-brown snake-skin, heavily tapered, 'winkle-picker' type as was written onto the tag (which I'd always remove), with a near glossy black upper stretch. Very cool, I had to admit, yet anything but inconspicuous. Practice at this had aided me in conjuring up the proper size for my feet (and, my only preparation, the thick socks I wore). I kicked off my old loafers, feeling not a little wistful, but also somehow proud, that these inglorious examples of twentieth century footwear would dwell on in this world. Maybe even start a shoe revolution, an idea which got me suddenly thinking: might my actions here have repercussions for the future? It was a sobering thought to have as you were putting on boots, that every tread of my feet might leave an imprint on the very matrix of the future world… It was almost all too much for me, I decided, and then also decided that if I could just keep to the rule of being as inconspicuous as possible, I would be ok, and the twentieth century, too. This rationale brought me back to earth, and to the serious business of conjuring clothes that would help me meld in.

My jeans I let be, as they already blended in fine, but I'd need a good shirt and a waistcoat and a hat, and, before I could stop myself, a gun. These all came out in a blur of activity, as I felt more and more worried that someone might see me, materializing stuff out of nothing, and call all blue hell. I certainly felt like I was doing something extremely nefarious, my eyes now shooting round me, like a man afraid his plot to do some evil deed will be undone by discovery before he can do it. I was sweating. It was a hot day, indeed, and I was feeling pressure, and so, before I could stop it, out flew the gun, a Colt .45. Why would I need this? was my immediate reaction. This could be trouble, I felt. Yet, there it lay in the dust, shining and alluring, beckoning the cowboy in me to fall into the trap, reasoning with me that, hey, if you want to blend in, this is the Wild West (even if it's not particularly Wild), and a gun's just part of your normal apparel, everyone has one, so come on there boy, pick me up, pick me up! *You wanna blend in after all, don'cha?* Then another slightly more coherent reason drifted into view: my mind went back to the door of Poly's Pots & Pans, and the scribbled note, and the possibility that Poly had been abducted... Whether I was convinced that he had, or that having a gun would make me blend in all the better, now that it was 'out', and now lying just right there before me on the ground, glimmering in the afternoon sun, it could hardly be put back. And I couldn't just leave it there, so, laying the shirt and waistcoat over the fence at my side, I reached down, picked up the Colt, and then conjured up an ammo-loaded belt and a holster, hoping to God in heaven that I'd never have to use this instrument of death & destruction.

Placing the gun-belt on the other side of me over the fence, I then picked up the shirt and the waistcoat, and examined them. They looked very snazzy indeed, but, it then struck me, because they were new, might appear a little bit stand-outish. 'Be Inconspicuous' was my motto, after all. My solution was simple. I reached down once again, and this time took a handful of dirt and sprinkled it lightly over both, then patted the dirt in very lightly, adding a few creases here and there, with some rigorous shaking. Anyone looking at me would think I was mad, sitting there in the hot sun, consciously messing up my own clothes. I could hardly disagree: why I thought I had to work in a little wear and tear I couldn't rightly say, but, like most things that passed through my grey matter these days as excuses for thoughts, it just seemed to be right. For sure, anyone watching me would think I was crazier than a rattlesnake. I soon discovered that my reasoning along these lines was quite accurate, as, unbeknownst to me as I was doing all this, I heard a tiny voice say precisely that: 'Mister, you're crazier than a rattlesnake.'

I looked up and around. A little girl, not more than

seven I guessed, looked down from the corner of a window in the opposite building. She was unmoving, her arms crossed and leaning on the sill, as though she'd been watching me all along. Had she been? Long flaxen hair over a face that was as cute as it was mock-serious. Immediately I stood up, shook off the waistcoat and shirt. 'Bugs,' I retorted thinking on my feet, literally. 'Little bugs, nasty little things!' and then I made a play of shaking them more fiercely, sometimes slapping the clothes with the palm of my hand. 'That oughtta do it,' I pronounced, after I had delivered one last smack to them as they dangled from my outstretched left hand. A quick glance at the girl told me she wasn't impressed. And then she said: 'Mister, you some kind of magician, or sum'pin?' This was bad, I concluded. This was potentially lethal: discovery of my powers by anyone, even this teeny weeny not-yet-eight years old little girl, could spell disaster for my mission, and even, although I did not know how, the future of the world as I'd known it. I hadn't worked all this out, of course, hadn't gone into the fine detail on what it mattered if someone were to discover my magical powers, but something told me it couldn't be good. At the very least I might get arrested, or investigated, examined, or put away until they could find out what to do with me, and then there was the possibility that I could mess up the future. Yet none of this had really been processed, and so it just remained as a dim feeling of possible doom that my presence here could be precarious for not only myself, but the world at large. Yet, might this all be upset by a not-yet-eight years old girl? Hardly the spirit on which to embark on my adventure, I told myself, so I shot back, adopting as confident a tone as I could muster: 'Indeed, young lady, I am! What would you like?' At this, I knew I had her: she brought a cute finger up to her forehead, eyes rolling up. Then from her tiny wee mouth: 'Some flowers!' It was not what I wanted to hear. Indeed, it had been a risky proposition from the start: how could I hope to imagine that she would ask for some item that would certainly have been for sale in Poly's shop? And flowers were definitely not on the inventory! I would have to think fast. 'Flowers, young lady? I can give you something better than little old flowers. Anyone can summon up *flowers*!' (The last word was delivered in a deliciously disdainful tone.) And there, over the upright palm of my left hand, the fingers of my right did a twirl, and out popped a flower-designed silver brooch, suddenly shining in the midday sun. 'Voilà!' I called out. The little girl showed more than a trace of surprise, her palms splayed out either side of her face, as she audibly gulped. She might not have been able to see what it was, but that something, something shiny, had popped into existence produced a definite buzz. Now it was my chance to turn events in my favour. I walked over to the space under her window, and said in a voice that suggested confidentiality: 'Now, little Miss, you can have this right now, but don't tell a soul,' I said, raising the index finger of my right hand to my lips, 'or it'll *disappear* on you.' (I might add, as I said all this I adopted a mock-Americana accent; it was the beginning of my play-acting in this new-found old world.) The little girl, unable to speak, nodded fiercely once up and down, and then, in one smooth action, I threw the piece up, and she caught it at once. 'Now, go inside now, and keep that there piece to yourself. Be seeing ya.' The girl peeked at the brooch inside her palm, then looked down on me one last time, nodded once more, and then closed the window with both hands, and drew both lace curtains as well. I sighed with relief and returned to the fence.

Time, or something, was against me, I felt. I'd spent too much time already and the incident with the flaxen haired kid had put the wind up my sails. How long before I was discovered being nefarious by an adult? So, I spent as little time as humanly possible changing into the shirt and flinging on the waistcoat, followed by the latching round of the gun-belt, and holstering of my trusty (if brand spanking new) Colt .45. The discarded clothes, however, summoned incipient panic as I wondered precisely what to do with the leather jacket, the flabby shoes and the casual long-sleeved shirt with, I noticed now with unaccustomed horror, its 'Made in China' tag sown into the very material and not easily defaced or detached. I damned myself for my cheap tastes, my inveterate tackiness, wondering what I had learned at all from having had a catalogue of the finest Western clothes at my disposal for so long. (Indeed, why had I even bothered to retrieve these excuses for clothes from that alleyway long ago when I had made my first transformation?! Ah, paternal education runs deep!) A fire, I wondered, perhaps if I light a small fire? No? Stuff them under that pile of stacked wood over there? Oh, for a rubbish bin somewhere, I moaned, internally. And, then, with typical practicality, and no particular connection to what I'd just been worrying about, I felt the sudden need for a hat. Maybe it was the sun, which was beating down fast, like a hammer on my iron head. And, at the drop of a hat, so to speak, out dropped a hat. Then another, having decided it didn't quite match. Upon the appearance of hat three my temper began to noticeably rise, hat in one hand, bunched up unwanted clothes in the other. Hat four, which fell down over my eyes, had me jumping almost with fury, as I cursed the near-tragic proportions of my lot. But anger's a lens on a hot summer's day, a channeling conduit of energy, a crucible of power, sensibility and purpose in one, and so, in one moment of flash-blinding brilliance (and random chance), all things were suddenly resolved! Hat five was perfect and then smoke filled my nostrils, alerting me to a (somewhat mysteriously) free-standing iron brazier a few steps further back, well-stoked with coals. Oh, happy chance! A quick glance told me this was the rear end of a blacksmiths. I peered in a little to the dark of the small barn-like building where I expected to see the smith in action. Nobody there, thank Jesus. So, rolling each item into a loose ball, tucking the shoes in too, allowing each to catch fire nicely, until all were safely ablaze, in went the detritus and out went the stress. *Au revoir* to rubbish! I placed a loose horseshoe or two on top, just to keep the stuff down. I then straightened my clothes, tugged lightly at the rim of my hat, jiggled my gun-belt and jeans, plucked at the wings of my waistcoat and turned myself round, to stride into the future. Or was it the past?

I could hear the clothes crackle as I walked away, and the sound gave me comfort that my mission would work. All I had to do was to keep out of trouble, find my old 'friend' Poly, and get back to the world that was truly mine... and the girl that was waiting there, too. My new clothes gave me comfort, I had to admit, as I walked back up through this narrow channel of buildings. Little by little I could feel myself grow into the role they afforded me, as a cowboy for real, in the land and the time of the cowboys. Damn, I could feel myself swagger.

I re-entered the main street with a pause; I needed to take in the scene. It was as though I was seeing it properly for the first time. Figures aplenty walked up and down the street right before me, and before long, I had spied my first character mounted on a horse, trotting leisurely to the right. He was a character because he was wearing a three-cornered hat, smoked a big fat cigar and sported the longest beard I'd ever seen on a chin. Then, over on the other side of the street I saw a bowler-hatted pair of blokes in long coats, one portly, the other slim; they had a funny way of communicating with each other, which I found myself watching intently. I soon caught myself on, though, following the precept: don't stare at the locals too long, and so soon looked away, and around. The predominant colour here was brown. Buildings were gradations of brown, of course because they were wooden, although one or two, now I looked a little more concentratedly, seemed constructed of brick. The bank on the opposite corner was brick. It announced it was a bank with huge capitals, BANK, with additional words below: EST. 1848, and, my eye scanned, above: TWENTY FIRST NATIONAL. (This age had a love affair with capital lettering and no mistake.) Each building, or shop-front, screamed out its name in a similar way (which I quickly punned as 'Capitalist!', harf harf): DRY GOODS, VICTUALERS, DENTIST and GROCERS, and the effect for each was further enhanced by the height of the façades, which seemed at times preposterously high, if never quite imposing: there was too much of an impression of wide-open space for that. Be-hatted men and women were going about their business, some passing time standing on board-walks, chatting away heartily, some solitary, like myself, taking things in, or, smoking a cheroot, or consulting a fob-watch, maybe thinking of some appointment they had to keep, while others were looking in windows, others were entering or leaving establishments, creating a fine bustle of activity everywhere I could see. The street was a dusty, not-quite even expanse, scored with mysterious lines and the indecorous marks of passing feet, both bi- and quadrupedal.

Thinking, no doubt rightly, that my solitary fixed-point staring might bring me attention, I broke from my moment of awe -because that's what it felt like to stand there and stare at this old Western town, my heels dug in the dirt- and proceeded to amble my way into their world. It was still very bright, and not a bit cool, and yet I'd chosen correctly in terms of attire, and felt at ease as I walked, with each step becoming at one with my role, and my growing place among the inhabitants. I had taken a turn to the left, away from the direction I'd come from, feeling the need to explore, telling myself Poly could wait for a few minutes yet. The sounds once again filled me with wonder, because they were the sounds that had existed a hundred years before, so even the smells and the moments of startle, like when a mounted horse riding near me suddenly snorted and bucked, struck me as magical. The far-off trebly sound of a piano attracted me. The sound of chance conversations almost forced me to stop and listen in. Even the yelping of dogs running free pulled at my sense that all I was seeing and all I was hearing was as real as could be.

I soon learned that I really should keep to the boardwalk, not the street, with its dirt and its droppings, and its sudden intrusions of horses, and one time, almost dangerously, a wagon, and so I sidled away from the dirt and onto the wood, which had the added advantage of allowing me to stop now and then, as natural as pie, and peruse the wares of various shops through their occasional windows. It was as I was doing this, mingling among the good townsfolk, sometimes noticeably swerving to let past some lady or gent, that I noticed a slight alteration in people's apparent awareness of me. It took a moment or two for me register this as part of a pattern, but considering I had been kind of invisible up to now, I took it in good faith, as a sign, perhaps, that I'd truly entered their universe. After a moment or two, indeed, it was others who were making way for me as I strolled, with the odd moment here and there in which I'd be attempting to give way to someone and yet they appeared anxious to let me do the passing. The eyes of the passersby would find mine, and what the looks I was getting appeared to communicate was somehow not entirely positive. Was it fear? Was it being unused to my face? Perhaps it was such a tight-knit community a stranger would stick out. I found it most strange, whatever it was, even faintly disturbing, as it played distant havoc, as it was still only a potentiality, with my creed of inconspicuousness. Was I starting to make waves?

Wondering where this all might lead to, I deemed it prudent to forget about window-shopping for now, to take refuge somewhere and just get my bearings. Perhaps, after all, I had no time for leisure: I'd have to find Poly and get the hell out. The sound of the trebly piano had grown both in my ears and in my consciousness, as somehow providing me with the chance that I needed. Old habits die hard, so the thought of a cold one to drink the stress off came perfectly natural. With something like glee, I beheld the SALOON, only paces away on the other side of the street. A Wild West SALOON! I could hardly contain my delight. I paused to let a fully-fledged stagecoach pass just right by. It was a truly wondrous thing to behold, and it took me completely by surprise. First the horses at a synchronized gallop, maybe (quite a blur, don't ya know?) three tiers of two, all reined-up and attached to their harness and buckles, made a thunder of sorts, as dust billowed up. The whoops and the shouts of the riders at the front of the coach broke into the mix, and then there was the sight of them, sat high up on the front of the coach, all wearing hats, all sporting generous moustaches, in their rough brown jackets and long boots, one holding dearly onto the reins as another man surveyed all around him, holding a rifle -or was that a shotgun?- pointed upwards. Shouts issued freely from these and a third, and possibly a fourth, who sat along with them but were now all a blur or an overload of the senses to take in. Then the coach itself blossomed before us: a flaming red, with curlicue twirls in yellow (what a colour-combination that was!) all over the body and door. I could catch only the briefest of moments to peek in at the passengers inside, but I could swear by my grandmother's grave that the lady I'd seen earlier, the one with the huge bustle, was there, and... she was smiling at me! Definite eye-contact! Apart from the thrill of seeing this grand thing pass, I consoled myself with the thought that at least one human being here could lend me some cheer, even if it was obvious she was hightailing it out. What, I wondered briefly and mischievously, did it feel like to be sitting on that bustle at all, at all?

The dust kicked up by the commotion was matched only

by the flurry of attention the passing stagecoach had received from those around me. Young and old alike were passing comments, shouting out cheers, slapping backs and issuing 'hollers' of words I found technically unintelligible but perfectly graspable. Personally, I was glad as it drew all eyes off me, or rather created a sudden commune of souls, as I was accepted briefly into their world: 'Man, what a sight!' said one bystander middle-aged man directly to me, 'Man, what a sight!' he said once again. So, I reciprocated with what I thought would pass muster round here: 'Indeedy, Sir, indeedy it was!' By the look on my interlocutor's face it wasn't clear to me whether this phrase was quite the done thing or not, but it garnered a smile. I wondered myself then where I had come up with the phrase, realizing ever so slightly that my consciousness appeared to be slipping, as it often did when in the company of others, toward imitation, whether successful or not, of those all around me. It was my habit of old, as little by little -and it was a natural process- my mind came to terms with how I imagined they thought and sought to be like them in gesture and word. Essential, of course, to help me blend in. This explains why I then took off my hat, held it high and shouted out with a conviction that surprised even me: 'Yeeee-Haw!' Unfortunately, either my timing was off, the main event now finished, or just that no-one was that much impressed, so reaction to my 'holler' was not quite what I'd hoped, as others began to turn back to their business of doing whatever it was they were doing before the coach passed. While this allowed me a moment to suffer the anti-climax alone, it also allowed me to subsume it, ignore it, and to pass on. In fact, I had to admit, with this consciousness thing manifesting itself like this, I was beginning to change little by little, too. I was beginning to get into my role, feeling more comfortable with each passing moment, or the role was beginning to get into me. So, I brushed off the moment, taking a significant step toward feeling part of this world and yet not caring a whit.

It was certainly the spirit to be in as I contemplated my trip to the saloon. I pulled up my jeans with both hands, and jiggled the gun-belt till it hung right, my right hand imparting a brief pat to the butt of the Colt, to make sure it was snug, and then took steps to get off the boardwalk. Somehow these minimalist actions, as I thought them to be, had once again engendered that feeling, that those around me felt somehow wary of me. The smiles and the bonhomie were gone, replaced with brief glances of eyes seemingly lacking in warmth. As I proceeded, whoever happened to be in my way shifted quick, allowing me passage to get where I wanted, onto the dirt and over the street. I needed that beer more than ever, I thought. And yet, I felt good about this. The rationale of being inconspicuous was being slowly, or actually quite quickly, eroded by my growing contentment at being a 'cowboy', decked out in duds, ambling through this Wild West town in the middle of nowhere, floating in time. Yes, it was 'contentment', my acclimatization to cowboy-ness, but it was also the return of that ego I'd lived with for weeks and weeks now, and, only with Ruby, had tried to repress. I'd lived all those weeks wearing two guns (that everyone thought were just replicas). I'd lived all those weeks conjuring whatever came into my head, usually booze, or some 'trinkets', or jewels or food, if only beef jerky or apples, or great cobs of bread. But also wearables, except for the jeans (the prospect of having to turn them *up* always a turn-*off*), dolling myself out in the latest late 19th C fashion. I'd lived all those weeks... and then there were guns... And there were rifles... And there were knives... and with these came something I could never quite see, perhaps because I'd souse myself stupid on 'Jack Salter Rye' or 'Sixty Slugs Malt'. It was what filled my mind now, and not just my mind but my limbs and my hands, injecting swagger into my gait and, yes, cockiness, into my being. *But was it me?*

The sun battered down like a hammer as I got to the middle of the street. I could take it. My nostrils filled with the dust that had not yet settled from the coach's passing. I could take that, too. The feeling that everyone had abandoned their normalcy because of me entered my head. But I could take it. The sense that all eyes were on me was almost overpowering. But I could take it. I could take all this because I had sights set on my goal, the swing doors before me, under the shade of the generous porch, calling wordlessly out to me to come in and sample a taste of the West. I could take that for sure. So, I stepped up onto the wooden boardwalk and into the shade of that generous porch, and swung the doors open.

CHAPTER FOUR

Swing doors are funny things, of course. You push them open and they swing right back. You do it a second time with greater force and they just come back even stronger and then everyone's looking at you, wondering what you're doing playing with the damned doors. Actually only a few heads turned round, and none seemed too concerned anyway. But what heads they were! Few were be-hatted, as I was; most were seated on wooden chairs around wooden tables, on which themselves sat bottles and glasses and quite often cards, even the occasional book. Many were men, those that were seated, for sure, decked out in duds of a piece with the era: leather waistcoats and stitched shirts, bandannas, of all colours and design, round necks, generous moustaches under most noses. (Brief memory of myself with bandanna over nose, in a cold field, yikes...) Not all those noses were white, I now noticed. There were at least three black cowboys among them, and one chap who looked East European at least. But no segregation here!

Black and white cowboys rubbed elbows, table to table. The few women that were there were mostly on foot, decked out in wear that suggested their main function was to look easy on the eye: from elegant blouses of crushed crepe to frilled laces bordering the under-edge of their dress. One gal was pouring a drink and laughing uproariously with the male holder of the glass. He was slapping the table, and hollering: 'Stop, stop, stop!', but it seemed like he in fact didn't want things to stop, stop, stop. Anyone who glanced in my direction did so furtively and quickly, unwilling to countenance any interruption to the day's entertainment, which was boozing, gambling, and flirting with women. Smoke from cigarettes and cigars filled the air. And, over on the left-side corner of the quite spacious room, a bowler-hatted piano player tapped out, with more enthusiasm than skill, some upbeat melody I couldn't quite place. After taking all this in, I then thought about entering further, approaching the grand counter, with its recessed arches and sparkling collection of bottles, beyond the sea of occupied tables, where two aproned barmen, either side of a pair of glorious brass taps, stood impassive, unmoving, and, I now noticed, with their two sets of eyes locked precisely on me.

There was enough space between tables for me to improvise a path to the bar, doing my level best to appear inconspicuous as I walked. Yet I enjoyed the clack of my heels on the hard wooden floor. I cupped my hands round my belt buckle (which, by the way, was plain, and didn't have TEXAS or any such nonsense emblazoned on it) as I walked. I drank in the passive smoke from each table. I listened in to every swear word and cuss. I stole glances down at these characters as I was skirting them, wondering about what they did in their lives every day, apart from all this. The dust and the caked dirt on some of their dungarees and their boots told its own story of days on the horse, driving steers from one state to the next, under a punishing sun. The way one man grabbed at the upper arm of one of the gals and pulled her face down to his lips told its own story of institutional sexism and low education. No-one cared less, some even hollered with glee. Another slapped down his cards in obvious fury, issuing a string of cusses, before grabbing his glass and downing the entire contents in one furious gulp. At one table, I caught sight of a curious book which was held open by one man for discussion with another: beautifully rendered graphic drawings of said steers, each branded with symbols, like inverted crosses and plus signs and even a heart shape or two. Very strange! Tabletops were either covered in green felt or were plain wood, glossy but for the odd spill of foam or of ash. The backs of each chair were tooled in the most elegant way. Customers spat now and then in the direction of dull-metal spittoons placed here and there, and some even succeeded in hitting them. The floor was hard wood, but overlain, inconsistently, with sawdust. And by now, I was just about right at the counter, from which, down below, hung whitish towels, some looking moist and unpleasant. I placed my hands on the bar, and did my best to come across real.

'Howdy,' I said to the barman who was closest. He broke from his immobility and returned the greeting, asking 'What'll it be?' 'A beer' was my answer, having noticed the taps previously (distant memories of Monahan's floating back), and having cherished the hope of a 'cold one' out there in the heat. His eyes seemed awfully close together, in the sense that he seemed somehow unfriendly, or suspicious of me, but his manner and tone were the opposite, as he set about taking care of my order, pulling back slowly on the tap to release the beer into the large handled glass. 'Mighty hot, I must say,' said the barman, his delivery a little bit slurred, in my humble opinion, by the weight of his moustache, which obscured part of his mouth. I was enjoying myself: 'Indeedy it is, indeedy it is.' Whether I had coined a new phrase for the West was still unsure as he didn't bat an eyelid, his actions all concentrated on gently lopping off the overflow head on the beer with a small wooden paddle. After then releasing some more of the nectar into the glass he seemed to feel satisfied with all and then transported it, almost gingerly, smack damn right before me on the counter, quickly, however, slipping in under it a plain cloth-knit coaster, and turning it round so the handle was easy for me to grasp. 'On the house!' 'Why, thank you, kind sir!' I retorted, getting into my role, and my adlibbed American accent, too. Just to take advantage of the moment, and perhaps also to state my credentials for all to see, I slugged back the beer, which was warm, and not particularly delicious, in one long, languorous draught, smashing it empty back on the hard glossy counter for everyone to see. 'Yeehah!' I 'hollered' for all I was worth, lost in my acting, and not a bit reeling from the strength of the alcohol, which I could now see was unlike anything I'd been used to in the good ole twentieth century. 'Now, give me a whiskey!' I called. The barman had returned to his aproned impassive statue-like stance but soon broke back into professional subservience, grabbing a bottle and slug glass and sweeping round to place both before me. Not wishing to offend him, but somehow impelled to do so, as though by some force of my acting, I reached out and stopped the man's hand from pouring the jigger, grabbing the bottle myself and saying roughly: 'Here, gimme that here!' I had somehow intuited that cowboys can get away with such forwardness, that a barman can take anything, as long as he ends up taking your money too. Perhaps he could see it was my way of telling my audience that, hell, I was here, don't no-one forget it. Or something like that. I threw in the brown liquid with a force and roughness that inevitably led to some spill, but that, too, was all part of the show, I reckoned. Slugging it back in one was another, but, I soon realized, as the alcohol delivered a double-punch behind the whites of my eyes, if I carried on like this I'd keel over, and collapse on the floor. So, I subsumed the punches and took the decision to go easy, not wishing to undo myself. I must have been hoping for some sort of audience, however, as I made sure to then turn round, lean my back on the thick brass rail of the counter, and take in the sights, perhaps hoping to catch the eye of a gal.

In fact what I got was a shock, a particularly nasty one in the shape of a gun barrel pointed my way, from a distance of twenty yards or so, the distance I'd walked to get here inside the saloon. Right over there, from the swing doors, now held open in suspended animation, stood a tall man with a straight-brimmed hat, fancy waistcoat and long jacket, and all black, or dark. Was he going to a funeral? Not mine, by any chance? He held his pistol in his right hand, with his finger clearly on the trigger and his thumb hovering dangerously over the hammer. I was not a bit mortified that my dumbshow had ended in something like ignominy. 'Mister,' called the man at the swing doors, the man with pistol pointed at me, 'I'll gun you down here and now like a dog if you like. Put a hole in you the size of Texas from here. Or you can come easy now, Mister, dropping your belt, like…' I had to admit I didn't really think I would like to be gunned down like a dog here and now, or in fact that anyone would -what a stupid proposition!- especially in front of all these fine people, so I knew I would have to comply. As for putting a hole the size of Texas in me, I had a few quibbles with that on the basis of how that might be accomplished, but decided there and then it was best not to raise them right now. It had occurred to me pretty quickly that I really didn't have an alternative. I further wondered, however, why he couldn't just have asked me nicely, not trying to make a big fuss and showing me up? That didn't seem much of a way to treat a complete stranger… So, it was with some consternation, which I of course internalized, not wishing to give him any cause to shoot, but also not wanting to be seen grovelling, that I answered: 'Man, not a problem, not a problem,' and brought my hands slowly, oh so slowly, down to my buckle and proceeded to think how I might unlatch it. If my hands appeared to move just a fraction of an inch toward the Colt, I knew I'd be meat, so I did things real slowly, with fingers splayed out for the best possible view. All activity had stopped at the tables, and all eyes were on me. Somehow this was to my liking, working against everything my first rule had spelt out so clearly: Be Inconspicuous! Dib-Dib! This was clearly not that, and yet my 'consternation' or innate dislike at being meted out such treatment brought me some comfort... if only the comfort of knowing I'd been wronged... with the distant thought that... *I might fight back yet.*

Another distant thought was a question or two: Was this me talking? I wondered. Where was my fear? I had plenty of space to consider these things as, I only now noted, the noisome piano player (begging your pardon, mister) had stopped his dreadful performance. Not only that, the player had in fact deserted his post. Scarpered. Was this all prelude to something he didn't want to witness?

I let the belt fall with a thud and a clatter onto the ground, a sound amplified greatly by the hush that had fallen over the room. I held up my hands. This seemed enough to satisfy the man with the gun, who then began to relieve the swing doors of their tension by taking his first step toward me and into the saloon proper. I could see he was tall, very tall, and his steps were nothing if not declarations of some manly claim upon righteous authority. I could see I was in for a beating, at best. Yet I dared not move an inch. Not yet anyway.

Thump. Thump. Thump. His steps felt like the heartbeat of some evil beast. I began to feel dread. I was immobile, just waiting, like a deer watching an on-coming car. No, make that a truck. His pistol was still drawn, if not pointed at arm's length toward me, the business-end was still visible, easily brought up. His face, under an imposingly well-shaped round-brimmed hat, was long and lean, the high-cheekbones-look, eyes dark and -sorry for the cliché-piercing; his black moustache -to match the hair visible under his hat- was the loudest feature on his face, and bespoke a man who didn't have the words 'timid', 'shy' or 'mealy-mouthed' in his vocabulary. Sweat was beginning to form on my forehead. Partly it was the general warmth of the day, partly it was the effect of the alcohol, which was starting to thump by itself, but mostly it was the fear that the man with the gun would put paid to my uprightness with a well-delivered blow to my face, if not some other vulnerable part of my anatomy. Yet, what had I done? I found myself asking. What had I done? Was this connected to my reception outside? What was I doing that was attracting such negative vibes? In answer, like a furtive animal aware that time's running out, and choices are few, my eyes scanned the fellows within the establishment for some sign or way out of this. It was a sea of wide eyes. It would make a great photo I thought. And then as I looked I began to see more. My eyes roved from their eyes to their whole being, personae, emitting that aura which shouted out 'Cowboys we are!' I could vouch for that. 'We're rootin' tootin' cowboys, one and all, and we've been on the ole trail since Noah was a lad! We want entertaining, and you're gonna give it us! We'll drink to ya, fella, and then go back to our gals!' And yet there was something that jarred, something only now I was beginning to see: none of them had guns!

The instant I saw this, my eyes reeled back in my head, which, I believe, is the standard sign of a person attempting to recall what they've witnessed before. The old eyeballs seek out some plain surface, I've heard, usually the ceiling, to avoid all the clatter of what they see now, and use that old plainness to recover the imprint of what they had seen before. And as I looked up now, wishing the ceiling had been just a mite plainer, not gloss and not covered in curlicue flower patterns, I saw all them folks once again out in the street, and out on the boardwalks. Not one of them had guns either! Not one of them… I had figured it out!

'Kind Sir, forgive me!' I drawled to the man with the gun now only paces from me. 'I do beg your pardon! I hadn't known about the *ordinance* on weapons! ['ordinances prohibiting weapons': a bit of info I'd picked up from my stint in the library all those eons ago] Cross my heart and hope to die!' If only it had been just words, or if I'd only just not spoken… I reached out the index finger of my left hand, perhaps just too fast, as though to make the sign of the cross on my chest, and, to my horror the man raised his pistol, and shot. Correction. Somebody shot. 'A shot rang out' I believe is the phrase that suits in situations like this. He had raised his gun, that was for sure, but something wasn't quite right about angles and all… Never mind! Right behind me, bottles exploded, all shattering and sharding, like they were screaming. My whole body ducked, though it was more like collapsing or just dead-weight-falling, from the shock of it all, wondering why the tall man with gun had done such a thing, if not just to put the fear of the afterlife in me. I'd been so submissive, too. What the hell did he want? Then I remembered my gesture and imagined that that must have sparked it. But no. I'd misread the scene. For now he was turning, gun still in hand, reeling off - BLAM, BLAM, BLAM- shot after shot back to the swing doors, as he himself fell, or dived to the left, behind an occupied table. The occupiers of said table, four men and a gal, did not appear impressed with his strategy, however, and made like the seats of their chairs had suddenly become as comfortable as freshly smelted iron. Did they jump? Yes, they did, they certainly did, left-wise and right, buckleaping out of their seats in a flash and splaying out onto the floor. Their chaos appeared quite infectious, indeed, as now everyone there appeared to have decided *en masse* that sitting upright on their chairs was just about the last thing anyone wanted to do, especially since, as it was now becoming apparent, there was a madman with a gun firing in from just inside the entrance. For that's what it was. A genuine gun battle, occurring right now in front of my eyes, even if I was below the waterline, so to speak. I had no wish to raise up my head and confirm what I guessed was occurring.

It didn't last long, however, the shooting that is. Whoever it was -and whoever it was was not sure, as I only caught sight of a flash at the opening, and heard a strange holler, more like a speeded-up warble than anything- soon desisted. In the ensuing quiet, the man with the gun, the man who had threatened me, who had come into the saloon to upset my beautiful day, now stood up, still looking wary, and made for the entrance at speed. Before doing so, though, he'd motioned to the fellows behind me, the barmen, to come around quickly and keep watch over me. I was hardly in much state to move, but the sudden sight of a giant man in an apron, the other barman, wielding a suddenly-materialized shotgun impressed upon me the importance to move even less. Take me away, if you like, was my feeling. Lock me in prison, oh please, but don't shoot me in the chest with both barrels, *I would like to live just a little bit more.* It was then that I noticed my proximity to my unlatched gun-belt and gun. In the present circumstance, it seemed the tiniest action could have unforeseen consequences, as, for example, my eyeing the gun as it lay by the side of my head: that could mean death for sure. So, I was actually genuinely glad when the giant stepped in and kicked gun and belt out of my reach.

There on the ground, as I was, lying as horizontal, and hopefully as pathetic and unshootable as possible, under the shadow of the shotgun-toting barman, looking up at the woody legs of chairs and, to my left, the dangling white towels, with their splashes of Godknowswhat here and there, I thought about life. Not life in the general philosophical sense, but in the very particular sense related to now. Death had been close. *Had been? It still was!* It might strike any time now, even so. The tall man -the sheriff?- with the gun might be gunned down outside as he seeks out the attacker. Then he'd be dead. Or quite possibly, because he looked like he knew his way round all this stuff, he'd be the victor and he'd get his man, delivering one well-fired shot into the heart of the mysterious attacker. Third scenario: the madman with the gun would get the sheriff, then re-enter the saloon, fight it out with the barman and his shotgun, kill him, and then come for me. Or just shoot some bodies that got in his way. What all this meant, apart from being some form of hell, was that in the midst of it all, *I* might be key. Had I not been here, things could only have happened differently. Perhaps no-one would die, had I not been here, distracting the sheriff from his routine duties. The attacker might have been discovered, and thwarted, earlier. Yet, if he dies, I now wondered feverishly, will that change the future? If the sheriff dies will that change the future? If the barman dies, will that change the future? I concluded that I could be sure of only one thing: if *I* die, I can say for sure that *that* will change the future -for *me!*

As I contemplated these points, a panic awakened in me. Even in the best-case scenario, I'd be arrested and flung into jail. I couldn't just walk away from this, pronouncing a few well-chosen words, 'Sheriff, sorry for not seeing the sign, and upsetting your day, and about that other fella, I don't know him, no Sirree, I ain't never clept eyes on the man…' I was innocent, truly, an innocent abroad, but… I'd carried a gun like a gunman, swaggered uninvited into this peace-loving town and gone straight to the saloon for some fun. What had happened to me? And what had happened to my plan to 'Be Inconspicuous!'? I closed my eyes, feeling the weight of it all descend on my mind. I could be trapped in the nineteenth century for years! I might even get hung as an accomplice! The gloom of this fate fell upon me and, although it was hardly possible, I slumped even further, head lolling back like a doll, or like a puppet with the strings cut.

Moving was not an option. The giant above me kept staring down, the default 8 of the double-barrel pointed right at my head. So, I had to just wait. I interpreted the clatter of wood and the thump, thump, thump of the floorboards as the return of the 'sheriff', and then listened in as his disembodied voice boomed out: 'Got away. Off on his horse. Me and the boys gonna get up a posse.' A pause, then: 'So, how's our guest?' No response was made as the tall man now came into view, his gun safely holstered, and looked down: 'You one o' Tyler's men?' he spat at me in a vaguely venomous tone. I knew a slow answer might earn me a kick, so I shot back as quickly as possible, employing a tone you might hear from the mouth of a lowly private in the US Army: 'Please, Sir, No, Sir, I don't know no Mr Tyler, Sir!' Then I threw in just for luck: 'I am so sorry for coming in wearing a gun. I had no idea, Sir!' My response had the sheriff look at the giant as though for some clarification, and then back to me: 'Mister, you can't sweet-talk your way outta this! Now git up!' The last three words were barked out at me, and with all due compliance, I did my best to do as he said, pushing back with my elbows and hands as my legs bent, and this way and that, within a few seconds I'd clambered up till I was now standing before them, on my seriously shaky legs.

Instinctively, I put my hands up high as I did so. 'Turn around!' screamed the sheriff, reaching round to the rear of his belt and producing the most dread thing in the world: hand-cuffs! My eyes latched onto these as I just stood there, not moving, facing the sheriff and the huge aproned barman with the shotgun now pointing level with my chest. This was hardly compliance, I knew. In danger of kicks or a thump to be sure. 'Turn round and put your hands behind you!' screamed the sheriff once more. And yet I could feel something inside me resist. Doing as he commanded would land me in jail, and what happened after that was anyone's guess. Resistance, however, might lead to a sudden snap of his rage into a blunt punch to the head, or a dig in the mouth with the butt of the shotgun by the now temporarily deputized barman, hoping to impress his new employer. So, not quite sure if it would work, simply carried by pure instinct, not to mention all those weeks of 'practice', I splayed out the fingers of my raised hands in one tiny action that could hardly be interpreted as a 'move', and, hey presto, in both the left and the right appeared the only thing I could think of right now: apples, two bright red ones.

This caused my two rivals to stutter a moment with audible shock and surprise. I had also been lucky in that the assembled cowboys and gals, who'd now well recovered their poise, had been watching all this intently, to see things through to the end, no doubt as a kind of complimentary entertainment. A collective sigh could be heard at the sudden appearance of said fruits of the *malus pumila* variety. (Don't know where I picked that up, but education's a funny thing.) My face had changed, too, from that of the obedient loser to something a tad more in tune with the power I was now feeling. A confidence was beginning to course through my veins that I could outdo them with all their blunt ways. Surprise doesn't have a long shelf-life, however, so I let the first -pristine- apples tumble out of their pedestals, and down to the ground at our collective feet, as I conjured up two new ones, a red one perched on the fingertips of my left hand, and a green one perched on the tips of the upward-pointing fingers of my right. Raised eyebrows from my close interlocutors. These apples were then quickly displaced by other red ones and green ones, popping out magically from my still-rigid up-pointing fingers, standing there before the world and his wife, holding each one for only as long as it took for the next one to unthrone it. They seemed to come up from beneath at the base of the palm; I felt a tingling there. My immediate rivals looked on in solid amazement, both of them craning their necks forward as they did so, drawn by the sight of what was fast developing into a stream coming out from each hand, which now gained more momentum and speed, as apple after apple popped into existence, one after the other, flying out now, one not merely toppling the other one out ignominiously but acting with something like projectile force. The apples described two arcs, streaming in parallel, until it was actually more like two fountains of apples flowing out and up into the air, then, obeying the laws of Newton's Gravity (because Einstein hadn't published his corrections quite yet) cascading out wide and falling down to the ground, onto the bar counter, and onto the tables, the chairs, and even the heads of my rivals and, soon, the assembled cowboys and gals. Who of course were now shrieking and hollering, especially the gals.

And then it just stopped. I had not moved, not even the expression on my face, which remained locked in a grin, and we all listened in silence as the last of the apples completed their respective arcs and fell upon surfaces, wherever that was, bouncing out the last of their latent energies, until there was none.

Only silence. Then: 'Jesus, Mary and Joseph and all the saints and the sinners!' exclaimed the sheriff. 'Goddarn...' drawled the barman, slightly less interestingly, his shotgun now drooping and pointing down at his feet. I savoured the moment, enjoying the looks on their faces and then, still unmoving, pronounced, in -why I don't know- a suddenly-assumed German accent: 'Unt, now, for my next trick...' and -Pop!- in my right hand, appeared the self-same Nimschke Colt .44 revolver, complete with gloriously engraved ivory handle -suddenly cold to the touch- which I'd seen on the wall of P.P.P. all those weeks ago. A sleek, stunning piece, I couldn't help thinking, which I then promptly aimed in their general direction. I had the drop on them now. I had made sure that this one was loaded and ready to go. (I also told myself not to be distracted by the fine engravings on the barrel.) 'Please be so kind,' I began to request, transforming suddenly, as somehow seemed appropriate to how my mood took me, to a toff English accent, 'as to let the gun fall ever so gently to the ground, there's a good fellow.' The barman seemed willing to comply, although he came across a little unsure as to the way of doing so: dropping a weighty piece like that could hardly be done 'gently', and it might just go off in the process. So, responding to the question in his eyes, I chipped in: Okay, just *place* it down as slowly as you can, like a good chap…' This he did, bending his considerable trunk with some effort, 'slow' likely being his only speed. 'Now, Sheriff, if that's what you are, dear chap,' I said, playing up the English gent-thing as far as I could, and making sure, with the slightest of twirls of the barrel, that he noticed my pistol was directed his way, 'please unlatch your own gun-belt, and drop that down, too.' I was delighted that both were so eager to please, even if I was unsure what to do next. What I was at I was not able to say, putting on accents and all, but I suppose it was that old thing they say about tension in the air: it produces the most unexpected consequences, like laughing at the news of someone's unexpected death, or TV -which hadn't been invented yet-presenters getting the giggles on-air because they're trying too hard and know that fifteen million people are staring at them through the lens of that giant video camera plonked in front of them. But now it was time to revert to my main act, the American cowboy, in accent and poise, which, if it didn't fail me, might just get me out of this.

'Sheriff, believe me…' (*was I really addressing a sheriff in an old Wild West Town?*) 'I know nothing of the fella who attacked just here now. And I'll say it again, I am sorry for carrying a gun into this fine town, and among all you fine people, but, I'm sorry to say, I must take my leave of you all

and make my way out of here, as I've got business to do.'
This idea of having 'business to do' narrowed the eyes of
the sheriff, who said: 'Like the "business" of killing
innocents, mister, like your friends did last week? Mr
Wilkes, the town grocer, and Bobby, his son of ten years.'
Now my eyes narrowed, and my feeling grew cold, inviting
in doubts. How could I be standing here holding a gun on a
man who had experienced such an awful event? 'You think
we're gonna believe,' continued the sheriff, not three feet
before me, 'you ain't part of the Tyler gang come round last
Tuesday and shot up the town? You standing here with a
gun and the Ordinances up everywhere?' 'I swear it,' I
answered, 'I'm telling the truth, and I'm sorry for your
town's trouble, mister, truly I am.' The sheriff paused in
response, then said as slowly and deliberately as I have ever
heard a man speak: 'I don't know what you are, Mister, with
your magic tricks and all… You some kind o' spook?' He
was clearly hoping to get a rise out of me. I could now see
that he was indeed the sheriff, noting the five-pointed
cheap-metal star on his jacket lapel screaming out
'SHERIFF', and I knew he'd do anything to get back into
play. There was something about this, something inside me
said, something not right about me, standing here holding a
gun on a man sworn to protect this town from outlaws, or
mavericks like myself… Somehow I was beginning to feel
sorry for creating this situation, having barged into their
lives with only the pleasure principle directing my thoughts.
What a world to have to live in, with gunmen coming in
and shooting people up, leaving the town in tatters, people
just hoping to do their business, progressing to the future
and all… The more I dwelt on it, the more I was becoming
confused in my stance, half-wondering was I right to stand
there at all and seemingly add to their woes… 'Some kind
of spook, or some kind of *killer?*' said the sheriff once again,
the last word delivered with ice-cold contempt, and, ever so
slight though it was, his body now moving toward me, to

narrow the distance between his hand and mine, hoping to pounce, glimpsing my weakness… 'No!' I screamed out, and 'No!' once again, and my whole body shook, in a desperate attempt to reiterate not so much my authority but my innocence, leading to… because it was 'whole body' after all, a squeeze on the trigger I hadn't expected.

BLAM! went the gun, exploding in smoke as a bullet flew out and, thankfully, because I hadn't been pointing it right at the man, smashed onto the counter and careered off to the right and into the wall, where plaster flew. The sheriff flew too, toward me, seeing my surprise as all this was happening, be it a thing of split seconds, and past caring if he would be the recipient of the next speeding metal projectile or not. 'Things have gone beyond that' was the message I could read in his eyes. It was only with something like preternatural speed and an agility I've heard only comes to people in times of maximum danger, the fat and the slim (and I was somewhere in between) that I swerved to avoid him, flying right-wise myself, and, God of Ill-Luck strike me down dead if ye dare, dropping my beautifully-engraved piece as I did… My swerve landed me smack-damn right over a table which, because of the force of my flying body, began to skid freely over the floor, me on top of it. 'What a ridiculous sight I must be!' I thought as I held on and slid. I knew I was curtains unless I did something quick, so, even as I somehow part-enjoyed sailing away so precipitously from the centre of things, I used my two hands not merely to grip at the round edges, but to pull myself forward mightily, in one huge surge, throwing myself over the rim, to fall beyond what I was hoping would now be the protective surface of the table. I fell in a heap and a clatter, the last word in grace, but at least still alive. Though not for long I suspected, cheap tables in crappy Wild West saloons hardly affording much hope of stopping a metal bullet or three. And talking of three, I didn't have that many seconds to think. Sure, I could conjure another gun, or a rifle, but that would then be murder or death, a fate which held consequences not just for now, so as I landed abjectly beyond the round table, limbs all akimbo, be-hatted head hitting hard against wood, the world and wife still with their eyes firmly on me, I only thought big.

It was almost too late. The sheriff had swung to the ground and recovered his weapon, pulled it out from its holster and was bringing the barrel up. His actions were swift and the fact that he was silent spoke volumes: he was going to shoot me to death, right there in the middle of the saloon, because that was the law of the West. Cause a fuss with a gun and you're deader than dead. Having an essentially flimsy -when we're talking bullets, which travel eight hundred feet per second (so I once read)- over-turned table-top in front of me complicated matters, but memory's a funny old thing, and it had me recalling those grandfather clocks that I'd thought were attackers. For some silly reason I had wondered after that time what sort of a mess they would make were they ever to be launched into open space with considerable force. I now had my answer: 'quite a bit, I do hope!' Using both hands, palms brought together, I pointed my magic right in line where the sheriff was now standing, raising the barrel of his no doubt usually lethal weapon, and out, out, OUT came a beauty, a darling in ebony, handcrafted case, 8-day movement, mechanism crafted in Massachusetts, inlays of coloured flowers round the sides, glass sparkling in the afternoon sun, for the very last time in its short but exciting life. It flew out like a rocket, smashing through the up-turned table as though it were made of balsa or not there at all. Yet, as it poured out into the air, filling the space with its wood-bulk, I had a frightening insight of what it might do. I'd never done so before, so I wasn't sure it would work, but detaching my palms I moved the right out a tad, and, to my relief, gained the effect I was wanting. By the time the giant clock had fully emerged into space, it was now slightly swivelled around, with no great loss of momentum, and so it flew on, sideways not forwards, me having no wish to decapitate the son-of-a-bitch, gun or no gun. Flying like this, sideways, also gave me more cover, and if it took out the barman, then all the better for that.

Whatever people's general conception of chaos had been up till now, it was soon replaced by the event of the huge grandfather clock materializing out of nowhere in space and time (that's appropriate!), and flying, turning from nose-front to sideways, over the tables. A frightening beast; sudden blunt giant presence; and hurtling bar-ward. You could hear the collective shout of everyone there at the sudden appearance of the thing, a shout which then diversified into rising but various screams, punctuated with cuss words and warnings, at the prospect of it hitting the two standing men. Then into the audio mix came the gun-shots as the sheriff blasted his weapon at will: the splintering of wood, the breaking of glass, the inglorious notes of what sounded like long-pent-up springs and coils being released precipitously, or something like that! *Oh happy memory!* And then the touchdown: the sound of the crunch and the wails as the damaged beast smashed into the sheriff and the barman with force.

It hit them about chest-height. I could see the whole thing from where I still crouched. They both threw their hands out in protective gestures just before impact, which likely cushioned the blow. The sheriff's gun, and his hat, too, could be seen flying upwards just before impact, which probably sounded worse than it was. Although I'm sure it did hurt... 'Ahhhhhh!' sums it up, in stereo. And then the clock fell like a stone, the weight of a ton, and their bodies keeled forward and over the wreck. I felt a twinge of regret as this happened, and hoped they'd survive, if just not quite yet. I was also feeling glad *I'd* survived! Everyone else was just screaming and shouting and kicking to get as far away as was humanly possible from where I was, now, out of my crouch, standing up, my right hand fixing the hat into place on my head, as though even at a time like this fashion mattered... Looking round briefly, to take it all in one last time, with the saw-dust and smoke and the debris in free-fall, I could see flight had its merits, having come to this point. I was glad to hear only groans from the sheriff and barman, as though hurt but not dead, which, in the circumstances I felt showed considerable compassion on my part, if of the hard variety you get in the West. *Oh, the wisdom I was acquiring!* I turned on my heels and made straight for the doors, flinging away tables and chairs with my hands, with a strength that surprised me, and involuntarily kicking away apples and spittoons *(ugh!)* and glasses and bottles that got in my way. I dived through the swing doors ingloriously, as though expecting anytime now to be hit by a bullet, zig-zagging my body this way and that, until momentum caught up with me, and I tripped myself up with my non-standard movements and this sent me way past the boardwalk and out into the dirt. But, no time for this, I was telling myself, and so with a force beyond conscious instruction, I jumped to my feet and took off, right-wise, down the main street, destination completely unknown.

You could say I was kicking up dust, and then some.

CHAPTER FIVE

Why I chose right and not left was not down to an entirely conscious decision. Left-wise meant a clear dash back to where I'd come from, the twentieth century and all that, and that was where, really, I wanted to go at that particular moment, telling myself I can deal with the ole conjuring thing some other way. But instinct's a funny thing, and strong too, and mine was to find Poly and give back the 'gift'. How I then jumped on a horse that didn't belong to me -a hanging offence, so I'd read back in the ole municipal library- and 'hightailed it outta town', I couldn't quite tell you, but it sort of came natural, as though outlaw behaviour was now becoming hot-wired into my soul. It was only after what felt like an hour or so of hard riding, under a baking sun, through a landscape peopled only by enormous cacti, the odd bush or a tumbleweed rolling here and there, the occasional lizard sidling about, that I began to think about all this.

I was losing myself. That was sure. Not just on this

horse, which was hell to keep up on, but in terms of my soul. Precisely what was 'hot-wired into my soul'? I asked myself pointedly, even aggressively. How could I do what I did in the saloon? Well, there was a rational explanation for that, that of survival, but it didn't quite address the problem *in toto*. Surely, if I'd been as I was before all this happened, before I'd gotten Poly's 'gift/curse', I would have come quietly, in the hope of being able to have it all sorted out. Or rather, I simply would not have been there, in that 'den of iniquity', as the Preacher, another mainstay of the West, might call it. Going back further, why had I conjured that Colt .45 and the gun-belt in the first place? OK, it was down to a preconception that such was the norm way out West, but, guns have a meaning, and carrying one can lead to things, and the notion that Poly was in danger and only a good guy with a gun could 'git him out' was niggling at me. A sudden bout of extreme regression brought me back to the night with the biker in the bar, back in my hometown, where it had all started. So what if he'd been rude to me? Surely that had been an exposure of *his* shortcomings, not of *mine*. Better to have let it go at that and walk on, 'turn the other cheek', as the ole Preacher might also pipe up and say. And yet I'd provoked him into a fight. I hadn't walked on. Was that what this was all about then, I wondered, while privately asking: *why should I have to walk on?*

I rode on. If you could call it riding at all. I was holding on as I imagined you shouldn't, head and upper-torso down as far as possible, hands desperately clutching the beast's neck, not even thinking about the reins. Hat long gone in the flux. The horse galloped on, and I was glad no-one could see us, and that horses can't speak. 'I'd hate this to get round,' I confided to 'Horsey', as I'd imaginatively dubbed my steed for the day. Not that he likely cared one way or the other.

So, I can't easily back down, that's what it comes down to, I thought, as I returned to the questions nagging at me.

I'm not necessarily confrontational, but I have too much pride, I concluded, then privately asking: *how much is too much?* From this, then, getting the power I had been given was always going to be problematic to say the least. (This thinking was leading somewhere; I was gaining knowledge here…) Yes, I could see where it started, and in my mind drew a trajectory from that to the megalomania -that was the only word for it- that had grown with the gift/curse. From recently graduated nice Irish lad with no great determination to 'get on', living off the state's goodwill in an anonymous wee Northern Irish town to… swaggering cowboy-wannabe with a tendency to materialize all manner of 19th century goods out of thin air and then spend evening after evening just getting sloshed? What a trajectory! Plus, I added, assuming that role -or, more accurately speaking, *being subsumed by it*- had been a big part in all this. Once I had grown into this magicking cowboy alter ego thing, I was always going to change, and change considerably. I couldn't avoid that… First, as an ego-based supplement to my new-found powers in the land and era of my birth, and then as a necessity in this land and era, in order to meld in, and be seen as just another cowboy and all… If only they hadn't had that trouble the week before, or whenever it was when they made it against the law of the town to carry a weapon, I might have gotten through. I might have simply enjoyed the experience. At which point in my thoughts, my mind's eye filled with the images of the day, and the sounds, especially upon entering the saloon …all those gals… all that booze… the tinkling of piano keys… the smoke… the feeling that this has got to be a fun place to spend the afternoon. Not to mention the night… (*Oi!* said the Preacher at that.)

Somewhat despondently then, I rode on. One time I dismounted, feeling the need to part with the fluid I'd imbibed earlier and water the dry desert plants, watching carefully for rattlers, scorpions or any of the other delightful indigenous fauna. This is why they wear these high boots, then, I mused. The flora also left a lot to be desired. Knee-high gnarled bushes, spiky green outgrowths with razor-sharp-looking jagged leaves, and tumbleweed balls of annoyingly intricate interior design: I did my best to dapple as many of these as I could, countering their aridness with my life-affirming flow. I hadn't reckoned on the sudden subsequent feeling of aridness in my own body, especially in the area of the throat. The sun hadn't let up, and here I was expending fluid and energy, drinking nothing, becoming gradually dehydrated, and feeling shrivelled up inside. Having no hat didn't help, and yet I was too distracted to conjure a new one, which, anyway, would likely fall off when riding. So it was with great relief when I spied what I took as a body of water, shimmering out beyond the dirt and the sand of this dusty plain. Was it a mirage, or the real thing? My energy levels were getting so low now, I was beginning to question my perceptions themselves. Keep on like this, something warned me inside, and you'll never come back (to reality). *Ha... what a joke!*

Conjuring up relief didn't appeal to me somehow. First, it took energy, and second, I kind of liked being a shrunken insect in this vast wilderness, like this was something I thoroughly deserved. Conjuring up a big jar of ice-cube filled water, like Poly had done all those fantastical eons ago, and a lovely round table and chair to go with it, and a nice tumbler, now just seemed like sacrilege against nature. Of course, I was hardly the most respecting of beings when it came to my surroundings, but that was usually when I felt master of my own space, the doer of my grand will and general centre of the universe. It was difficult to feel I was the centre of the universe here, alone -apart from Horsey-with the scrubs, the dry plants, the bleached-out bones of dead animals and the cacti, which, I now noted, punctuated the plain with eerie regularity. Who the hell exactly was I in comparison to those green statuaries? What the hell exactly was I in comparison to the enormity of this great tract of land, this plain of dust, with, as I now noticed, its far-off guardian mountains glinting in the still-hot late afternoon sun? My sense answered that one right off: just another scorpion-like creature, scrambling, or was it 'scuttling' over the face of a hard, arid world. Somehow this insight brought me back to simpler times... the life of a dosser, far, far away, scuttling and scribbling away... not habouring too many dreams about what I'd become... certainly, though, something more elevated than a scorpion, or a crab.

Water, water...(another classic!)... and not a drop to drink. Unless we headed that way, mirage-way, now. So, up I tried to climb back onto Horsey, who certainly seemed the heart and soul of hospitality. It looked a cinch, until I came up close to the creature's remarkable dun-coloured flank. Raising up my cowboy-booted leg was problem number one, as my anatomical limitations dictated I'd have to pull a tendon to manage getting my winkle-pickled foot into that hanging metal stirrup. A full body heft, I soon discovered also, hands grasped onto the lower base of the leather fob at the front of the saddle, was also a no-no: I made so much commotion Horsey backed off real quick and I'd be spending minutes coaxing him back. Half-despairing how to do it, I reasoned, very reasonably, that I'd done it once before, in my panicked flight from town, and guessed I'd therefore have to do it as a jump, a leap and a bound and hope to hell the horse would catch my drift as not being some sort of manic attack on his person. OK, so eventually it worked, but not until I'd learnt the trick of whooping things up, and talking to the horse like he and I were partners and we had a job to do. The first few jumps saw me crash into the dirt as Horsey sidestepped with a grace I could never manage, and then I let the moment take me, that moment being the feeling that if didn't accomplish this, I'd collapse upon the ground properly, get stung to high heaven by an army of bleached-out exoskeleton multilegged poison-bearing crab-like monsters and then a great flock of buzzards would swoop down and pop out my eyes and other choice takings as appetizing snacks. 'C'mon, Mister Horsey!' spoken as I faced him, like you might face a teammate just before the final push in some great game of sport, thousands looking on and cheering that you can do it, only two minutes on the clock notwithstanding. 'C'mon, Horsey! We can do this! We gotta get that water!' Now in full belief the creature understood my every word, grasped the deep significance of all, the life-and-deathness of the moment, as I sidled round his flank, stepping back a ways to get a run in, shouting now: 'H2O, you dumb-assed fourlegged son-of-a-bitch! [feeling as I said that that I might have said too much but couldn't turn back now...] We're gonna kick that water's ass, we are! That's right, Buster, just you and me, we're gonna...' And at that I sprang. My feet lifted and I flew. It wasn't what you'd call a perfect landing, but neither of us spied any rodeo judges hiding behind the dry-assed break-my-heart-if-I-have-to-stay-here bushes and scrubs, so we didn't care a whit. We were back in town! Metaphorically, at least.

It felt good to be back on, and to be bounding forward, water-ward. I assumed the same daft and desperate posture as before, but occasionally lifted up my head to check we were indeed headed in the right way. Yes, ahead it shimmered, and I knew whatever it was we were at, we had to be doing something right. And yet, I'd raise my head again after what I considered a fairly long while, where time is counted by the number of bumps and thuds you have to put up with, your whole body undulating as the horse beneath gallops further and further through horizontal space and the only sound you can hear is the rude, crude thump of hooves on hard, hard ground, dust flying up and infiltrating nostrils and the sun beating down with its own harsh rhythms, sweat pouring out of face pores, built-up balls of sweat bursting every now and then and feeding salt right into your eyes, and yet the water seemed no goddamned closer! It was all getting too much.

The next time I put the ole bonce up and saw that not only were we no closer but that we appeared to have circled round, so that the whole enterprise was an exercise in futility, I let out a cry of despair. I then, unwisely, and precipitously, forced my body into an upright position, and promptly fell off old Horsey. At speed. Just possibly Horsey had buckleapt at something just at that precise moment, maybe a snake, or just according to the law of random actions, which states that 'Nuthin ever goes smooth', and off I did fall, with a thud to the ground, and one almighty smack on my hatless head. I was out for the count.

Blackness and quiet: such peace! Here was no sun and no thirst and no up-and-down movement or any movement at all. It occurred to me I could be happy with blackness and quiet like this. I was floating, it seemed, or suspended, no part of my body in touch with the world. It was lovely, I thought, to be like that, with no-one to bother me, and nothing to do. Just here seeing, and hearing, and feeling, and tasting, and smelling *no thing*, caring about *no thing* and *no one*; no cares in the world about life or about death or even of pain. Until… cracks appeared in the sea of the night, and sound filtered through from above.

'Fella! Is that you?' enquired a voice from above. 'What 'cha doing all splayed out on the ground there for?' was the next not very welcome question from the heavens above.

'Pardner?' it asked, and 'Pardner?' again. Then the tone changed from inquisitive to one that was nothing if not blatantly conclusive: 'Pardner!' Insistent and joyful, kind of like 'Eureka!' re-moulded. 'Eureka?' I asked, having projected my thoughts into my response, dry lips mouthing the word with some difficulty. Eyes still wide-shut. 'Eureka?' it called back from the depths of dark space, and so I threw out: 'Pardner?' 'Pardner! Eureka! whatever you want, I'm just glad to see you!' boomed the god-like voice from above. My eyes still firmly closed, and still thinking I was indeed talking to some Elevated Being (yet an Elevated Being of my acquaintance) in the pitch-black expanse, punctuated though with an ever increasing number of light-emitting stars, I instructed in a far-off voice of my own: 'You say "Eureka" and I'll say "Pardner"'. I paused to let that in. 'That's the "Call and Response" I was telling you about... Call and response... Now d'ya get it?' I mumbled on. '"Call and Response, Call and Response..."....'

Now hands were upon me, and I had to find out why, so I opened my peepers, only to be blinded by the light. Radiant light, but with shading, which steadily grew into shapes, if still beyond knowing. The handling was soft, though, so I guessed it was friendly whatever it was I was doing the Call and Response with. 'Pardner,' again I then murmured, and heard 'Pardner!' returned. We'd established rapport. And feeling we had, I made more of an effort to look at the greys and the browns and the odd line of black, until I could say that this was seeing, no longer dreaming... And, oh, what a sight! With that blanched-coppery head of hair, big jowls, the glint of his round glasses, shining white teeth and a moustache the size of a lorry, it could only be Poly! Eyes now fully open, eyebrows raised, I blurted out: 'POLY!' To which Poly then said, 'It certainly is, fella, none other than your old friend Poly Rhumboldt, here at your service once more!' A moment of straightening me up so I sat somewhat upright, my butt in the dirt, and he asked, innocently, but with an edge: 'What brings you here, fella? What brings you here?'

Before I could answer what I thought was an extremely hard one to answer, I just had to ask, having had a moment or two to take in the man and his bulk: 'Poly, what on earth is that long pole sticking out from your back? And what's with the string?' Yet, before he could answer, noticing all those hooks in his lapel, and a faint smell of fish, I had figured it out. And I smiled, closing my eyes once again.

Of all the good luck in the world, this had to be the bestest of all (even if it was resulting in the bit-by-bit demolition of my grammar). How I'd run into the bloke I'd been looking for all of this time out here in the wilderness was beyond understanding, unless it was Fate, that oul crock all us true pagans imagine exists. It wasn't long before I was standing, dusting myself down and exchanging pleasantries and gentle slaps on respective backs (which Poly extended a mite to help with the dusting). I also made mental note of how much my language was melding into the language of my adopted territory, as though I were, slowly, inexorably, becoming one with the populace, blending in so much I'd leave behind all that I ever was… if I didn't watch out.

Poly: C'mon with me, fella. Straight back this way.
Me: [looking 'back' where he'd motioned, back water-wise, the ole shimmering regained, and, scanning, what looked like a shack, very small, and what I took to be a thin whiff of smoke rising up from its top] That your… place [not wishing to say 'shack']?
P: 'Tis, indeed, young fella, 'tis indeed. That's where we're based at the mo'.
M: We?
P: The better part 'o me, Ha!
M: [remembering his predilection for shouting out 'Ha!' and also that it was always uninterpretable too] That a fact? Well, I sure am dying to meet… your better half, I surely am!
P: [seemingly taken aback a tad by my delivery, and newly-assumed accent] Boy, you done gone American!
M: [only momentarily self-conscious] Check out the duds!
P: You're a cowboy, I swear!
M: An outlaw, no less!
P: [assuming a mock-stern look in his eyes] Don't want no trouble, Mister! No, Siree!

And so we bantered and joshed as we strolled, Poly leading Horsey back by the dangling reins. It was no shack at all but a cross between a log-cabin and a free-standing house: wood beams for walls but tiles on the roof and a chimney. Chairs and tables outside to the left. A few trees either side, providing some shade, and, tucked in at the back, I could just see, some kind of pen, or enclosure. It seemed like a cow maundered there... and, now that I was looking just that bit more intently, a fair few chickens as well. There was even a small corral, out beyond, with a very humble barn attached. What a glorious place it was after all! Not ten yards from the door, however, Poly stopped in his tracks and motioned, ever so slightly, for me to do the same. He called out: 'Susanna! Yo, Susanna!' This had me thinking of the song of almost the same name, and I made a mental note to ask Poly if he knew that one, definitely pre-Blues. In the moments of waiting for a response, if not a call-and-response, I was wondering what Poly's idea was. It was still a nice day, if warm now rather than hot, so perhaps all the better to meet in the light than the dark. First impressions and all that. The door of the cabin had been open from the start, so I was just waiting to see his wife emerge over the threshold when from a ways to the left of the house came a voice calling 'Poly!' with glee. The two of us looked over and saw a lady I presumed was Susanna, and a teenage girl, standing next to her. Poly beamed back and then turned to me, announcing proudly: 'Susanna and Lizzie...' And he then looked in shock at my face, then back to his wife and his daughter, looking speechless and flustered, and then back to me and rasped, in a tone of clear mortification, but quiet enough so only I could hear: 'Mister, all that time we spent at my store, and gabbling on about everything under the sun and all, I never did ask your name proper... begging your pardon and all...' 'Quite all right, Poly, right as rain, right as rain!' I assured him, wondering however it was that

I'd not piped up my name at some point… But then wasn't that normal? Shopkeepers proclaiming their name from the street, the customer always a guest without name… 'I never told you!' I added, dragging out the moment out for all it was worth, as of course we looked like nothing if not buddies, then looking back to the girls as I slipped out the 'info' into his ear which he needed to complete the intros. (I'd actually just thought of it right there and then, after a brief purvey of my gear and an exchange of glances with Horsey.) 'Tex!' Poly announced with a kind of gleeful relief, which was then momentarily threaded with a doubt only I could pick up on, a single steely glance my direction. 'Tex' was good enough for me, I'd decided, just what I was coming to be, and to hell with Ireland and boring normality. 'TEX!' shouted Poly once more, having drunk in my wordless response to his glance, now big-voiced and joyous, pointing vigorously, and repeatedly, at me, as though to make sure they knew he was still doing introductions. I bowed, mock-graciously, but graciously even so, and Susanna and Lizzie just got the titters looking at that. These led to laughs, and briefly, for Susanna anyway, a short fit of coughing, all of which set me off laughing too, infected with gaiety. Poly looked on.

Strangely enough, Susanna and Lizzie chose not to come any closer, but moved to their left, and took their ease on the chairs, two at least which were long and low hung, like deck-chairs, both looking very glad to be doing so. Must have been some walk, was my thought. 'We'll meet them real soon,' confided Poly, but now he was pulling round by way of the back of the cabin and was soon directing me to chop up some wood, which I looked forward to doing with great relish, accepting the ways of the West in a flash (chop wood first, then be offered some tea, that's how they do things round here). 'I'll git your mount seen to,' assured Poly, imparting a friendly slap of his palm onto Horsey's shoulder. A moment or two later, still holding the reins, he very kindly handed me a pewter mug brimming with cold water he'd filled at the outside tap. It was the most delicious draught of cold water ever, slaking the thirst I'd built up in the desert. As for my fall, I was as right as rain now, and ready for work.

After what felt like about an hour of chopping, with the sweat pouring out of my pores in torrents of brine, we were done and ready to wash up, at a small wooden trough fed into by an iron faucet and pump contraption. The water felt great, needless to say. As I gloried in it, my eye was caught by an adjoining wooden rack covered with pots and pans, gleaming and dripping from Poly's recent hard work. I'd come full circle, it struck me, journeyed beyond the clutter of enticing goods that had decorated his store for the benefit of strangers and now entered fully into life out here on the range. The layout on the large outdoor table put the icing on that cake: a slap-up meal of some fresh-caught rainbow trout on a spit (Poly really had gone fishin!), potatoes in jackets bubbling with butter, boiled eggs, poached eggs, fried eggs and raw ones, too, mountains of chopped corncobs, steaming away on a giant-sized plain porcelain dish, leaves of boiled cabbage crossed over with strips of thick bacon, lightly peppered, cobs of brown bread and hunks of hard cheese, bowls filled with syrup or honey, and four pitchers of milk standing like guards at all points of the table, glasses for all. Poly'd been busier than me!

We then joined the ladies, who hadn't gotten up, it seemed, just sat there, while I was directed to be seated, I noted, at the opposite end of the long table, a feature I had to get used to, and to occasionally raising my voice so they could catch what I said. But it was such a great pleasure, and such a great feast, smiles all around. It being awkward to reach over all the time, I had my corn and potatoes and drink near my end, and they had theirs way over at their end, Poly in between, telling them how we had met. I kept to myself the impression that Susanna looked beat, and

Lizzie as though she could do with more sleep. Soon it was Poly and me doing all the talking anyway, between slurps of fresh milk and bites on that glorious fish. 'Now, I'd hoped we could fix you some pie,' confided Poly, 'but it seems we're all outta apples!' At this, Poly looked mock-stern at me once again, a forkful of butter-dripping potato suspended half-way to his mouth. Little globules dripped back onto his willow-patterned plate.

Up to this moment, I'd forgotten all about the (recent) past, and the (distant) future, savouring the tastes of the fare and enjoying the chat with them all. But I'd noticed things, too. Susanna was a fine lady indeed, very fine manners and beautiful, too, and I wondered how it was always the case that the slender ones always end up with huge bear-like husbands. Was there some law about that? And yet, she wasn't just thin, but a tad frail, and I found myself hoping she would eat more. Lizzie did, gulping it down with abandon, and ole Poly kept passing her plates, and filling both their glasses to full with the milk. A table laden down with the fruits of the earth... Yes, they had a cow and some chickens and a river nearby for the fish, but surely Poly would conjure up stuff all the time. That's how it worked, so I guessed. And then I clicked back to the quip about apples and opened my mouth, having seen what he was getting at: 'Ah, now you see...' I prevaricated. 'They... just sort of came out... like a *fountain*, if you must know...' I was answering, but skirting things too. I recalled the mad scene at the saloon, and re-saw the eyes of my impromptu audience all as they had looked on in absolute shock.

Seeing I was fluffing, Poly put down his fork, and shot straight: 'You mean you were using your magic round here?' My eyes met his briefly and then sought out the table-top, a furtiveness coming over me all of a sudden. I noted that he'd used the word 'magic' openly, so it was obviously no secret from his wife and daughter. This meant I could speak openly and do my tell-all. But first a long draught of the milk for my strength. 'Well,' I began, 'well, the day after I'd been to your shop… I…' I paused, looked up, noticed all eyes on me, nobody eating or drinking, or even moving at all. 'I… err…' Now I employed my hands in the act, rotating the fingers of both hands, first with some speed, as though feeling confident, then ever so slowly, as though in the throes of growing speechlessness. 'I…' My mouth attempted to form words, the words that I needed to explain what I'd done. At one point I did manage to say 'cha-ri-ty' (all broken and drawn out, like I had a fishbone stuck in my craw, so it was likely not understood), which garnered a narrowing of eyes all around, then, I thought to clarify, 'helping people!', but I did so without making sentences, and so however clear it was to myself, it must have just struck them as mystifying pieces of a puzzle they didn't even know the picture of. 'Err… not really me…' I proto-explained, scrunching up my eyebrows at that. I thought my utterance, combined with the facial gesture, quite coherent, but by the time I had gotten to '… dressed up… a little bit…the boots and all…' Poly reached out his large hand and cupped it round my bare forearm. 'Boy,' he said, looking me square in the eye, 'I think you needs a drink.' There was something in that, in the words and the tone, that brought me back through the ether of time and of space. It was like we were back in his shop, and I'd embarrassed myself with my presumptions and assertions, knowing basically nil. This was the same, with one proviso: the not knowing was the other way round. I was glad when he broke from his stare, and announced with a shrug: 'But let's finish this first!' The tension was broken and Susanna and Lizzie laughed out, Susanna exclaiming, in a softly sarcastic tone: 'Lordy! Ain't life simple!?' At which we all had to laugh. Susanna laughed so much she started to cough, about which Poly and Lizzie made a big fuss.

Sated and full, Poly asked to be excused from the table, and then promptly cleared up the plates, soon enlisting me.

The ladies were well taken care of, I thought, the opposite of my hometown in Ireland… Poly did everything -what a bloke! We carted the plates to the back of the cabin, and soaked them in a huge tin basin (very P.P.P.!), a cup of soap powder thrown in for good luck. 'I'll do them later,' he said. 'Let's go for a stroll.' So, he led and I followed, the sun now only a quarter-strength of what it had been, very pleasant indeed to walk in. We wandered vaguely river-wise. I took in the view as we did, and it was rich. A line of mountains in the far distance, threads of clouds over them, beginning to turn pink. And the vast expanse of the land was breathtaking. A desert of sorts, with green patches here and there, the odd isolated tree sticking up, and those beginning to grow silhouetted and stark. I saw an eagle fly over one, and pointed, but Poly's eyes seemed locked onto a spot in the closer foreground, where the river was flowing. So, I caught the direction of his look and did my best to make out what it was that was interesting for him. It didn't take long.

'We wanted it near the ole stream,' intoned Poly, looking down as we got there. 'Because, well… because water is life…' It was a beautiful cross, I could see. Some hardwood, like ebony, finely inscribed, too. Poly knelt down and read: 'Little Tom Rhumboldt, only just three, now in the arms of the Angels'. He paused. 'Have to inscribe a date on it, shoulda done that by now, but, as you can see from the dirt, it wasn't long ago.'

I was unable to speak, and just stood there like I was one of those motionless trees out there in the desert. I could feel strong emotion welling up somewhere, but I was desperate for it not to come out.

After a bit, Poly stood up. We backed up a little, and walked down to the riverbank proper, then sat ourselves down on the grass, watching the flowing and the shimmering, the life of this place.

Out of nowhere, Poly conjured up a bottle of

something, and two tiny glasses. He poured us out jiggers and we drank them now in synch. Then one more, just the same. After the second, I spoke: 'Uisce beatha,' I said. Poly inclined his head to catch that. '"Uisce beatha" is the Irish for whiskey. "Uisce" means "water", "beatha" means "of life": "Water of life".' 'I'll drink to that,' said Poly, so we did, long and slow. And then it was his turn to speak.

'Susanna's... poorly.' He said it without fuss, or even turning his head. I could tell he'd hesitated over what word to use, but 'poorly' spoke volumes. 'If the Lord have mercy, though,' he continued, 'Lizzie might make it.' He said this looking straight out ahead, over the water, out to the hills. I wanted to speak, but something told me no. 'I had to get them here as quick as I could, fella. I'm sorry I got you took in...' 'No...' I parried, but he wouldn't let me. 'Not fast enough, Lordy, not fast enough,' and as he said this his glance turned back to the grave we had visited and he was quiet for some moments. Poly resumed his talk. 'Don't know what I was thinking, I'm sure. Couldn't trust no-one round here to take care of the shop. My family's out East.' He broke into a slight smile: 'You can't get something for nothing, so the ole magic was... a li'l *gift*, I suppose... for anyone crazy enough to want to take on the job... Actually, I don't really know now myself...' Now he turned round, and, with a smile I was glad to see on his lips, amended: 'Oops, didn't mean to imply...' 'Not at all,' I rushed to reply. I was eager to simply be there with him, to listen to him, to share a quiet drink with him. I didn't understand what had happened, and why they had had to come out here all of a sudden, but I felt it was improper to ask, for the moment. He'd tell me in time. Now was just for him.

Then, after a moment or so, Poly spoke again: 'So...' he began, seeming a little uncomfortable to be raising a difficult topic at this time. He pointedly looked me up and down, me in my cowboy get-up, recently-conjured hat firmly plugged on my head -my little comfort blanket...

'You…' he was straining to formulate his question, clearly not wishing to offend, '…working there? In the shop? In that… get-up and all?' I looked flustered immediately, and he reached out with his palm, to assure: 'Don't get me wrong, fella, no obligation, remember?' Yet, I could *not* remember, and my face answered that. Poly smiled: 'The ole booze had you sozzled, that what you mean?' He said it with such cheer and such lack of incrimination I couldn't not assent to that. It was my let-out indeed, and I nodded. 'Livin'' it up, then, young fella? Well, why the hell not?!' And he burst into jollity right there and then. I was so glad to see it, I joined in the fun. Helped by another wee dram. But now I was thinking, under the laughing and drinking and all. I hadn't really considered it properly until now, but now I could see something else: that Poly really knew nothing of me. He couldn't know I was from his future, by one hundred years or more. He thought I was just in from the next town.

Poly: So, what d'ya do with all them apples?

Me: Had a bit of a run in with the sheriff.

P: Sheriff Hamilton? A hard man!

M: You can tell me! He wanted to arrest me!

P: What? For distributing apples?

M: Thought I was part of the Tyler gang…

P: Heard about them… bunch o' no-gooders.

M: Well, he pegged me as one, and pulled out his gun.

P: You don't say!

M: As large as life, I was shocked, wondered why I was getting the bad treatment. OK, I was packing an iron, against regulations…

P: Packing iron? Whatever for?

M: [looking flustered and lost for a quick answer] Thought… it was… standard…

P: [meting out another of his famous mock-stern stares] Boy, you's certainly from outta town!

M: You don't know the half of it!

P: [now a serious stare, like he was worried] How so?

M: No, it's OK... I just meant, like, I was just thinking your town's very different from mine.

P: [raised eyebrows] Go on.

M: Well, [feeling somehow unable to stop] we don't have no horses trotting down the street... we have us 'cars'...

P: Train cars! We have them too. You joshin' me?

M: No, I mean cars in the street. They go up and down, and they stop and people can drive them and go to the supermarket and buy groceries and put the groceries in the trunk...

P: [looking quizzical] I heard of one 'automobile', I think, over in Denver or somewhere... But, Mister, what on earth is a 'super-market'? Just a big one? And a trunk...?

M: [realizing I was saying too much, I had to back-track] Yeah, a big one, Poly, bigger than your shop anyhows, kind of outside, but inside at the same time...

P: [more intensely quizzical looks]

M: [feeling the pressure and wondering if I'd already done enough to alter the future of the planet...] I mean, inside, Poly, inside, just big, OK, stocked full of goodies... and we don't really have that many 'cars', just a few, really, you could probably walk all day and not see a one...

P: [looking distinctly unconvinced] Walk all day? Because you've no horses?

M: Well, we do have a few, actually, now that I think of it... yes, [dumbshow of counting, pretending to recall certain details] yes... Of course, what am I saying, we need them, too, to get around, here and there, yes, of course... there's gymkhanas and such...

P: [after a moment of looking at me as though I had three heads] ...Jim Kanas? Who or what in the world hell is that? [then, his tone and look losing its softness, until...] Mister, or Tex, or whatever you answer to, that's the biggest bunch o' horsecrap I ever heard!

M: [the features of my face assumed a look that could be described as 'hurt', pausing considerably] Indeedy... indeedy it is!

Pause. Then, Poly, yet again taken aback, this time no doubt by my made-up word, leading the way, we broke up into laughter which was as long as it was loud. Having allowed the merriment to continue as long as it could, and now building up my courage and hoping to capitalize on the good will, I decided to take the plunge: 'Poly,' I said, in a new and somewhat confident tone, 'I'd like to return ...*it*.'

P: Return what? The apples? [voiced sarcastically]
M: No, the... *gift*.
P: What gift? Did I give you a...? [at this point, a light seemed to go on behind Poly's eyes]
M: Yeah... the... 'gift'... you know what I mean... and I'm sorry for being so ungrateful...
P: [looking down in the dirt] Why ever for?
M: It's wonderful, I know. Incredible, in fact. But... Poly, having it makes me...
P: [having waited long to hear the last word, but in vain] Makes you *what*?
M: Crazy. [significant pause] And dangerous, too.
P: Carrying a gun... throwing apples at people...
M: Well, not just apples, actually.
P: [another serious stare into my eyes] Do tell.
M: [delivering the answer with a wince] Grandfather clocks.
P: [brief quizzical look] A longcase? Where? [a little more desperately]... At who?
M: At... well... at... the sheriff...
P: Sheriff Hamilton?
M: Mmmm, yes. But, just the one, actually. And I kind of swerved it... didn't want him... getting decapitated and all...
Poly exploded, raising his arms, bolting up straight onto his

feet and bluntly shouting out: 'Jesus, Mary and Joseph!'

M: That's what he said!

P: [firing a look that would burn a rattlesnake] Man! You are a *li-a-bility!* What in tarnation am I doing trusting a person like you? I must have bin CRAZY! You... [motioning with his hands the action he imagined I had perpetrated, and then gesturing what appeared to be a very large object]... you... [in exasperation] AGHHH!

M: [feeling crushed and as though shrinking into the earth] So sorry, Poly, so sorry for my craziness... but you see, it's the ... [shouting] GIFT ! It's not a gift, it's a.... It's a CURSE!

Now *I* stood up, feeling the urge to assert my rights as the one who was wronged, not the bad guy in this. I was suddenly possessed! 'Yes, it's a curse you gave me! It made me into a stupid, crazy, dangerous person! I was threatening people with guns... stuff would be coming out of my fingers as I slept at night! Tins, pans, bread, rice, knives, guns, rifles, even, as I just told you, Grandfather Clocks! I'd wake up and there'd be all this stuff everywhere! My girlfriend Ruby screamed once because I'd thrown Bowie knives up into the walls as I slept! She was terrified! And I was becoming a megalomaniac! A jumped-up hard man in a cowboy get-up: look at me the wrong way and watch OUT!' By this time tears were coming out of my eyes, I was virtually screaming out words, a flow of words to match the flow of apples, or whatever junk it happened to be that was sidling through my mind... I was falling apart! Poly, struck by the vehemence of my utterances and my actions, autonomic shakings and stutterings, not to mention the look of aghast self-pity and terror upon my face, said: 'Oh Lordy, Lordy, Lordy! My good friend, *I have done you a wrong!* I'm the one should be apologizing, not you!'

And just as the curtains were closing on this tragic spectacle, we suddenly found ourselves hugging in acceptance of the fault on both sides and the hope that from now on, we could fix it all up.

****

Much later, and much calmed down, I appreciated lying down on the 'guest bunk' inside the cabin. In the dim light (of the moon) my eyes picked out the odd detail: the stove with its iron chimney contraption, the modest gingham-clothed table and chairs, the comfy big sofa by the opposite wall, framed pics here and there for some décor. What a cozy and comfortable place old Poly had made! I'd even been impressed by the outhouse, which I visited with unfounded trepidation, but, when push came to shove, was glad of its separation from the cabin. Poly had certainly done a lot of work in a short time, and the dedication to his family touched something in me. I could hear his steady breathing now, with the occasional snore thrown in for good luck. My ears, though, were still a little bit red from the emotion of earlier, and from the ensuing few drams we'd consumed to smooth out the waters. But I could not sleep. I'd had a devil of a time trying not to disclose any more about me and where -and when- I was from. All the time, of course, I wanted to, but each time some dead hand of conscience came in and blocked me from opening up. Don't mess with the future of humanity, was the basic import. So, I'd been forced to tell barefaced lies, and it made me feel bad. It made me feel bad because I'd grown to like Poly very much, and he'd let me into his world, let me share time, and good food and drink, with his family. So, every time I told a porky, I'd shrink down a little further inside. But I couldn't show that as we chatted away.

I couldn't quite keep the lid perfectly down all the time, though. The ole booze has a lot to answer for. He'd gotten a 'dispensation' from his wife to *'enjoy the moment!'*, as the kind lady had put it, and 'Don't you bother about us!' she'd hollered gleefully. She was happy passing the time with Liz, them playing cards and all, coping with the odd coughing fit now and then. Anyway, I kind of recall, out of the haze, Poly giving me one of his looks, and, now that I think about it, it was after I'd let slip this time about flying. Flying! And 'planes'! 'Oh, yes, London to New York in six hours in one of *them*,' I'd stupidly said, then retracted in panic, burbling away to blur the import of what I had let slip. 'I mean "flying" like "going real fast" in one of them *plain* ships, oh yes…', speaking too fast myself as I said it. 'Six hours? I meant it would *feel* like just six hours…!' Poly had given me a long look that time, with eyes that expressed more than a touch of suspicion, but after a while I felt I'd done a pretty good job of covering my tracks, as he soon recycled the flying concept himself to talk about his long ago family leaving Ireland. Because of the famine, he said, which was 'something shocking by all accounts', the Great-Great Granddaddy 'had to fly himsel' to 'scape the misery of them having no spuds to stick in their craw', as he put it. I'd pressed for a date, and he threw out something about the mid-seventeen hundreds, which was *a hundred years before* the date I'd been thinking of all that time. It was a famine I knew little about, so I made a mental note to check up on it whenever I might get back to civilization. Assuming, wrongly, that Poly had been talking about the 1845 famine when he talked about his ancestor, that first time I'd met him, had played its part in making me believe ole Poly was my contemporary, before I knew better, up on the hill…

That got me thinking right there and then. I wanted to know what year we were in 'now', but asking that straight would have struck Poly as just too strange altogether. I was playing at being his 19th century contemporary, if from outta town, and that involved digging deeper into my role and hopefully never letting out the true state of things. The closest I got was to ask if he had a newspaper handy, to which he replied 'Sure' and pointed to the outhouse, and then slapped his thigh and chortled a bit. The outhouse… The outhouse! I tried to dampen the look in my eyes as I responded to this with what no doubt looked like a mysteriously developing glee. A trip to the outhouse, with its strips of torn newspaper, ready for wiping backsides, was all that was needed to fill in the blank of when it was that was now! Unfortunately, however, it was as dark as it gets on the plains, which is pretty damn dark I can tell you, at least when the moon fell prey to the odd ambush by clouds. I was not to be put off, though, and excused myself, forcing myself to look as unexcited as I thought it reasonable to look for a man about to wander off and empty his bowels. Yet, rather than that, I would grab a few sheets and examine them by the light of the pale moon. And I did, for all they were worth, which wasn't very much: no page heads I could see, just sheet after sheet of news about town affairs, classified ads and the odd drawn picture here and there. It was all very furtive and quick, there at the outhouse door, the vague smell of excrement wafting around, my eyes straining to check on the contents of flimsy inked paper, to anyone who saw me, a study in absurdity for sure…

Absurd or crazy. 'Crazy' is what he called himself for trusting me, and he wasn't too happy about me conjuring up dollar coins from the cash register, either! He'd retracted that, though, then apologized over and over, but I knew it was me, rather than him, who'd been crazy to accept. And even crazier to keep at it, and then, well, allowing it to take over me… Now where was I, and when? I had no real idea… We'd resumed our chat and talked this and that till I'd learnt all I could about life for a shopkeeper on the ole Wild West Frontier. Oh, the wonders, oh, the wonders, and the horrors too, I could have told him, of wars and more wars in the good ole Twentieth Century… Well, the art and the writing, too, and, oh my, the technology, too. But every time the latter idea came into my head, it wasn't the moon landings I saw, or skyscrapers shooting up everywhere, but a giant, menacing cloud I saw, expanding and lifting, expanding and lifting, obliterating everything below...

Still I could not sleep. Although it was a warm enough climate, being summer, I thought of Susanna and Lizzie still stuck out on the porch. A regular enough arrangement, so I'd been told. There was always the night sky to take in, however: such a sight, I was stunned. Ten thousand stars twinkling did I behold! Did me and Poly both, as we did our final watering of the soil before turning in. And the fire, with the logs I had chopped, kept the wolves right away. Yet, I still thought about them, tucked up in their blankets, suppressing the odd cough, keeping themselves company all the long, cool night. 'Consumption,' he'd explained. 'Only cure's to be out in the air... and there's plenty out here.' Good for the old 'atmospheric influence', as he termed it, away as far as possible from the town. Good food and fresh milk were essential, too. He said he was sorry he had to separate us at the table, but it was 'just a precaution'. I could see how good a man ole Poly was to his family, how great was his sadness, his loss, his fears, and yet his hopes, too. He was doing his damnedest, and there I was acting out fantasies, playing around like an eejit, unaware of so much in the world. Maybe it wasn't the gift after all, I concluded. It was me. Me that was wrong. I was childish and wrong. Perhaps someone else could handle such power, or... even me, if I grew up at all... It was too risky, and anyway, greater things were at stake. This wasn't my time or my land. I had to get back, to get back to Ruby, to what I was born to, not get stuck in a world not my own. Maybe then, I'd be very changed when that happened. That could only be good. Yet, no, my mind baulked, I'd still not want to work in a regular shop, pretending to show concern for the customers, or licking envelopes at the post office, or handling 'claims' in the civil service. Where was the mystery in that?

Yet, look at me now, I suddenly asked I. I'm living a dream... Yet, what a dream! (Was that a coyote I heard howl out there?) I felt a pang of sadness as I reflected: I will relinquish this soon... How can I do that? And yet...

I was confused, conflicted, and sad, but something was telling me there's only one end, and it has to come soon. I can cherish this world wherever I go, within my own heart and my mind.

And thinking like that, I then slept.

****

Breakfast was outside once more, and it was plentiful and hearty and good. Susanna remained seated, just taking it easy, while Poly was brushing crumbs off the table, and looking generally busy. Lizzie was up and about soon after our fine repast, taking care of my horse. 'Where did you get him?' she asked. I hadn't expected that, and so blurted out: 'I just jumped on him in the main street... That's where we met, so to speak...' All eyes were on me at that. A sudden uncomfortableness rose. 'Horse-thief!' I heard in my mind's ear. But Lizzie broke the encroaching ice with a glorious slap of her hands and the following: 'Tex, you're a flippity-floppity outlaw and no mistakin!' and she roared it out so fast, if with remarkable good cheer, I was shocked, and also just a bit gladdened. With energy like that, it struck me, she'd do just alright. Poly looked shocked too, with me, and with himself. He'd never thought to ask how I'd come by my four-legged friend. But he desisted from speaking out, no doubt as he'd heard quite enough. I was looking embarrassed enough to serve as punishment for my doings anyways...

Anyhow, this was a distraction it seemed Poly could do without right then. Rather, he was anxious for us to take a wee dander, as I guessed, because we needed to talk business, and needed the space. Despite all our talk the evening previous, we'd not made a plan: he'd told me at the start: 'Sleep on it'. So I had.

Poly: [us walking out round the back of the cabin, toward the river] You made up your mind there?

Me: I got to get back.

P: You don't want the gift?

M: I... don't... want... the gift... [tone and delivery halting, hardly convincing]

P: [reaching his hand round the back of his trousers he pulled out what looked like a very small and very flimsy piece of paper, and handed it to me as we kept pacing] You remember this?

M: [I took what was offered and gave it a look]
    MAGICIAN WANTED
  NO EXPERIENCE NEEDED
   off-off-off Curtis Street,
   P.P.P., General Store, P.E.C. Rhumboldt'
This is the ad which started it all! [I'd almost jumped on first sight]

P: You bet.

M: ['quizzical' written all over my eyes, now trained on Poly] ...

P: Well, you were about the tenth to answer.

M: The tenth? But I came just the day after I saw it.

P: Tenth? Eleventh, twentieth, it's all the same thing. Only *you* passed muster.

M: [a new bout of 'quizzical' engraved itself on my wide-open peepers] ...

P: Boy, you sure do look funny at times.

M: [eyes widening further] ...

P: Oh, Jimmy-Jack Cracker, don't you know *any*thing?

M: [face all scrunched up now, head swivelling this way and that] No…

Poly's own head started to swivel with mine, and so there we were, two sad, sorry sights, swivelling our heads in tandem in the bright morning sun. What could I say to him? Of course, I didn't know *any*thing. How could I? I wanted to ask that, right now, my answer to his question, another question. And yet… I wanted to ask lots of things. Or two most of all: what did it mean I could 'pass muster', and just how the hell did it all work, this conjuring lark, after all? That would do for now, but each time I thought I could broach either of these hot potatoes, I'd catch sight of his eyes, which smiled as they watched me, beneficent and simple.

It was like we were back to shopkeeper and customer. Asking him straight questions just didn't feel right, or it felt like the 'sacrilege' I thought I might be committing out there on the plains, summoning up whatever luxuries I needed to sate my appetite. To ask Poly what it was all about, really, was like tampering with the very fabric of life. Like I couldn't ask what year it was because to do so would be as strange as asking why the sun shines every day (if not quite in Ireland…). Stranger even. I wanted to know, but asking just didn't seem right. So, I just smiled right back at him, telling myself we were quits. If he wasn't taking the hint and opening up about the magic behind it all, well, I was doing the same in regard to the details of everything I was. And everything I'd come from: the sad, mad, bad, great, amazing, astounding, and yet also horrendous, Twentieth Century. Asking, speaking, telling: that would spoil all the fun, like when you're forced to explain a joke. Worse. It'd just unravel everything. On both sides. Ignorance, I had finally come to see, really is bliss.

'Keep it,' he said. 'You might need it just to get back,' he explained. I looked down at the slip of paper once again, noting its febrile condition and then beginning to place it as carefully and reverently as I could into the front pocket of my shirt. 'Nope,' Poly then said, clicking his fingers and summoning up a very slim leather palm-sized case, which he handed to me. I duly received it and slipped in the paper, and then not knowing quite what to do, followed Poly's eyes as he checked out my denims and then pointed to the right front pocket. Tapping his nose, as in a nod's as good as a wink, I then dutifully followed the hint and slid the case in till it was held tight and secure, and Poly smiled once again. 'Once you get through, burn it and you will be free, my friend, you will be free.' To complete the scene, I reached out my hand and we shook. The hug that ensued made it feel even better, like buddies who'd come to the end of a long journey together. Breaking, it was Poly who spoke, looking out at the glimmering stream right before us: 'Uisce beatha, a chara, uisce beatha...'

A bright fish jumped.

****

We returned to the front of the cabin. It was time for goodbyes. I passed a few polite words with Liz, as I'd come to abbreviate her, and told her how fine she looked, and that I was 'gunning for you', which brought a laugh from her, and momentarily worried glances from Poly and his wife. 'Tex, I can believe it! It's a rootin' tootin' cowboy you are!' Liz then exclaimed, and I blushed, said 'Ah, shucks...' and mixed in a smile, which came real natural, too. (My sublimation of folksy American English, with all the concomitant gestures and behavioural idiosyncrasies was becoming complete. *Was it all just an act?* a little voice inside me enquired.) Susanna was up out of her chair, too, and I bowed to her, showing as much gratefulness as I could, and wishing her the very best, and then, out of nowhere, just taking the notion, I started singing: 'Oh Susanna, don't you cry for me, for I'm going to Alabama, with a banjo on my knee!' It was quite a moment for her, and she clapped, saying: 'Oh, how delightful you are!' with a real Southern (Alabama?) drawl that to hear was a delight for me, too. Then Poly stepped in, out of nowhere it seemed, and took Susanna by the hand. He smiled a broad smile and then he let rip, with a delivery you wouldn't find anywhere except on the stage:

I came from Alabama
Wid my ban-jo on my knee,
I'm gwyne to Louisiana,
My true love for to see;
It rain'd all night the day I left,
The weather it was dry,
The sun so hot I froze to death,
Su..san..na, don't you cry.

Oh! Su....san..na,
Oh don't you cry for me,
I've come from Alabama,
Wid my ban-jo on my knee!

He virtually exploded in the chorus, and having taken Susanna by the hand already, now led her on a kind of barn-dance sort of thing, with him doing most of the skipping about, holding her in the centre, so to speak. It all happened in a whirl. It wasn't enough though, it seemed, and he suddenly raised the index finger of his right hand and exclaimed: 'Waitee here now, don't go away, folks!' And with that he scarpered back into the cabin, as we all looked at each other wondering had he flipped out or what. Well, he had, but in the best possible way. Now out he came again, proudly holding one long shining thing it took my breath away to behold: a banjo! In one fluid move, Poly'd thrown the strap over his shoulder and begun to pluck, and as he did so, he sang the sweet words, soft and slow:

I had a dream de odder night
When ebery ting was still,
I thought I saw Susanna dear
A-coming down the hill.
The buck-wheat cake was in her mouth,
The tear was in her eye;
Said I, "I'm coming from de south,
Susanna don't you cry.

Then, with a pause filled with expectation, he launched into the chorus with abandon, and we all joined in.

Oh! Su….san..na,
Oh don't you cry for me,
I've come from Alabama,
Wid my ban-jo on my knee!

The cheer this created among us was stayed only by an added-on bit of solo plucking we didn't notice quite at first, but then, as we did, we started to stare at the speed and the fluency of his fingers playing white hot on the strings. Paul E. Clarence Rhumboldt, Banjo Player Extraordinaire! I only noticed as I stared, that, presumably prior to picking it up, he'd somehow slipped on little extensions to his three main plucking fingers: it was a bit of a blur, mind. After his final flourish, his fingers going so fast you could hardly tell them apart, we exploded in clapping and whooping and hollering and even me and Liz jumping up and down a little, too.

I should have just let things go, but I never can do, so I reached out my right and stole the instrument from Poly, who unlatched as gracefully as he could from a man grabbing at the thing: 'Now I can play you the Blues!' I hollered. I had never held or played a banjo before in my life, but it sure felt good as I strapped it up, to have it hanging there, with its circular body looking radiant white. Yet, I've always played guitar, and the tuning is different, and the sound and the sensitivity was scary. After fooling around with it a few moments, I soon realized I would have to make do with only the two treble strings, or it'd be a real mess. They didn't care: whatever I did got them smiling and 'Woooing'. After some more fiddling around with the strings and the frets, not to mention the little steel extensions I'd stuck onto my first and second fingers and thumb of my playing hand, I was ready to play, primitive though it would be. Then, something else struck me, like a thunderbolt: might this not be, I almost swooned to think, the very first appearance of the Blues in the world? *God forgive me, BB King! Muddy Waters! Blind Lemon Jefferson!* I prayed.

'Woke up this morning,' I sang out, with a thunk-a-thunk-a-thunk-a-thunk-a-thunk 'at a quarter past after three' (not able to fill the line, I improvised and in doing so took liberties whenever I needed), thunk-a-thunk-a-thunk-a-thunk-a-thunk, 'I called my baby,' thunk-a-thunk-a-thunk-thunk-a-thunk, 'she was mad at me' (but had the telephone been invented yet?), thunk-a-thunk-a-thunk-a-thunk-a-thunk. 'Picked up ma banjo', thunk-a-thunk, 'Gonna play ma self to sleep!' Now I was executing the descending resolution bit, brokenly, I soon realized, as I was involving a third string in the mix and it just wasn't working, and so... I sang all the louder over that: *'plinkety-plinkety-plinkety-plinkety-thunk!'* What a mess, but it didn't matter: I got nothing but hollers and whoops from my highly appreciative audience of three! 'Yeehaw!' I shrieked out for all I was worth.

And yet that thunderbolt came back: 'the first appearance of the Blues in the world'. What was I up to at all? Who the hell was *I*, incompetent whitey, stealing a march on the real pioneers? I was playing not with a banjo but with Time itself, throwing in a little piece of the future before it had come. My face clouded over. What was I at? 'Kind folks, do me a favour,' I spoke haltingly, 'you're all very kind, but, begging your pardon, so to speak, don't mention what I just played... to a soul...' I'd scrunched up my face like it was caught in a sidewise vise, hoping to communicate not only the import of what I was saying but also my discomfort, too. 'Just forget it, if you will...' Moment of awkwardness, the seconds dripping by... 'But we can't forget you!' exclaimed Liz, breaking the stillness and the ice in one go. 'You're just so rootin' tootin', I tell you you are!' This animated everyone and they all crowded round me, slapping me gently by turns on the shoulders and head. Poly said it for all: 'Man, God threw away the mould when he made you!' Cheers, hollers, applause! And, on my part, oh such relief!

I got on my horse, which Poly kindly held for me so that I could so without drama, and turned to them all. 'Be seeing y'all now...' I said with a trace of almost unbearable sadness, as I would not, not ever, be seeing them again. It was mighty hard breaking eye contact with ole Poly, who called out: 'Stay outta trouble, for pity's sake. But...' he seemed almost reluctant to add, '...if you ever need me, just holler!' You could hear a break in his voice.

'*Adieu, mes amis*,' I called back, wondering if they knew French at all, and then off I rode, into the sun and the vast land stretching out before me.

CHAPTER SIX

Poly'd made it real simple, if grammatically dodgy: 'Scoot right over there, between *them* two peaks.' So I did. Watered and fed, Horsey was as glad as I was to get going. Perhaps he sensed he'd get back to his owner and have done with the frolics of this damn amateur. I'd washed up myself and was looking every bit the rootin' tootin' cowboy Lizzie had me pegged as. As for the details, I'd thought it best not to burden Poly too much, just giving vague reassurances on how I'd get through unscathed and back to 'my own town'. Which, though I didn't of course say, happened to be a little bit further away than Poly could ever know. I was now happy with that, my deception, as the more I had thought on it the more I had convinced myself that my presence here was fraught with danger for the very future of the planet. Best not to think on that too much, I had concluded, just get on with the final stage of this mad adventure and get back to where I belonged.

Where I belonged, however, also had its drawbacks, not

the least of that being having to sit opposite a pencil-pusher, as happened one glorious day not too long ago (give or take a hundred years), and answer questions about what I had been doing that week in order to find 'gainful employment'. Memories of the first encounter had been enough to depress a penguin: after a barrage of Qs on who and what I was, the male interviewer, whose skill of enclosing documents in plastic bands (extending the band out so far that it would thwack back onto the paper like a pandybat on a bum) was positively frightening, surely designed to intimidate, turned the computer monitor round for me to check that everything was in order. All very nice but below the line entitled 'Date of Birth', now filled in, sat 'Date of Death', not filled in. Yet, I thought. And 'yet' I vocalized: 'Why is *that* there?' I had remonstrated right off. 'What?' he had asked somewhat pointedly, like I was breaking protocol. 'Why do you need to have that "Date of Death" there on the screen? It's hardly going to make anyone feel very good, is it?' 'It's just regulation,' he robot-explained, like it was immaterial to him how anyone felt about it and why was I wasting his time... I looked at him in as pointed a way as I could, knowing an argument was futile, that this guy was a cog in a clankingly huge machine and I was at best a long not-easy-to-remember number in the midst of a whole trayful of documents, and that in a filing-cabinet the size of a new fridge, in the midst of an office bursting with docs, all wired up to info centres situated all round the country, where I could be tracked and categorized and sent on my way with a flea in my ear if need be. In fact, I was the flea.

'Not many filing-cabinets out here' I said to myself, as we flew through the landscape of brown rocks and dust and cacti. 'No stupid computers, either!' I shouted. Horsey reacted, minimally, but oh, if he'd known what I was on about, *oh my!*

The absence of things flying about up in the sky was

another of the things I liked about where I was now -in contrast to (or was it in concert with?) the things I didn't like about back there. We'd stop now and again for a short rest and a drink, and at times like that, I could take it all in as a natural man, at one with the land: the sound of the breeze, the sound of the odd bird, a buzzing insect, or a wild dog, the sound of ole Horsey as he made the occasional snort, but, for ages on end, indeed never-ending, no sound of a jet or a helicopter. And no white lines in the sky. It was enchanting, that silence, that simplicity, and yet I had to resist: I'd made up my mind, I had to go back. *Enjoy it just now*, went the mantra, *enjoy it just now...*

So, what was my strategy? This I also dwelt on, ruminated on even, like I was a cow and my problem was a mouthful of grass. Idea number one: build up speed as I approached the town and belt on through like a fury from hell. Great, but hardly foolproof, as a number of things could go wrong: Horsey might stall being back in his territory, or seeing his owner, get all misty-eyed and nostalgic. Alternatively, the owner might just spy Horsey and get all fury-eyed with the rider, being me, and pull out a concealed Derringer and do his best damage. Just flying through like a Valkyrie was likely to draw the attention of just about everyone, and not least Sheriff Hamilton, whom I had no desire to re-meet. Idea number two: wait until dark. Nope: no patience. Idea three: be all cagey upon my approach, and see when was best to return at a trot, trying to look nonchalant and as uninteresting as possible to all prying eyes. Yes, but then if someone recognized Horsey, I'd be a sitting duck, with no momentum to fall back on. It then struck me that perhaps I'd have to ditch Horsey! Not just in the middle of the desert, of course. I couldn't be callous. No, I'd have to engineer things so I could have the horse wander back into town (would he do that?), and then I'd make my stage-entrance separately, and, it would have to be the most inconspicuous stage-entrance in history. Tiptoeing if need be. (But then, re-thinking that, being horseless might be just as suspicious, even attract all manner of questions. 'Mister, you walked all the way here? Through the desert?' 'In them boots?' Memories of Shaolin Priest Kwai Chang Kaine filtered through to my frazzled brain, and I couldn't get that sonorous TV theme song out of my head for an hour.)

And, now… there it was… Just up ahead. The town, shimmering in the distance of another hot one. After a half a day's riding, we had journeyed our way back, going as straight as a die, guided by the sight of the two peaks Poly had pointed out. And what was this particular outpost of humanity called? I still didn't know, or even care very much, as my thoughts tapered into one intense point: how to get through.

Idea number four surfaced next, born of a growing anxiety for my steed: I couldn't just abandon him here in a place where all manner of snakes and things that bite crawl about. It just wasn't on. Personally, I'd need a make-over of sorts. Be a traveller, stocked up with enough goods to obscure the saddle, and therefore minimize recognition. I'd somehow cottoned on to the idea that it was the saddle which would give us away. I'd also have to re-clothe and then dirty the new duds as before, to make it look like I had ridden long and far to get here. (Well, I had, but…) I'd ride in, a huge Texan Stetson on my head, or possibly something less conspicuous, just something to obscure my face, and then tie up ole Horsey, trying to look as nonchalant as can be. Someone, I hoped, would take care of him later. The next step was a dilly: I'd tie up not outside the first place I came to, but outside a hotel, or even a saloon. Just not the one I'd been in, of course. I'd been thinking hard on this one and come to the conclusion that I needed to stage-manage a trip to the back part of the hotel, or bar, where, somehow, I'd quietly exit and then disappear into backstreets, slipping 'n sliding this way and that, until I'd threaded my way back down through the town, beyond prying eyes. (What was 19th C American for 'Where's the jacks?') The clothes, being different, would be half the battle, and, I saw as my ace, my very gait and comportment would do all the rest: goodbye to the swagger and bluff of my previous self. Forsake the American braggadocio and assume the mantle of The Quiet Man -Irish-American, then! Yes, I'd project a quiet normality, and then be outta here, not with a bang but with something more like a glorious whimper!

That was the plan anyway.

****

I'd retained the boots, flash though they were, and the denims, but replaced the flowery cowboy-style shirt with something soberer, and a longish coat that seemed suitably drab. Not quite a Stetson, I plumped for a sun-stopper the size of a small state, which happily, if annoyingly, drooped over the face quite a bit. I'd conjured up a few blankets, some canvas and a lariat or three, and then fastened them onto Horsey's back so as to obscure the saddle as best as I could. No guns, of course, this time. I'd want to stay away from those items as far as I could. I was a failed farmer, now seeking my long-lost brother (likely attributable, I only realized later, to Caine's quest in the *Kung Fu* programme I'd always loved), and I'd been riding all day and was 'tuckered' and in need of a drink and bath, if you don't mind the dust I'm trailing in here... I would mimic the manner I'd noticed here and there, a preference for minimal utterances and not too much eye-contact, except at the very start, to show I was honest and good. Over-expression was not the way to go in nineteenth century Americay. Being so intent on playing my role, I had my head hung down, expressing tiredness for any who were watching, and so missed the sign announcing the town. No matter, I thought. I'm only wonderin' where in Bejaysus my darn brother has gone… or, done gone, in the vernacular.

Similarly, I paid little attention to their Boot Hill. A mound with some crosses surrounded by light bush, stark against the blue sky, some stones silhouetted. Actually, I wanted to wander over there and go through the tombstones, having always been an avid cemetery-lover, and partly as a consequence of my nationality… There was nothing glorious about this place I could tell at a glance, but then maybe that's best when it comes to death. Somehow, in a sudden whim, I felt I wanted to pluck that pencil-pusher from back in Ireland, with his rubber bands and his hulking computer, with its not-so-fancy swivelling monitor, and just plonk him down right in the middle of all those grey slabs and twists of thorny twigs: 'Get typing!' I'd say.

We ambled on, Horsey and me, growing closer to the town, and, I reflected wistfully, to the end of our brief but eventful acquaintance. I never knew how much horses smelt until I had the pleasure of sitting on one for hours and hours under a piping hot sun. Horsey now smelt good to me, but it had taken some time to acclimatize. It was a deep waft I was imbibing in those first fretful hours just yesterday, a heady concoction for the olfactory senses, only made palatable by the extremeness of the situation I'd been in: fleeing from the law! And, to make matters worse, I hadn't been as riders usually are, head up and nose to the wind: oh, no, I'd been hanging onto ole Horsey's neck, nose to the flanks, his hair actually commingling with my own nose hair. You don't get much closer than that! Furthermore, I'd been in denial-mode. Not denial in the usual sense of not believing, but rather not allowing myself the luxury of… well, anything. To be prey to the most pungent horse-scent with not even a handkerchief between us was precisely what I'd wanted most just then. You see, I'd been shocked to my core at my own outrageousness, causing all that mess, all that madness in the little sleepy town I'd wandered into. That's why I'd been all monk-like in the desert, feeling it 'sacrilege' to conjure items up again. I wanted to kill that part of myself, or at least subject it to anything vile and unpalatable I might come across. Maybe, I then reflected, there was hope for me yet. So, now, as we ambled on, I recalled the mad flight of the day before, and the feeling I'd gone through to the depths of my soul, and concluded that, yes, now Horsey smelled just great to me. Peaches and pie on a Sunday afternoon, a beautiful stink. Hell, I probably smelt just like him now.

Approaching.... trot by trot by trot...

Occasionally peering out from under the lip of my enormous hat, I took in the initial buildings either side as we made our slow but steady progress. Well, the buildings proper were preceded by wooden pens, holding pens for horses or whatever, a sign announcing it as the O'KEEFE CORRAL, which, I amused myself by noting, was just four letters longer than the famous one. There was even a pair of steeds inside them I now noticed, and the odd stableboy tending to long containers I supposed were troughs for meal or water; they were partly stocked with hay right now, I could see that. I didn't want to look too closely, however. I was doing my very best to show no hint of the wonder that still dwelt in me, that of being actually here in the world of the Old West. On the left, the wooden building was tall but anonymous, no sign saying what it was for, unless you took in the front, which had huge doors, and, just glimpsed in the shadows, a horse standing there: a barn or a smith's. On the right was what seemed to be a three-storied house, the top windows fully open and the lace curtains flowing out and flapping in the wind. I caught sight of my first street pedestrians after only a few moments: a trio of what had to be Chinese boyos, each kitted out in identical, classic, silky Chinese tunics, head to foot, or foot to little cute caps. They seemed to be making for the three-storied house. What interested me was that they showed no interest in me. It was working, then, I hoped. I'm just another visitant in a long line of drifters and cowboys and what-not to come here.

Past a few dwellings, it seemed, and then the signs started, to the left and the right, high-up façades announcing their trade: MASON, Prop. K.C.DAVIS, then, HARDWARE, TIMBER & LUMBERWARE, Prop. M.BROOKS in standard elegant capitals, above a slanting porch roof of rough brown tiles, and, below, the shop-front proper, enjoying the shade, with its match-stick-like pillars holding things up, and wooden walkway below. This you could walk all the way down the street without pause, but the rooves of each structure were at different levels, and you could tell each building had been just slotted in. MICHALOVIC & BEJA: DRY GOODS & SUNDRY CLOTHING announced one on the right, and I wondered if I'd find what I needed at all (nothing these places could offer me, that was for sure). TREWIN'S FURNITURE STORE. Nah, don't need that. Or, GUNS, NEW & USED. D.J. MEALOR. Not right now. Next to that, O.G.HARA MERCANTILES. Nope, not today, bro. JULIUS HENRY: SURVEYOR. Psha! Hardly. Then, intriguingly, C. JONES. GENERAL STORE. I wondered if it was as glorious inside as P.P.P.. But even so, it was all getting a bit worrying, for I knew we would soon trot our way to the area I'd been in yesterday, and that was not good. Then I saw it: GRAND HOTEL, on the left-side of the street. I was saved!

Meanwhile, below us, pedestrian traffic had increased. We were still not being noticed, so I was thankful for that, but wondered how long it would last. An elderly black man, with bright, curiously orange hair, pushed a kind of wheelbarrow contraption loaded with what looked like mattresses right down past us. He certainly didn't have time to waste on us. A quartet of girls, all wearing one-piece patterned body-length dresses and in pigtails, ran wildly along the walkway on the right, if not quite singing, then chanting some words, in a state of some glee. Two other children I noticed looked less free and easy: one boy was straining under the weight of a younger boy he was carrying, whom I guessed was disabled. Here and there, shopkeepers, mostly in plain white aprons (over neat, sober duds), were standing by their doors, some sweeping, some chatting with folk, either passing the time with them or trying to persuade them to enter, I couldn't tell which. But whomever I noticed I was glad of one thing only: we weren't being noticed, beyond the odd glance.

I stopped Horsey with an improvised 'Gee-haa!' and what I hoped was a comforting slap to his rump with my right hand, and got down. (I had never got the old spurs in the rump thing. I hated the idea of sticking them in and so I'd only done so either by accident or when it had seemed the last chance I had of stopping Horsey's forward momentum out there on the plains. I hoped this had earned me Brownie points in Horsey's estimation of me.) I wasn't too fussed that my alighting may have looked more like falling off, but I was glad no-one seemed to have looked. Reins in hand, I then realized I'd never tied up a horse. We'd come to the front of the GRAND HOTEL, and there was the horizontal post, but my first attempt was pathetic: the reins soon came unravelled and Horsey started to drift. I eventually got it, bringing the doubled rein round and then pulling the end through so it caught and seemed tight, but, as I watched it, I wondered if once I was inside it wouldn't come undone again. It was then that I looked into the horse's eyes and did my very best at equine telepathy: *You've been there for me, pal, and I appreciate all your help. Just don't go wandering off now at this time, I do beg you.* I did what I thought was holding his gaze, like we were bonding, and I was rewarded with... a snort, and then, a sudden thump, thump, thump. Horsey had spoken his true feelings, and there they were on the ground behind him, for all to purvey.

I stepped up onto the walkway and took a deep breath: I had been here before. Not at this establishment, of course, but here, at the threshold of not just viewing but actually participating in the West. And something had changed, I was sure. Something in me. I had a plan, to escape and return. I'd sloughed off the swagger and was happily ensconced in my ordinariness now, even if it was part of the ploy. I had no wish to make any flap, any stir of the air, if you like. Just to take a last look, combined with a celebratory draught, at the world I had been lucky enough to fall into. I was two steps away, from the portal of the GRAND HOTEL, and from my freedom and soon-to-be reinstatement as a young Irish man, just graduated but not quite decided on what he will do, not properly a waster, just a bit of a thinker, a man with a future in books, or in music, perhaps. I was that, a young rapscallion, yes, but just for the moment, I was the -not entirely euphonious- Friz Zimmerman (I'd made that one up in the saddle), farmer who'd decided farming just wasn't his thing, and was now in search of his long-lost brother JimBob, God keep him safe.

I dusted myself down, as, after all, it was a hotel I was entering, and I had intentionally dusted-up my duds quite a bit out there in the desert, at one point, no doubt to the bewilderment of Horsey, even rolling around in the dirt. What a sight it must have been for him... I'd then spent a good five minutes slapping myself down, palms doing two things at the same time: attempting to brush the dust off and, simultaneously, work it right in, too. Yes, my companion must have been as confused as an equine being can be. Anyhow, now I was here, and I passed my own standard of muster, as the well-travelled man, ready to flop for a half hour with a cold one, enjoy a little leisure after all the hard riding. I did indeed feel tuckered.

I took in the signs either side of the inset doorway, with its swing double-doors just waiting for me to push. One read: J.T.FERGUSON, HOTELIER, EST. 1879, PRIDE O' THE WEST-, and the other was a little poem:

"COME IN WEARY STRANGER
AND REST YOURSELF HERE.
YOU MAY NOT BE HOME
BUT THIS IS DAMN NEAR"

It seemed 'DAMN' had been tampered with, like someone had painted over it, but it had then been re-done, if in a slightly different shade of black from the other letters. Again, I noted, this is the age of the upper-case letter. Talking of upper, I bent back a little and took in the façade, all done in horizontal whitewashed wooden slats until your eye met the porch roof, which only extended out just a foot or so. The day was still quite sunny, so every detail stood out, even the small blemishes here and there, the occasional dent in the slats, and even a hole or two, sprayed round the edges, suggesting gunplay. But you had to squint to see these, the whole showing a marvellous face to the street, that spoke luxury and glamour and wealth, in almost subdued tones. A brief turnaround revealed the street once again, in its browns, and its whites (of the sun) and its blacks (of the shade). The contrasts made it hard for the eye to take it all in. Folks walking upways and down, in various fashions, a lady passing, elegant, under her parasol, a gent passing by her and tipping his top hat, oh such courtesy! Across from the GRAND was the BANK and the TEA MERCHANTS, both looking busy with those going in, and those coming out, their minds on various transactions, remembering all the teas they had tasted, maybe some of that Pu-erh or Golden Monkey I'd seen in Poly's way back when. And then in the foreground there was Horsey, still looking at me. I'd have to be quick. Half an hour was way out of bounds. They hang horse-thieves, I'd heard.

Feeling sufficiently dusted off, and having now gotten back in role, I advanced to the doors and pushed them aside. Before even doing so, I could see over the tops of them that this was a plush establishment. Walking through, I could see it was a lot more spacious than the saloon I'd been in down the street. And tailored for a higher class of customer. Well, it was a hotel first and foremost, with the bar and saloon area over to the right and the RECEPTION over to the left, and a fancy dark wooden staircase in between, directly opposite. Customers as such were few, fewer by far than in the other place, and those that were there were well-dressed and respectable-looking. No fancy dames. No cowboys. Gents only, it seemed, or the odd businessman-type, in drab greys. No-one looked up except the man at RECEPTION, to whom I tipped my hat, half-unsure what to do. I'd spied the glorious bar and, thinking the simplest action is the best, proceeded to amble right-wise, hoping that my tip of the hat sufficed as a greeting and a release for me to get some refreshment. The receptionist's business-like smile heaped relief on my soul.

Feeling quite the least well-dressed, I tried to make my body language communicate some bearing at least, that I was a *bona fide* traveller, just paying a quick visit and willing to mind my business if you were. It all went like clockwork. I skirted the tables in an arc around them and made my way to the bar, placing a brief smile on my lips as I caught the barman's eye. We exchanged our Howdies and I placed my hands on the wood counter and surveyed the choices. 'Mighty fine bar you got here,' I threw out, as my way of allowing me to continue to purvey the sight of the arches and bottles and bibs and bobs hanging down here and there. The sheen of the wood, of the counter and of the arches, was a deep radiant brown: 'Ebony?' I enquired. 'Cherry wood,' retorted the barman, with obvious pride. 'Mighty fine, mighty fine,' I then said once again, enjoying the acceptance the barman's answer seemed to imprint on my mind. I could speak American all day, I almost chortled. 'A beer, if you don't mind, I'm as thirsty as sin,' I then said, and immediately wondered if that hadn't been hasty. 'As thirsty as sin' struck me as potentially dodgy, as though I'd revealed a rough side, or been overly forward with my words. The smooth and speechless fulfilling of my request by the fellow bought me relief, but I felt I was on thin ice, and better to keep my mouth shut.

So I did, except for a 'thankee' -why I didn't say 'thank you' I wasn't sure-, and took my beer to a small unoccupied table, for fear of more chat. (By the time I sat down, I had it: 'thankee' was just that extra bit countrified-sounding: *my acting was directing me*...) Now, this beer was colder than that last one I'd had in the other place, and it felt great. Here I was sitting and enjoying a beer in FERGUSON'S 'WILD WEST' HOTEL, surrounded by people who'd been dead for decades and decades... That was a funny thought just at that moment, because it didn't seem real I could be here. Alternatively, *I* wouldn't exist for decades and decades and so we were doomed never to meet... And yet here I was, sat at a table by myself, enjoying a pint, but, I realized with some regret, not availing of my last chance to exchange some words with the people of the here and now. Of course, I'd been through this already, with Poly: there were limitations to what we could say, either one. But, surely inquiring after a gentleman's business, or where he was from, or if he'd seen any action out on the plains, surely that would be fun, without jeopardizing the future of mankind?

It was then that I realized one aspect I'd missed in my journey to the Wild West: no Injuns! Oops, Native Americans... But of course, I soon realized, that term was invented later. It was a nice term, I suppose, showing, eventually, recognition that those boys were first. And yet, where were they now, in the time of the West? I hadn't seen a one the whole time I'd been here. I'd actually seen a wooden statue or sculpture of an Indian Chief, half-size, outside some shop, I now recalled, but no flesh-and-blood ones, anywhere. Ah, let it be, said a voice inside me, as I slugged a fair draught and looked up at the gilt chandeliers. There are a million things I haven't seen here: so much to explore, actually, so much to subsume… But no time! I have to be moving, a voice inside me insisted. And yet, somehow I couldn't, like something was niggling me, about learning all you can before you get out of town. Not being able to decide quick enough, I clicked my fingers and out of nowhere a waiter came to me. I'd tried that old trick many times back in Ireland, but it either took ages or people would look at me like I was Lord Muck. Here I was king. As soon as I'd said it I regretted my words: 'A bottle of your finest Bordeaux, my man!' Regretted it not because I couldn't pay for it -I had a stack of silver dollars- but because it signalled a loss of focus, when I should have been making plans to sidle away. Not a problem, another voice inside then piped up: I'll enjoy a few moments in this great Western dream, and then I'll be out and away like Little Jack Rabbit. When he returned with the bottle and glass on a gleaming silver tray, I flipped him a silver dollar, and then, thinking quickly, another as a tip. His eyes -he looked Mexican, about my age- studied the coins in his palm for a few moments. Was he pleased? Was it enough? I couldn't tell, so I threw one more out, 'for the barman chap' I explained, to pay for the order so far. I didn't want to leave the Old West with debts to my name.

And talking of names, very shortly after that what should occur but a man I'd not noticed, or had but not much, perhaps because he was one of the businessmen types in drab greys, leaned back from his chair at the adjacent table and said: 'Elmer Worthington, gentleman salesman. I can see you're a man of fine tastes!' He'd obviously noticed the arrival of my Bordeaux and seemed one of those types who don't mind getting all friendly with someone as long as there's a chance they might join the party. Perhaps he'd also picked up on my generous ways. Well, it was Elmer's lucky day: I couldn't drink all this on my own and, glory of glories, I'd get to interface with a real nineteenth century bloke! 'Friz Zimmerman,' I parried back, extending my hand and throwing in: 'Welcome to join me!' at which Elmer did.

Elmer was not much older than me, definitely under thirty, but he had me on flesh, which filled out his chin, and had rounded his shoulders, too. Not much up top, either, but a pleasant smile with it. Elmer came across as nothing if not a kind-hearted man, and a lover of good food and wine to boot. To wit: 'Let me have a look here, Mister, if you don't mind,' and Elmer then reached over, swiftly fishing out a pair of wire-rimmed glasses to examine the label, and read slowly: 'Château Lafite, Rothschild... 1889...! Hell of a year!' I was delighted with his enthusiasm, but not quite as much as I was with the revelation that 'now' was clearly sometime later than 1889. But when? My smile of realization chimed in with his concerning the quality enshrined in the bottle and I thought of following it up with the convoluted: 'Yes, but what is their *latest* best wine?' or having the waiter return so I could order the *latest vintage* they had. But that might look strange with a perfectly good bottle here, and anyway, Elmer, re-pocketing his glasses, was speaking again. Or rather he wasn't, but his seemingly frozen posture spoke volumes to me: it said, 'Well, ain't ya gonna offer me a drink?' So, in compensation for not noticing straight off, I shuddered into action and clicked my two fingers again, calling 'Waiter', to request a second glass. (It was with some relief, I then realized, I had managed not to conjure the damn thing out of thin air.) (Furthermore, it now came back to me... the ole Winchester had been 1894, which pushed things closer to the big one nine zero zero, the end of the Wild West...)

Now well equipped, Elmer and I drank a toast impromptu: 'To the day that is in it!' I piped and Elmer, learning quickly, repeated the phrase, if haltingly. Now, when two complete strangers meet and then drink a toast together in a bar the silence afterward can be deafening. Questions like 'Well, just who are you?' and 'What shall we talk about?' abound in the consciousness, or *so I had thought*: in America, however, no such awkwardness exists, it was becoming clear to me. White to white, at least, we were all one big family. And, hell, apart from a few pounds and a handful of years we might almost be twins. You might have thought we were related or had been acquainted afore had you heard us go at it, or Elmer at least -I was happy to take the back seat to his apparently endless run of stories. Elmer was a seller of 'junk' as he told me, but 'junk people wanted', for scrubbing the floors or painting the eaves of the house, or tidying up gardens, lassoing cattle, even, and 'well, just about anything'. And then, with a chuckle: 'Oh, we also sell food, I forgot!' He was an employee of something called 'Haas, Baruch & Co.', and was 'really just finding my feet', but had 'just closed a deal' and was now 'just sitting easy and letting the bones have a rest'. (He was very fond of saying 'just'!) All very interesting, but now it was my turn, and yet somehow I'd become tired in the process, which had stretched to fifteen minutes or more. (There was a wall-mounted clock with a large easily readable face over the RECEPTION, which lay directly beyond ole Elmer's pate.) (Talking of pates, I'd long removed my annoying hat and placed it on the chair next to me. The waiter, seeing this, had kindly asked if I wanted it hung up, so I'd assented and thanked him. Nice establishment!) It was clear why Elmer had become what he'd become: he could talk the hind leg off a blind donkey. He'd stretch out a story just when you thought it was ending and then import a host of new details and then re-start again just to make sure I wouldn't be lost. It was all very entertaining, but also a bit draining. I wondered if I could find out anything more interesting about the present times. Yet, I was also feeling just a little bit anxious, like perhaps I'd overstayed. There was a limit to my being fascinated by Elmer and the Old West in general and I was approaching it fast. Feeling under some obligation, I mumbled something about having to leave 'the old farmstead', 'not able to pull my weight', but 'I wasn't born to it', and was 'hoping to forge a new career in something... exciting and new... if I could find something like that'. That got Elmer recruiting me for 'Horse & Barack' or whatever it was called, and me waving 'no' and smiling a lot, wondering how to get out of this. 'Let me think on it there, pardner,' I said, in my best folksy voice. And we drank to that. I also found myself explaining -getting into my role- how I'd come here searching for my long-lost brother JimBob, a name which, once I had said it, feeling its cozy-down-home-Mamma-cooking-cherry-pie-ness on my tongue, nearly had me in giggles. I covered it up, though, as a cough, then chugged back a full glass. If this all looked a bit strange, it had the welcome effect of seeming to impress on Elmer the emotional distress I must have been feeling right now, and so, very nicely of him, he changed the subject.

'How was it out there? Any action out on the plains?' Elmer had to ask me that twice, as I'd been in a reverie of what might happen if I were not able to make it away. I was thinking I could be caught, even right here, Sheriff Hamilton coming in fast, kicking my chair out from under me, and pointing his six-shooter right in my face, saying 'Gotcha, you scum!' I might never escape! What was I doing here, sat in this saloon-area of some goddamned Wild West Hotel, chatting with Elmer about junk and about eaves and what year was vintage, how little I cared, and poor old lost JimBob, the brother I never had? And yet, I couldn't be rude. 'No, smooth as you like, not a soul did I see.' 'No Injuns, then?' 'No, not a one!', I responded, a slight glimmer of interest in me stirring, cajoling me into asking about something I'd been just thinking of: 'Actually, Elmer, where are they all, for crying out loud? The Injuns, I mean,' with a chortle and Bordeaux-inspired slap of the tabletop. It'd just struck me I was actually quite interested in that side of life here: here was my chance for some enlightening. 'Oh, don't worry about them. We're well off without them, my friend… Well off without them!' he shot back.

Now, chat between strangers is a curious thing, because if things are going well, it's awful at some point to hear something you'd rather not. A bit like drinking a glass of champagne and then discovering a hair in it. This was the moment we'd come to just now. Call it my ingrained Irish anti-Imperialism, if you like, but I'd always been sympathetic to the fate of the indigenous people of America, feeling they were treated pretty poorly. My facial muscles were still carrying the traces of my enthusiasm, and yet now they were battling contrary ones. And yet, as I said once before, I couldn't be rude. 'How so?' seemed innocuous, but it was the least I could do, not able to shrug it all off as I should have. Perhaps my look of unhappy concentration said more. Elmer had things down pat: 'How so? Cause they ain't Christian-living, my friend Friz, they ain't Christian-living!'

'Well, Elmer, yes,' I stammered, not really wishing to get into it all, 'but that's just not their religion… I'm sure they believe in whatever they believe in…' By the look of understanding on Elmer's face, he was appreciative of my comments and willing to move on, so, only lightly he said: 'Just saying is all…' I was glad to hear this, glad this seemed to put an end to this line of inquiry. I'd glimpsed a vast chasm of prejudice, but I'd no desire to pursue, hoping, at best, I'd at least signalled an opposite idea, whether or not it had impact or not. Yet again, even though I was here in the midst of a time not my own, a place not my own, I had

soon reached the limit of what I could learn. I could, but I
wouldn't, probe further. It might just get ugly. It was the
same as with Poly and the ole magic thing. Human relations
forbade it.

And yet, the topic wasn't quite over. Elmer had suddenly
become animated once again: 'I know of one Injun alright!'
'Who?' I shot back, and then, wondering if that was
question enough: 'What? Where?' 'How about "When"?'
fired off Elmer, 'how about "When"?' he repeated, looking
delighted. 'OK, then: WHEN?' I obliged. 'When there's a
full moon!' exclaimed Elmer, then, beaming, laughing a little
into the bargain, seemingly enjoying my continuing
befuddlement. Then: 'Yesterday!' 'Yesterday?' I echoed,
wondering when exactly ole Elmer'd get into making actual
sentences. 'Indeedy it was!' Elmer confirmed. Now, all of a
sudden, having been hoping for sentences so much it was
now a single word which had my attention: *so 'indeedy' did
exist after all!* (How had I known that, on my first sortie into
town? I wondered. My assimilation had been deeper than I
knew!) However, as I was warming once again to ole Elmer,
albeit of the limited mind-set, he jumped in and delivered
the news: 'Yesterday, afternoon sometime, the ole Apache
attacked once again.' Eager for more, I pounced: 'Tell me
more, tell me more.' 'Well, Friz, before I do that, I think I
need this,' and he poured out some more of the purple
nectar into his glass, and, me, seeing mine was half done,
downed the dregs, and motioned for a sympathetic fill-up,
too. He obliged. We were back on track, kind of.

Elmer raised his eyebrows just an inch, bent his head
down just an inch, and motioned for me to do something
similar, if only just an inch. This, I was thinking, was
CONFIDENTIAL mode. After a less-than-casual look
around, Elmer then leaned a little more into the small space
between us and said: 'Things been a bit crazy round here
recently…' I didn't let on, but I could definitely second
that. 'Don't know if you know…' Elmer enunciated his

words with great care, clearly relishing my attentiveness. '…but ole Sheriff Hamilton…' seeing something in my eyes which he interpreted as confusion (well feigned), '…he's the Sheriff of this here oasis in the desert…' and now seeing my mock appreciation for his explanation and interpreting it as welcome enlightenment, continued: '… well, ole Sheriff Hamilton's got his plate full, yes, Siree. His plate is done loaded with fare!' He'd rushed the last part, like all good showmen might, sat back in his chair and tapped the tabletop for maximum effect. My face said I was none the wiser, so, seeing this, Elmer returned to the small space between us, which was now getting smaller, as he'd motioned me to move closer, too. This, I suspected, was his BETWEEN-US-TWO-ONLY mode. 'You'd think just having the Tyler gang after you, wanting your skin u'd be enough, but oh no,' Elmer was running with the ball now, 'No! He has to have this…' and here he paused, maybe out of deference to me and my liberal ways, 'cray…' but, clearly searching, but unable to deliver a softer word, '…crazy Injun out to get even, shooting and hollering his war dance in front of good Christian folk.' I was still looking as enlightened as a dead pig, so he threw me a lifeline: '…Ole Hammy, as we affectionately call him, out of ear-shot, mind, well, he's ex-Cavalry, and, well,' (Elmer's 'wells' seemed to be his way of delivering what he thought might be sensitive/offensive info to yours truly), '…well, he was involved in one of them clear-out operations a little south o' here... well, I won't go into details…' (I kind of hoped he would, but then time was short and so was tolerance for this doozy) '…all above board and all, but, darn it, thon Apache, well, he done escaped from the round-up and been looking ever since for to get even with any involved… and ever since is over a year, boy!' Elmer shot me a look that demanded sympathy but wasn't getting it, so he rushed on: 'OK… Yesterday, sometime in the afternoon, th'Apache came looking for Hamilton, guns out and murder in his eye.

Quick as a flash, he sees the Sheriff, who, I will inform you presently, was busy right at that time, and fires off a shot: BLAM!' In order to communicate its effect, Elmer's left hand now gripped his right, which had obediently formed the shape of a gun. 'BLAM! BLAM!' once again, both his voice and his actions big. *What, it then struck me, had all the BETWEEN-US-TWO-ONLY whispering been for?*

Heads turned round, if only briefly, but it didn't stop Elmer from re-assuming, with a speed that surprised me, intimate mode, his head now brought so close to my own I thought he might butt me. '"Busy", I said,' said ole Elmer, fired up now, and determined to deliver the *coup de grâce*. 'Talk o' the town, apparently...' he said. My eyes were widening, as though I knew what was coming, like I wanted to stop it and I half-didn't. 'Madder than Tyler! Madder than thon ole Apache! Some kind of spook, so they're saying. Some kind of SPOOK!'

I was hearing about...*ME!*

The whole world now was reduced to the words coming out of Elmer Fudd's mouth: '...this crazy guy... throwing apples -apples, yes, but, Lord, what a lot!' his eyes, which I just realized had always been too close together, narrowed further, 'the gals all there said they spent ages picking them up, and, get this, apples wasn't all he was throwing...' pausing, as though, this time, unable to bring himself to say it out straight, 'get this', again, another sharp look into my eyes, eyebrows suspended, '... one o' them big...' seemingly unsure how to describe it, '...*Regulator timepieces!*" Elmer made a motion with his hands to suggest a stand-up something of considerable size, and continued, his eyes showing fatigue at his own telling, '...at the Sheriff, and...' again pausing dramatically, his 'and' weighted down like a bomb ticking down towards zero, as he now went into ABSOLUTE-TOP-SECRET mode, motioning me yet even closer, and whispering at half the level he'd been whispering before, eyes shifting round him briefly once more, to check no-one could hear: '...they say he used...' (chortling, almost gasping) '...magic, or some kind of conjuring power... say he's a Necromancer, a witch... a veritable Child of the Devil, I do declare! Oh, Dear Lord in Heaven, Bless my Soul!' Elmer slapped his right hand down on the table and I jumped with the suddenness of it. And maybe the realization that, yes, perhaps, I had overstayed my welcome. In this bar. In this cray... well, crazy -but *I* was actually the craziest thing in it- world!

As if that wasn't enough... behind me I could hear the sudden entry of a customer through the swing doors. It was likely a regular occurrence, but this one seemed just a little different. Perhaps it was due to the noise of the doors hitting the side walls a tad violently, coupled with the double clack of what I gathered right then must be a huge pair of boots, made either from wood, or metal. Whoever had done this was breaking some rules, I was sure. Before looking round, I stared Elmer in the eye as though to communicate that I thought just that, about someone breaking the rules in this fine establishment, and also, considering where we had gotten to in the story, that the entering person's timing had really sucked! Elmer had, after all, spent such great energy on telling his tale, and I had similarly spent such great emotion hearing what I had done (what *I* had done!), as though it was a story entirely unconnected to me, a bit like those times back in Ireland when I'd have to just grin and bear it, listening to tales of what I had done the evening previous *as drunk as a lord*... But Elmer's eyes were now staring past me, and onto the annoying intruder, a look of growing awe -or was that actual fear?- etched into his pudgy features. Worried, suddenly, my head flipped around, and just in time, too, to see a truly giant be-hatted bear-man open his giant mouth, which was surrounded by more hair than is usually seen on a barber shop's floor at closing time, and say: 'WHAT SON-OF-A-BITCH IN THIS PROPERTY DONE STOLE MY DEAR HORSE?'

It was time to get out!

'Jesus Christ! Bye, Elmer!' I blurted and literally jumped out of my chair and into my own JUST-PATENTED FLY-PAST-THE-TABLE mode, yet, because it was 'Just-Patented', I couldn't quite get the physics right, and so my definition of 'past' the table might be combined with 'through', to arrive at something closer to 'grazing' the damn thing. With the result that... my sudden action tipped it sideways a tad, a tad which became a tad more, so that, sadly, the wonderful 1889 Château Lafite Bordeaux, with its fine ink representation of the ole winery's lordly, iron-gated house on the label wobbled, and then wobbled again, and, despite the best efforts of Elmer Worthington, employee of 'Arse & Buttock', teller-of-tall-tales (which were true), lover of life and fine wines, and yet also, it had to be said, racist hater of Indians, the last one third of its delicious (and extremely pricey) contents egressed from the neck as it now became horizontal and... -'Yahhh!' he exclaimed- ruined ole Elmer's clothes for the day. I was gone.

On past the table and then past the bar did I fly, unimpeded, eyes now all front-facing and examining what lay before me. And what did? Well, beyond the bar, past the fancy staircase, and just right of RECEPTION, I could see two wooden doors, and that, I decided there and then, was where I was headed now. Neither were signposted as far as I could tell, but my future depended on which one I would choose. I half-thought to enquire of the barman, as he strained his neck round to watch my retreating steps, 'Which one is the restroom? (the jacks?)', but desisted. I now heard the Bear-man, as opposed to the Barman, calling out once more, shouting how he would 'get' me and 'mangle' me and 'pull my insides out' and how I would 'hang', each phrase growing louder, meaning only one thing: he was gaining! Seeing the universe as a series of two doors, where even the wrong one leads somewhere, and not always to death, I plumped for the right, it being closest, and barrelled my way through (no locks and no handles), hoping to high heaven I'd chosen correct. I had! There was sunlight just up ahead! I was going to just make it. And yet alarm bells were ringing, if only inside my own head. Aghast, as the door slammed violently against the wall, because I'd hit it with force, and rebounded, dislodging flower pots and some flimsy shelves, I stared in some horror at what awaited my rocketing form: a tall window, no less! Would I have to jump through plate-glass?

It was time for quick thinking, so I halted a sec, turned back briefly and grabbed at what I reckoned was just about the last flower pot still upright (albeit wobbling a bit too) and threw it as precisely as I imagined the best baseball player in the country might throw his ball (had it started here yet?): and, well, SMASH! What a sound it did make as it dispatched the large pane, which, following the shock of the hole, cracked into large pieces and fell one by one onto the sill and the ground. Then, with sudden curiosity, I watched the projectile, with its purple and yellow blooms adding colour to the day that was in it, sail on out beyond the window as though that was just water off a duck's back, only to then smash once again, this time by violent explosion, against the opposite wall outside. Inspired by the success of my work, and drawing on energy I didn't know that I had, I ran to that space and, with the first-ever pounce in my life, not counting P.E. class all those years ago (in the far future), launched myself through the blessed portal to outside. All very well, but I'd put in too much, and so there was little I could do to avoid the same fate as the pot. BLAM! I hit the wall, just as the flowerpot had done, hands out, but not enough to stop my head from making contact with unforgiving brick. And, alas, I was out for the count. Blackness and quiet and thoughts of a soft beach at night and the lapping of waves… All is bliss, all is bliss…

My first thought upon waking was that I must have been out for some hours, as now it was dark. Was I alive? Was I OK? Had they all just left me alone here in a heap, thinking I was dead, or no fun? And while it was dark, however, I discerned light around the edges of the black hole before me. And if I just listened I could hear something, too. It sounded like waves for the first two or three seconds of regaining consciousness, but this soon changed to thunder, I noticed with shock. Then I felt pain in my cheek and my head whipped to the right. Why was that? I set myself to enquire. I also suddenly felt incredibly light, as though I was levitating. I was! Was this someone else's magic trick? Certainly I was rising up, but, I now noticed, with chagrin, by a force less than supernatural: the features of dark resolved before me: I was in the steely grip of the Bear-man. His face was resolving into a bush-like mass with two pools of off-white flecked with red for his eyes and a toothless abyss for a mouth, not to mention a gnarled and scarred fleshly lump for a nose in the middle of all this. He'd slapped my face once (I'd now figured that much out) and was gearing up for another, and there was little I could do about it. 'Horse thief! See how you like this!' and one of his giant arms detached itself from holding duty and then bent horribly back, making me wonder again if baseball had begun yet, and wouldn't this guy be great as a batter. Another part of my brain said: 'Forget the baseball, if ole Bear-man can hold me suspended with one single hand, I'm doomed!' I waited for the thwack to end all thwacks.

It was then I heard 'Click'.

'Click', it seemed, had an unseen power of its own. It arrested all movement in one. I wondered if it might be accompanied by Click Two and Click Three, but actually what came next was a voice saying: 'Steady there, fella.' Decidedly feminine, too. Even sexy. I was still like a doll, hanging there in the shade, but I was beginning to think, or to hope, I'd been saved. 'Now, put him down nice, and no sudden moves... or you're a dead man, big and all as you are.' Sexy but authoritative, my favourite kind, said a voice within me. And it was, authoritative, that is, as slowly I was being lowered back down to the ground, till my head touched the wall and my body did its awkward best to assume the perpendicular of the where the wall meets the ground. 'Step away, fella,' the voice then said, and I could see where it came from, but it was all in silhouette, teasing me. Without being prompted, I clambered back to my feet and stood up as best as I could. Dressed in as elegant a number as one might ever see out on the street in this town, bustle and all at the back (which first had me thinking of the mysterious stagecoach gal...), stood -and I had to shake my head once or twice, because the shock was almost too much to take in- the one and only... Ruby, my Gal, come to save me in my hour of need! 'Rubes!' I exclaimed, and raising just one small smile from her lips, she flashed 'Hi!' from her eyes, but, addressing Bear-man with something less than cheerfulness, barked: 'Get in there!' motioning to a wooden compartment I'd only just seen. The outhouse? Oh, I forgot to mention: Ruby was wielding a Colt .45 in her two hands, as steady as stone. Hence the click.

'I'll git you both for this,' mumbled Bear-man but did as he was told, shuffling into the dark wooden space as Ruby then sprang into action, running a stake she had found on the ground through the door handles, making egress unlikely, for now. I was just about saying 'Ruby...' and putting my hands to her cherubic face, when she cast me a look that said: 'Not now, let's get out of here!' So, we did, with my heart beating like crazy, we ran down the alley and got out of sight.

CHAPTER SEVEN

'Keep running!' I shouted, but Ruby was adamant: 'No!', dragging me bodily in through a door she had just spied half open. It looked like a barn, and the darkness inside seemed safe. A strong smell of horses and, listening, the odd snort or two. She kicked the door to, and instructed me, in the faint ambient light, to keep quiet with a 'shush!'. To keep quiet *and* still, for fear of disturbing our four-legged friends. 'Quite a barn,' I enthused, buoyant with all the excitement, the thrill of seeing Rubes again, escaping from death, or just getting 'mangled', not to mention the effects of the Château Lafite. 'Could this really be true?' I couldn't help asking my confused brain. I'd been through so much, of course, I had expanded expectations on what might just happen at any one time, but this was a bonus I had never seen coming, and even in the dim light before us, I fell in love once again. I leant my head to her head, and soon, my lips to hers -mine wine-flavoured and rough to hers wine-coloured and smooth. She reciprocated easily, obviously as

174

relieved as me. If not quite as lost in the moment... alas! She broke, whispering: 'We don't have much time. We've got to get out and not make a fuss... try to look...' 'Inconspicuous?' I chipped in, '...yes, I've tried that. It's never worked!' Her eyes caught mine for an interlude of three microseconds, more or less, as we both exchanged worry about what to do.

Then questions: 'How can you be here?' I half-whispered-barked. I'd thought only *I* could visit this marvellous land, but no, Rubes put me right, 'I just did what you did, and followed the cobblestone road.' 'Follow the Cobblestone Road! Follow the Cobblestone Road!' I began to sing-song to the old melody from *The Wizard of Oz*, till Ruby forcibly put her palm on my mouth, until I'd desisted. 'Well, I suppose curiosity got the better of me,' she said, looking round, eyes wide, a twinkle or two discernible even in the dim light, 'but then I was a little bit worried about you, too,' she confessed (archly), throwing me a (wry) look. I made my best attempt at a reassuring smile, but Ruby wasn't convinced: 'I think I was right to be!' I then pitched in: 'You came well prepared anyway!' Smiling somewhat bashfully, she answered: 'Well, you can hide a lot in a bustle!' At that we both tittered, and only when it seemed our sound was affecting the equine brigade did we stop. 'Well, now we have to get out, Rubes. We have to get out. Bear-man's after me, and so is Sheriff Hamilton. I'm Foe Number One. They probably have WANTED POSTERS all over showing my mug.' [Note: said in a discernibly hopeful tone] 'Then,' spoke up Ruby, 'you'll have to disguise yourself! Conjure up something and let's get the hell out of here.'

A moment to think. Then, hey presto!, assisted ably by my lovely escort Ruby, I flicked out my fingers and out came a hat (which, mercy to heavens, was the right size). I didn't much care for the one I'd left at Ferguson's Hotel. This one looked cool, lightish brown, it seemed, a lovely

Martin Connolly

felty feel, and, divesting myself of my farmer's travel coat,
next summoned up a suede waistcoat, to cover the drab
shirt I'd plunked for as dreaded Friz Zimmerman, hapless
farmer. 'Hide in plain sight,' I explained. 'Not for me the
ole ordinary. Live it up to the end!' My upbeat idea was let
down by the implication of what I'd just said, so I followed
up quickly: 'Don't you fear: the end of this nightmare, and
start of our dream.' Somehow these words, even if they
were a bit melodramatic, did the trick and Ruby's eyes
shone, and we even briefly embraced. Which of course
turned into another kiss, one that didn't end till she broke
forcibly from me and mock-slapped my face. It was a call to
arms, the moment of truth, the last gasp of quiet before the
big storm.

Actually, not so fast there, pardner! it struck me all of a
sudden. I had to conjure up gear for the lady, too, as she
might be recognized, too. So, off with the bustle and into,
well… 'What do ya want?' Ruby was as in the dark, literally
and metaphorically, as myself. 'How about a double-
breasted gretchen?' I suggested, a memory of that item
surfacing from somewhere. 'Don't like the sound of that,
Buster!' Here, Ruby caught herself momentarily thinking
about what she'd just said and then hit me: 'You've always
said "Buster", and that's what I call you, but that can't be
your real name, can it? I've asked you about this before!'
'Darlin',' I replied with aplomb, 'How about "Tex"? Or
even "Friz"? That was my last nomenclature…' She seemed
determined to continue but I'd gone into work-mode,
bringing to bear all the concentration I had left to summon
up clothes for the loveliest body in town. 'Shazam!' I
exclaimed, and near spooked the horses, as out of my hands
bolt straight at the end of my two extended arms flowed a
veritable sea of knitted fabrics and cut-and-sewn cloth of all
colours (our eyes now well accustomed to the low-light):
one-piece dresses in greens and in blues and in cream,
pleated skirts, round gowns and bodices, shawls and snoods

176

(yeah, them pesky things again), patterned frocks and flowery blouses, radiant satins and bright crimson silks and pastel cheese-cloths. Petticoats next and garters and hose, socks, too, and then piped up Ruby: 'Just stop!' and I did, with an almost audible screech. A vast sea of cloth was now covering the space between us up to our shins, and the horses were indeed spooked, neighing, snorting and clicking their hooves. 'Someone'll come soon, quick, make a decision!' I half-shouted. 'Lordy, don't you know women, boy? I'll be here half the day!' But she wasn't, thank Jesus. She honed in on a blouse (low-cut, I approved) and fancy skirt arrangement, and a dainty wee shawl (in homely contrast), and I turned, gentlemanly, as she extricated herself out of one outfit and into the next, and we were done.

Easy does it, and easy did it: we peeked out, relieved to have gone undiscovered all this time (I conjured up a few nuggets of sugar for the four-legged lads, who hadn't given us away: they seemed very glad to gobble them up). From here, we were perfect models of caginess, tiptoeing lightly and feeling our way up the side-street to bring us out of the alley and into the main street. 'You take the right and I'll take the left,' I instructed and, -whether it was the cowboy in me, or not- barely restraining myself from patting her butt, I gestured a heart shape with my two hands on my chest, which she answered with a smile that would melt butter. We were parting, briefly, in order to make our escape: we might not have such a peaceful moment again, until all this was done. I hoped it would be as easy as my present confidence -no doubt aided by the residue of the Lafite- suggested... Once she'd made it across, dodging the traffic of folk threading through, horses and one wagon lumbering past, I stepped onto the boardwalk next to me and made a brief check. Looking around me, I was relieved to see no-one looking remotely like the Sheriff, or Bearman, or anyone even interested in what I was at, which was, now, with the slightest of cues from my dame across the way, to simply amble left-wise and keep ambling, walking as steady as steady could be, not a care in the world and no business to do -a bit like my old self back in the ole Emerald Isle, I reflected. Oh, soon to be there!

What a remarkable gal, I also reflected at length, as I ambled. Come all this way, into dangerous territory, and all to save me! Kind of... I wondered if once all this was over, and I'd dispensed with the magic, would she still feel the same? Whether she did or she didn't, of course, there was no other choice, and no other way to find out than to do just that. Get along without gimmicks, so to speak, play it all straight, get a job, maybe, and see how we rocked and rolled when we did. After all, most folks got on with whatever they had, and possessing some awesome physics-defying super-power didn't usually figure in the mix. And... did it matter, I further questioned myself, that we'd be living back there and not here, back in the drab real 'now' of late-80s North of Ireland, and not in the thrills and spills of the late nineteenth century American Wild West? (Not that back there didn't have its own thrills & spills, of course...) What's an environment after all, I asked philosophically now, if not just a series of façades, like these huge wooden jobs declaring the wares and the services of all and sundry? Place -what was that? Did it really matter *where* you lived? Or was it *how you lived?* The latter of course. Take this place, after all. Exciting it was, and colourful, too. And yet just a mite dangerous, too. No, that's not the point. I mean, if I lived here, would I have to become part of it? Was that always true? I was wandering... meandering... but, as I ambled on, my cowboy boots clacking lightly along the hard boards, these thoughts kept on coming, in between glances stolen over at Ruby, and her delectable gait. Assimilation. Sublimation. God, it was happening to me, and I'd been here only two days! I didn't just look like a cowboy, I swaggered! Even my accent had gone all

American, even the vocab, the grammar... Indeedy it had!

Through Poly, I'd come to fall in love with this place just a bit, or even more than a bit. No longer a fetish with goods and surface qualities; I could see he was real. I could see he lived well, in that he lived from his heart and his soul. He gave his family everything he could, and it wouldn't matter where the hell he was doing it, or, thinking of the occasional magic he would use, how. Then, as I dwelt on that, the image of poor ole Elmer's face descended and obscured Poly's noble features. Another well-meaning man, a man of good intentions, a bit of dozer, maybe, but hardly so bad, and yet, he was blind. Blind to the hate he harboured inside, like it was just part of him, an organ of feeling, like his lungs or his liver, needed for life. It sure was easy to kill humans if you told yourself they weren't really human... or Christian... Question was: was Elmer in a minority or was that what helped make all this flurry of activity out here in the desert? Was that what built this 'great country'? Jesus, I suddenly stopped: was Poly like that, too?

The thought depressed me somewhat and I decided to halt the barrage. And anyway, we were making significant progress, the most significant part of which was just now, as I passed the same saloon where the trouble had begun. At this point I made sure to keep my face angled away from the entrance, and brought my left hand to my hat, obscuring my visage as best as I could. I made sure not to alter the swing of my hips, or to detract in any way from my confident, but not-too-confident stride. I was just another inhabitant of whatever-the-hell they called this town, in whatever-the-hell year it might be. I was beyond caring by now. Phew, I was now safely past the dreaded place of my madness, my transformation into the 'Child of the Devil!', yet the sound of the tinkling piano followed me still...

Oh, what joy awaits them! (it suddenly hit me, being a music-loving Child o' the Devil and all...). The Blues is coming, fellas! The Blues! Followed by... Jazz! I felt like shouting it out into the old dusty street. Yes, Jazz, that amazing cultural phenomenon I had attempted to sum up to Poly all those weeks ago, not aware he hadn't a clue. How could he? It hadn't happened yet! Then... R 'n B, Ruth Brown, Big Mama Thornton and then Rock 'n Roll, duckwalking Chuck Berry and ole Elvis Presley shaking his hips *and* the joint. Then onto... the Beatles! They'll take this place by storm! The Stones! The Doors! CSN (&Y)! Steely Dan! Bowie! YES! (The music I grew up with...) Rock, in its multifarious forms, and, funk, and Ray Charles, James Brown, Stevie Wonder, Gil-Scott Heron and whoever, whatever, the rest is -as yet unwritten- history! It'll take time, but, people, you're gonna love it! I felt like I was addressing the ladies and gentlemen all around me, on the street, passing me by on the boardwalk, random bodies in hats and shawls and double-breasted gretchens. I pictured how they might look wearing Walkmans, the earphone wires over their 19th C finery. Visions of a young slick-and-shiny black-haired Elvis belting out 'Blue Suede Shoes' into his angular chrome mic in the middle of the dusty street, 'A One for the money, a Two for the show!' Then, Hendrix, in white jacket and its trailing threads, playing his white Fender Strat and the Marshall stacks behind him blasting out the 'Star-Spangled Banner' with max distortion and wailing feedback...

It occurred to me there, as I kept to my steady pace, following the pace of Ruby on the other side, and trying my damnedest to be inconspicuous, perhaps just right now it was happening, out there in the cotton fields, down south, among the poorest of the poor, the lowest in society, the oppressed, the black people, stolen from Africa, stolen from all they had ever known... Some ole buzzard, hoarding the thought of a tune his Daddy had sung him, and *his* father before that, and rhythms and beats in strange tempos, and then hollering out in the fields to his toiling partner, fellow slaves under the thumb, but keeping the heart going with stories in song, voicings and whistles, a call and, then, a response, then a restatement again. Oh, I'm sure it was happening *right now!* as my boots hit these boards in a rhythm of their own... The beginnings of everything sweet and swinging in music, which, I now saw, had broken way out of *its* environment. Surely it had...

Environments are like mothers, nursing their children, coddling them and helping them along in life. But children are children, and they can't stay where they're put. And won't be told. Even the most affectionate get to walking around, walking off, on out of the safe zone, on and on, exploring. Popular music was like someone's child, and it started right here... and just at this time... it had walked long and far, long and far, even to my home country of Ireland, where I'd heard it on obscure radio stations, jazz and blues emanating from the giant Waltham speakers in our bedroom, ole Robert Johnson, ole Charlie Christian (neither of whom were old at all when they died), Wes, Miles, Mingus, Monk, Chet, Coltrane, and Django & Stephane, or as the stylus scratched its lonely way round and round the vinyl, and I'd be listening intently to all these other musical magicians, too, conjurors in sound and rhythm, architects of weird worlds, jazzers for the most part, Messrs McLaughlin, Coryell, Pass, Benson, Scofield, Abercrombie, Holdsworth, Zappa, Stern, Tropea, Stevie Ray, Metheny, or Chick & Herbie, or that grand triumvirate of wizards, Jaco, Wayne & Joe Z... Listening to the world, and other worlds, too, exotic places... Jazz on windswept, rainy Irish streets, an entirely different vista opening up to the one on offer through the window of the No.45 bus... Now Blues was firmly Irish, too, with Rory Gallagher, and Van the Man! Blues, Jazz, R 'n B and Rock 'n Roll lived everywhere! Place meant very little! England, France, Spain (Paco!), Holland, Brazil, Japan! Sure it had walked, the music had escaped from its moorings, flown like a bird...

like Bird, chasing some mad fevered dream... We could do that, Ruby & me... *wherever we were...*

I wasn't quite sure where I'd now come in my thoughts, but somehow I felt better, about something, perhaps about this country I'd been adventuring in, perhaps about Ruby and me, and about the future. Ruby and me. That was all that mattered right now. We had to get back, we had to survive. Just like the magical music that was on the verge of appearing. Just like the music, I kept telling myself. All You Need Is...

A voice awoke me from my intense reverie. It was a child's voice, but shrill enough to attract my attention, and, I noted distressingly, that of others all around. 'Mom!' it shouted. 'Look! Mom!' it shouted again, this time with a tiny accusatorial finger pointed in my direction. Mom was beginning to take notice, too, looking, however, only at her daughter, seemingly chiding her for pointing at people: 'Jody, that's rude...' But her daughter had more to tell, and so, as I watched, my walk now stilled by the suddenness of all this and actually curious as to why this tiny little girl could possibly find me, out of all the colourful characters ambling this way and that, an interesting study, I listened to the rest of what she had to say. 'He's the magic-man, Mom! He's the magic-man who gave me the brooch!' This statement brought about a change in her mother, who suddenly desisted from chiding her charge, and instead adopted a stern look and lobbed it in my direction. Surrounding passers-by, some be-hatted men, a few ladies in plain dress, also stopped their ambulations and, one by one, directed their eyes toward little ole me. Little Jody's words also effected a change in me, as the features of my face underwent a subtle transformation not unlike the way the surface of a lake changes before a storm: from smooth and placid to prey to ripples and wafts. My cover was blown! Now, if my observers had only numbered those just mentioned I wouldn't have felt so bad, but, alas, the general interruption to people's activities just now had been noticed by one more figure, just lying on the periphery of my visual perspective. I looked up just a smidge to confirm. Indeed. Above where Ruby was walking, who was as yet unaware of any change in the air, on the second floor of the building she was walking under, I could see one be-hatted man, looking very tall and, it had to be said, a mite authoritative, too, now standing up from where he'd been sitting, on a rocking chair on the balcony. I noticed also that he'd been cradling something long and dark and thin in his arms, something he now handled into a position that was more like meaningful holding, as though it might just come in use, anytime now.

'Good afternoon, Jody!' I called to the little'un, tipping my hat, and then said, with all the politeness I could muster, given my pressing needs to get the hell out as quick as I could, to her mother: 'You have a wonderful little daughter there, Ma'am,' and I raised my hat, 'Be seeing ya!' I had thought to blunder my way forward in the same direction I'd been going, and sure it wouldn't be much further to the end of the town and eventual escape, but I now saw that the man on the second floor was shouting down instructions, furiously it seemed, to his fellows -his deputies?- to block my way off, and to... catch me! A moment of indecision passed through my being, as I thought of my options. By now, a brief scan informed me, Ruby had become aware that something was up and was looking over at me concernedly, her eyes pleading with me to do something, whatever it was that I needed to do to get the hell out. My eyes turned left. BARBER SHOP. I was standing outside the town barber shop.

It would have to do. I did my best to make it look like I now wanted a shave -bringing my right hand to my chin and making a face that said: 'Boy, do these bristles need taking care of, or what?' and then sidled over to the front door like a regular customer. Regular customers, however, don't usually have half the town, as it now seemed, looking at them as they enter an establishment. I resisted the impulse to do a wee bow of farewell, and just turned my back and reached out for the brass door knob. I liked the feel of the brass on my palm, its smooth coolness and the thing about it which seemed to say: 'Brother, feel me, I am real. I was forged in a melting pot at six hundred degrees and I've been chilling ever since. You holding me is the best evidence you got that this ain't no dream. I'm real, boy, and you are holding reality!' Yes, I reflected, I was holding reality, but it was a reality that refused to bend to my will. It was only after a few attempts at turning the damn thing that I noticed the sign hung precisely at head-height, yes, right in front of my eyes, behind the glass which constituted the main part of the door: CLOSED. Yet again, that wonderfully quaint upper-case lettering! I was screwed! I could see the deputies coming right now! Hard heads in black hats, moustaches like iron bars sewn over their lips. A quick look behind me did little to help: men were approaching there, too!

Nothing for it, I told myself, turning back to the little girl and her mother, I threw out my right hand in a kind of ostentatiously casual way, and, with a pretty perfunctory 'Hey Presto!' conjured up the largest iron skillet in existence. It was certainly a heavy mother, and, as it popped out of my fingers, I had to use both hands in a sudden, fierce grip to make sure it didn't do as it clearly wanted to do -follow the dictates of gravity and sink to the floor, or even through it. Its sudden appearance caused a collective reflexive retreat, and audible sigh, from those all around. My audience! The general feeling I got from them might be encapsulated as one of shock, followed by intense curiosity, a collective: 'What ya gonna do with that, mister?' 'Well, I had thought to use it to beat off my opponents,' I answered in my mind, 'but, you know, on second thoughts, people, I think it would be better put to...' and as I left the rest of the sentence dwindle into (unvoiced) silence I lugged the thing -the black-as-sin deep-panned thick-walled thing that shouted 'I am made of iron' from its very soul- round with huge force and into the door behind me, choosing the very spot where the CLOSED sign hung, shattering the glass, which then -very obediently I thought- fell backwards into the shop, and not near the feet of any of these kind and wonderful people who had gathered to see my demise. I then reached in my hand, actually after dropping the iron thing with an almighty clatter onto the wood floor, and twisted the inside doorknob and, hey presto indeed, I had accomplished my goal. The shock of this happening had created a flutter of keen dismay among the crowd round me, with one notable exception, which, even though I was hardly taking it all in at this point, did catch my fleeting attention: the little girl had a look of bright wonder on her face and was now even clapping her hands. In the dying seconds before I flew into the shop, I couldn't resist the sudden impulse to conjure up a parting gift, a pair of rinky-dinky roller skates and tossed them her way: 'Have fun, Jody,' I called, 'but don't scuff your knees!' I was gone.

Gone into the barber shop and looking round like a man up against it, and no mistakin'!

CHAPTER EIGHT

The barbershop was at once wondrous and barbarous. Okay, that's a cheap attempt at punning, but the implements arrayed on the sill before each black-leather seat-contraption under the wall-length mirror fairly shone with a gleam somewhere between beauty and menace. Shining-white scissors standing in scintillating shafts of sheen-giving glass (okay, and that was a cheap attempt at alliteration, but this place *was* something special). Little corked bottle-ettes topped up with transparent liquids and oils, some without labels, some with: White Alloy, Canada Balsa, whatever. Immaculate wooden-handled brushes, some round and some flat as your palm, their soft, wavy bristles inviting and warm; brown ceramic pots, white (soap?) blocks in each. Face-down oval hand mirrors (I surmised), handles plain polished black, the back of each mirror a little world of hand-tooled engravings and in-lays. Various razors, each flat, lithe even, bodies of ivory, blades sometimes in, snug, out of reach, others half-out, the thin burr of the edge glinting here and there, and that's where the menace resided, I felt. There, and in the giant black leather recliners, redwood frames with chrome knobs here and there, each with a footrest that might double as a means to clamp the feet. They looked like nothing other than *loci* of torture, even execution, be damned. And damned is what I was fast becoming, here, when I should have been rushing toward the door at the back, instead of taking it all in, the allure and the magic of the trappings of the Old West. Darn it.

The door at the back now commanded my attention for a different reason altogether as out popped the barber himself, aproned and very barber-like indeed, but looking daggers at me, and past me, at the mess I had made: 'Mein Got!' he exclaimed. And then once again, 'Mein Got!' And elaborated: 'Verrückt! Scheisse! Wer bist du?' I didn't need the translation: 'upset' is universally understandable, even if it has regional variations in the way it's expressed. And, to be honest, I was upset, too, or sorry, rather, sorry for the mess I'd made in this man's nice shop, all that glass I'd spilled onto the floor. I'd done my best to tiptoe through it, mind, because I hate that myself, walking a mess all round a joint. So much for my plans to be inconspicuous and not be a burden to the already put-upon inhabitants of this little town in the middle of the desert, somewhere out in the plains of a world I didn't belong in... Before I knew it, I was stretching out my hands toward him, by way of supplication: 'I'm awfully sorry, Mister, Sir...' And then, feverishly wondering how to make amends right there and then, no doubt aided by the fact that I had extended my hands out, it struck me that conjuring up a gift of some sort might be more concrete. Then again, something told me that to do so right there and then -to suddenly materialize a solid object out of the empty space between us- might just ratchet up the poor man's anxiety even more. And so, with as positive a face as I could summon, accompanied by as positive-sounding noises as I could make, I improvised, swiping a folded white cloth from the top of the nearest black recliner, and shaking it out before me. 'Was jetzt?' 'What's this?' is what I imagined he said, but it was the way that he said it, a new tone of curiosity in there now, that convinced me that I was on the right track. Thinking back to ole P.P.P., my mind wandering through the woody rooms and vaults of wonders, I knew what it was that might smooth out relations, in my fumbling, best-intentioned way. I swallowed the 'Voilà!' I was just about to let out, because I was hiding the magic as best as I could, and lo and behold - and yet he couldn't quite behold a great deal for the moment- under the billowing white sheet there seemed to appear some darned giant… thing.

Its bulk near had me losing grip on it, but after a fumble, I'd gripped it and looked up at my German-speaking interlocutor, my eyes hoping to say: 'This is for you!' and me hoping that the language of eyes was universal, too. I threw in, adlibbing: 'Diss iz for … du!' just in case. The barber, bald-headed, but well compensated for round the sides, widened his already widened eyes, locked his peepers first onto the now-apparent shape beneath the cloth, then onto me, and uttered a non-linguistic, and so then an even more universally understandable, gasp. Just then, however, his wife (I presumed) then showed her face, peeking over his shoulder. Fine-looking lady, too, high cheekbones and a fine head of golden hair, pinned up and shapely. 'Simon! Ist dies es?' And with that, she passed round past her hubby in a state of something like glee, her whole being, it seemed, intent on the shape under the sheet. Slowly, almost like it was a dangerous thing to do, she extended her -fine bone-china- right hand, until it hovered above the centre of the sheet. Then, with a quick glance at both me and her husband, she pinched the sheet at the mid-point on the top, and, having extracted maximum drama from the moment, pulled it back, swiftly, wordlessly, to reveal… one rather enormous velvety dark-blue clam-shaped…thing! 'Gerade was ich wollte!' she exclaimed and then she just whooped for joy and delight, and scooped it right out of my hands. Hubby was now looking even more confused than before, if the upset had faded a touch. She plonked the thing down on his arms, which she had to command him to hold out, as I'd gathered, and, gingerly, almost timidly, half shaking with the excitement of it all, undid the lid, as we could all now see that that was what it was. And what that thing that it was was a set of the most adorable items you'd ever want to pull through your hair, dip under your fingernails, or look at your face in, all gleamy smooth silver, and couched in exotic waves of the most glorious blue satin and silk. A fine clam-shaped Toilet Set! 'Wunderschön! Wunderschön!' proclaimed the lady, half-fainting from the emotion of it all. Mr Barber smiled sheepishly or coyly or however it is you smile when you're getting credit for something you don't deserve. I was happy, too, happy that I'd passed through the trial of confronting a perfectly nice couple after having trashed their front door glass with an iron skillet. I was now accepted, for the moment.

And what a moment it was, as I allowed them their space and angled round slightly to take in the scene via the wall-length mirror, which reflected us all, and, I was only now beginning to notice, a figure far at our backs, or at my back at least. Before I turned round to face said figure, I drank in the image of me facing myself in my Old West duds: light-brown felty hat still firmly planted up-top, brushed suede waistcoat and faded dark-blue denims and my trusty snake-skin winklepickers, looking well cool, I had to admit. And then there were those eyes of mine looking back, glinting with a sense that this here was some place I could get used to, yes, indeedy, if I wasn't to be dragged to the jail and be hung by the neck until I was dead in the morning. That was likely my fate, I'd kinda come to accept. The sight of these two happy people dissuaded me from any attempt to push rudely past them, as, I felt it now, I just had no right to do. No right to go where I wasn't asked, no right to mess up people's lives, break their doors, windows, whatever, no right to cause people grief and be some kind of nuisance they just didn't need. I'd become all passive now, and so it was feeling like that when I eventually decided to turn around and face the music, here, or rather there, still near the doorway, in the form of a not particularly threatening-looking deputy, as I guessed him to be, approaching slowly, his own hat in his hand.

'Begging your pardon, Mr and Mrs Beeker,' drawled the man, who one couldn't not notice was a tad portly and, with his open necked checked shirt of dubious shape and condition, and denims as baggy as a half-filled sack of coffee beans, not the most fastidious of dressers. His face was a crusty, but beaming, smiling moon though, and it was only because he was packing a gun-belt and pistol, that he might be taken for one of Hamilton's deputies. 'Mister Dodie,' ('Doe-dee' it sounded like, even if 'dowdy' was how he looked, harf harf) exclaimed Mr Beeker, 'Good day to you, sir!' Mr Beeker said, to my surprise, in good, accented English. 'Good day to your good selves, too!' responded Mr Dodie in return, in a kind of high-pitched drawl (even if that sounds like a contradiction in terms…), twisting his hat now, his smile straining slightly as he looked purposefully past me, and then pointedly at me, and proceeded with, coming ever closer, step by tremulous step, 'Sorry to bother you 'n'all, but it seems this here fella,' he said unloosing his hat and tipping it my way, 'is wanted by Mr Hamilton…' He let that just drag there, and hoped that was enough. It was, and it wasn't. Mrs Beeker had words to say: 'Dear Mr Doe-dee,' she pronounced, turning away from the object of her devotion up till then, and taking a few steps his way, in her best Teutonic English: 'Vat do you vant wiz zees man, I begging your pardon?' Dodie motioned to the broken glass down below his own boots, and said: 'This here fella's done something he shouldn't, I reckon, Ma'am, we gotta take him in now.' Mrs Beeker looked aghast at the mess (obviously her first time to notice it), then at me. 'Sorry, Ma'am,' I said, and, with my best sheepish eyes, 'I was at th'end o'my tether...' Not getting it, I could tell from her eyes, I re-phrased and re-set: 'It's OK, Ma'am, they think I done bad, but I ain't.' (Why did I have to fall into uneducated grammar at the drop of a hat? But, it was part of the way I was feeling right then, abject and fated to lose this one battle, ever more assimilated into my role as a real 19th C cowboy who'd left school at the age of 9, knowing the chips were against me...) I tipped her my hat and made a step toward ole Dodie, who was huffing and wheezing, I now noticed. Mrs Beeker almost spoke, then she stopped, but her face had a cast that could only mean sympathy. 'Begging your pardon, Ma'am,' I then countered, reaching out to unloose the white sheet she was still holding. I took it, whooshed it out like I'd done just a few moments previous, and threw out a 'Lo!' as yet another shape showed itself under the now settling sheet. Frau Beeker watched. Herr Beeker approached a few steps, looking rapt. Deputy Dodie, I could tell, was looking mighty hard, too. I held out the sheet, and the china-bone hand swooped in once again, in a pincher movement to end all pincher movements: whoosh! A Grand Set of Finest Soaps, Manufactured in Louisville, Kentucky. 'Oh!' cried poor Frau Beeker, moved almost to tears. I handed the case to her and tipped my hat once again. Time for my exit.

Deputy Dodie looked relieved and astonished in one. He looked at me funny, like he wanted to say something but thought it best to desist, but I was willing to go with him and that was all that mattered right now. Just as we passed over the broken shards on the ground, I heard a plaintive, heart-felt 'Danke schön!' from Madame Beeker, which then morphed into a coordinated 'Tank yuuu!' from both. It felt good to have done something nice for once.

The crowd, which I'd forgotten about all this time, had not diminished at all, but had gotten larger, and, again, all eyes were on me, being led, almost half-heartedly, by Deputy Dodie, both of us with our heads slightly down, like we'd been on the losing team but everyone wanted to cheer anyway. But I sometimes looked up and into the glare of outside, expecting the worse. And yet, in the midst of all that noise and bustle, and the fact that ole Hammy was at the centre of it all, waiting for me, I suddenly realized there was one person there who would be looking out for me. I'd almost given up on getting away, in feeling at least, but not on the hope that one soul would shower me with a sweet and spirit-enhancing smile... Ruby, my dear...

Actually, the crowd was a lot friendlier than I thought they would be. First off, the little girl who'd innocently betrayed me was right there next to her 'Mom' (as they say it here, even though you have to make a longface to do so, or move your jaws up and down like a fish...), beaming a smile at me that would dissipate a whole skyful of clouds. Then there were the others, a mixture of menfolk and womenfolk, vibing me with all their late nineteenth century small town American values: moral concern edging into moral outrage, tempered only by the fact that the varmin was under escort and destined to get what's coming to 'im. Nah, that's harsh: I couldn't tell what they were thinking. Many looked at me with a curiosity bordering on concern for my welfare. I didn't look like an outlaw, and the body language of Depu'dy Dodie was doing wonders for my disposition. I could hardly tell, but it seemed the Beekers had come to their doorway, and I suspect their visages helped to disarm the onlookers of suspicions I was this mad, bad, dangerous critter. Hell, I was almost among friends! They parted very considerately anyhow, tipping hats to me, some of them, and what seemed like a half-hearted bow from a teenage girl in ponytails. Was she one of the four I'd seen when riding in? Then, still being escorted, ole

Dodie lightly touching my elbow just now and again, I thought I recognized the boy with the freckles I'd bumped into at the very beginning of this whole adventure: he sure beamed a smile right at me. He'd be telling his friends later on how he'd actually spoken to me and all... Yet, it was a friendly enough smile even so, so I forced a brief one back. More people parted, and as they did so, they closed up right behind us, in our wake, so the further we walked into the street the further I was being led into the middle of the crowd, forming a circle, a ring of people... to the inevitable showdown I couldn't escape from. Poor Elmer's missing all the fun, though, it occurred to me. He'll be kicking himself he missed this event. That's when I saw Rubes, on the far side at the front. She was looking aghast at me, and yet, I had to admit, looking mighty fine even so. Such a figure, such a face, what a doll she is was all I could say to myself. Her hair, so radiant in the hot sun, looked like the strands of an auburn waterfall on a mid-summer's day. Just over there now... our eyes locked, her aghastment compounded by the fact that my face and my eyes said it all: 'Yeah, I'm caught, Ruby, there's nothing you can do. You go back the way you came. I'm sure it'll be alright after a while. Love ya.' I could tell that she loved me, too, though we'd never walked down that particular linguistic sidestreet, mind.

The dust and the noise of people chattering was getting to me, now. I hung my head as we stopped in the dead centre of all those surrounding us. I could have used tricks, I suppose, but that didn't appeal. I knew I had to amend for my ways. (Was this me thinking this, or was it the role taking over? I couldn't decide.) Meanwhile, Dodie'd passed onto my right side, apparently following a nod from someone to do so. Just then, to our left, there was a jostling of onlookers and raised voices and before I knew what was happening, what I knew had to happen happened: ole Hammy strode into the arena with us. Pushed his way in, more like. Oh, the man looked beat up if ever a man did! A horizontal bruise at his forehead (must have been when he fell forward), a corset arrangement securing his chest (where the grandfather clock had struck) and visible blood smears still on his nose and his face, from out of which stared two burning-hot eyes lasering into my own, even if lasers hadn't been quite invented yet. I was in for a beating. 'Boy,' shouted Hammy, visibly quaking with anger, but an anger that seemed to fill in some hole in his soul, 'Boy, I been waiting to meet up wi'cha again! We's gonna have us a nice, long chat, oh Lordy yes! I thank the Lord! I really do!' Of course, I was silent. I didn't want to point out that he'd gotten all preacher-like in his utterances, as it seemed to me he'd been pushed over the edge of whatever it was he'd been sitting on when we'd last locked horns. Now Sheriff Hamilton was addressing the crowd, who were about as attentive as children at Sunday School during the first five minutes, his face larger than life, a menacing smile plastered all over it, beginning to look manic indeed: 'What we have here is a man who don't respect the law, people!' A brief mumbling of assent rose, but I could tell it wasn't quite as enthusiastic as he would have liked. So, he reached into the deepest chasm of his soul, and his phrasebook of high-sounding (if grammatically suspect) things, and finding no better way to say what he'd said, said it again, only with more conviction, the conviction of a man who's found Jesus in the desert: 'WHAT WE HAVE HERE IS A MAN WHO DON'T RESPECT THE LAW, PEOPLE!' That got them going! The tone of assent was definitely increased a few notches, as particularly the be-hatted men, probably business types, made sure that Sheriff Hamilton could see they were with him, *a hundred percent!* Interestingly, just at that moment, adjacent to a batch of said business-types, I recognized two gals from yesterday's saloon: they were beaming delectable smiles at me, as my eyes briefly took in their busty fronts and the fact that one was holding an apple out to me (there had to be symbolism in there somewhere). Then Hamilton turned round, throwing his gaze onto me, and shouted out: 'Grab him!' and before I could move up my arms to do anything, magical or otherwise, ole Dodie, against all expectations had transformed into Hamilton's robot and grabbed my right arm so hard and sudden that it felt like it was in a vise. Simultaneously, out of nowhere, but actually via a temporary gap in the ring of onlookers, out jumped another deputy, who then captured my left arm, too, in an unbreakable clamp. This was a short, squat, balding man, his eyes intense, miserable and unkind. So I was now firmly held on both sides, helpless to fight, unable to conjure anything, either. As I saw Sheriff Hamilton begin to step over toward me, my stomach tightened up. When he arrived, I could picture him delivering a vicious blow to my solar plexus. I could see he'd enjoy that.

It was just then, with the timing of an angel from heaven, that another deputy, also quite short, it seemed, pushed through to this hallowed space (ha!), his face all lit up, mouth opening and closing and uttering sounds that only after ole Hammy had shouted the man down became half-intelligible at last. '…got him… was sneaking around… Ferdy's bringing him now… ole creased face hisself… th'ole Patchee hisself!' This was enough to get Hamilton's attention for sure. With a 'Just hold him there tight' to my two buddy depps, he bent down to the height-challenged deputy who'd just broken the news and together they gabbled away, unintelligibly, to me at least. Unintelligently, too, I scoffed in my mind. In the relief of the moment, I threw a glance Ruby's way: she was still looking fearful and anxious, but now there was something new in the mix, where any interruption of proceedings had to be something, if only something to just defer the punch I had surely been about to receive, for a moment or two… In my mind, though, I wondered what 'th'ole Patchee' meant, rolled it around like you do a good wine on your tongue, trying to assess the palate, the bouquet, the nose… Whatever it was, it wasn't just talk. They were bringing 'th'ole Patchee' here, so it seemed, as with even greater commotion and bustle, soon I could see three men burst through, with considerable bluster, into this magic circle of hell. Two, either side, were grinning like idiots, while the man in between had his head down. But even with his head down, it was clear this wasn't just a man, a man like these other people stood around: no siree, this was a genuine Plains 'Injun', as ole Elmer might say, the very same he'd told me about. The 'th'ole Patchee': the old *Apache!*

His handlers held him firmly, but you could see they hardly needed to. Looked like he'd been on the end of a severe beating already, cuts or signs of violence on his bare shoulders and chest. He wore a red cloth round his head, and that's all we could see, his head firmly down, arms held back, standing more by the support of his handlers than anything else. On a nod from their master, they forced him down to his knees; it wasn't difficult. Hamilton looked on, but seemingly unsatisfied, directed them to do more. They did. In tandem, the two holders then pushed him forward roughly, so that he fell prostrate into the dust, his hands, now released, blindly coming up to cushion the blow, without much success. It was time for Sheriff Hamilton to assert his moral authority. 'Oh, happy day, people,' he announced to the onlookers all around, 'Oh, happy day! The Lord blesses us today with not one, but two…' he seemed to search around for *le mot juste*… 'Infidels!' He then raised his right boot, as though to deliver a kick to the Indian's head, but retracted it immediately at the sound of a sigh from the crowd. No, I thought to myself, I knew his type. He wouldn't want to get blood on the nice people's finery, not out here in broad daylight. Better to do all the beating indoors, with a rope over the mouth to stifle the screams.

It was horrible to see. I was growing to dislike Hamilton

more and more by the second. He then reached down, and, rudely pulled off the red cloth from the Apache's head. It was actually an attempt to grab at his hair. After tossing away the cloth with something like disgust on his face for having touched something so weatherworn and sweat-encrusted, he repeated the action, grabbing his hair, this time with force enough not merely to pull back the man's head, but, with an adlibbed support from the two men either side, who grabbed his upper arms, to drag him back up into a staggeringly standing position, his handlers holding him firm on both sides. It was an ugly operation from any point of view. 'Take a good look, people, take a good look at this filthy excuse for a human!' Again, Hamilton didn't seem quite satisfied with the reaction, so he continued: 'This here Injun's been wreaking havoc in this town, sniping out of the dark, taking pot shots at me, bringing his *evil* ways into you *good* people's midst!' This last sentiment seemed to get a more than adequate reaction: with a big stress on 'evil' and then a big stress on 'good', he knew how to appeal to the crowd. That always gets them! So, we followed Sheriff Hamilton's great words of wisdom, and looked.

The Apache man was naked down to his waist. He wore pale leather leggings below, and moccasins. His skin was a human brown I'd never quite seen before, a radiant brown, even if covered with dust and with the signs of a man viciously beaten by thugs. His face was a patchwork of wrinkles, and of scars, some old, some bleeding and new. But with his high cheekbones, and long, noble nose, his face, I thought, might be that of a chief, a leader of men, not a follower. His hair, though ragged and dirtied, flowed magnificently down to his shoulders (well, being hardly the most follicle-endowed being on the planet, it looked magnificent to me). The pupils of his eyes were as yet hidden from view, the creased lids still down partially, his head inclined partially, too, as if looking down to the earth at his feet. The creases were not reserved for his eye lids alone; you could trace a system of creases and wrinkles all through his face, like a map in *bas relief*, mountains veined by a network of rivers and streams. No moisture here, though, no tears for the white man, I thought. He was probably fifty years old, but he looked ancient, and wearied of life, or, more like, wearied of pain.

You could tell the crowd weren't sure how to react. It was like this was enough for one day's viewing, time to go home, which, funnily enough, is what ole Hammy then said: 'OK, folks, you've seen enough, time to go home!' And he started to direct his drone-fellows to move things along. This is when the Indian's head noticeably reared up, the lids on his eyes suddenly flashed open fully, and his lips parted: 'You killed my family, Hamilton!' It was a voice of thunder and of power. The crowd stopped in their tracks. Heads all turned back to look at the half-naked Injun in their midst. 'You!' said the Indian, his head now turning swiftly toward the Sheriff, his eyes staring into Hamilton's. 'You killed my wife! You killed my children!'

These words were delivered with such force and such passion no-one could speak, no-one could move. No-one but Hammy, who, without more ado, strode over to the 'filthy excuse for a human' and, unlatching his gun, and clasping it sideways, brought down the barrel hard on his head. Blood spewed from the wound and he went down, his body falling forward heavily, into the dirt once again. I struggled against being held as this happened. What I'd just witnessed gave me all the motivation I needed to get free. It seemed the people gathered round us in a circle were none too impressed either with Hamilton's behaviour, the women taking the lead in expressing dismay at the sight of a public beating of a defenceless man, even a defenceless Injun, moving as though to encourage others to back away and get out of this place, but the men outnumbered the women, and the men, being men, were hotwired to watch the violence of others, blow by hard blow if need be.

Hamilton, after swiftly holstering his piece, knelt down and bent his head down to the Apache man's head, now in the dust of the street, his hands free, the right reaching up to the wound, blindly. 'You're a dirty, filthy scum and your people don't deserve to exist,' spat Sheriff Hamilton into the ear of the man, and yet, as it was like an arena and the sound carried, it could be heard by everyone all around, in a moment of still that spoke volumes itself. Maybe there was compassion out here in the Old West after all, compassion for the Injun, as the hush that fell on the onlookers was palpable. Compassion, I felt, but sadly, it would never translate into action, because what did it mean after all? My mind started free-forming ideas... Us whiteys had taken your land, hadn't we? We'd killed all your buffalo, and starved you to near extinction, broken every promise that we'd made, and shipped all the miserable survivors out from the arable life-giving land and onto the arid, the barren, the desert, where only iguanas and cacti could flourish, to become one with the snakes and the scorpions, bellies dragging through the dust. Now I was sure becoming assimilated. This was the price of becoming one with the Wild, Wild, White West, as I was now carrying the social conscience of the race I'd fallen into. No longer 'I', but 'We, the people...'

Then out of this stasis something happened. RUBY: Ruby happened!

She shot like a body on fire out from the ranks of the others, uttering a shriek that would put the wind up a bear. It certainly got her noticed by everyone there, if not by the object of her attentions, over whom she now, having taken three swift strides in that direction, raised what it was she was holding throughout this whole ordeal. Now a parasol doesn't have much mass, but combined with a full-body attack, Ruby fell upon Hamilton with a force way beyond her. 'Fascist pig!' she screamed out (anachronistically!), as, the parasol now unloosed and lost in the tussle, she slapped with her hands on the 'law & order' man's head, knocking off his hat, ruffling up his hair and his dignity, too. The deputy who'd spoken to Hamilton first soon sprang into action; he grabbed her round by the waist and threw her back generally the way she had come, sending her into the dirt. I prayed for some supernatural strength to unlatch me from these two gorillas, who now held even stronger, as I visibly kicked up the dirt and the dust in fury, desperation.

Hamilton now had recovered, wiped the back of his mouth with his hand as he knelt, then threw a glance at the bedraggled specimen who'd attacked him, now thrown back onto the ground, at the feet of the first-tier onlookers, who seemed unsure what to do with her. He smiled, cheerlessly, and, given the circumstances, with something less than gallantry; then he launched a glance over at me, and smiled, once again, his best bad-guy smile. It was at that point that I knew I would do *it* if I could. Do what? asked the voice upon my virtual shoulder, shaking, along with the rest of my writhing body. Shoot, said the man I was transforming into. Shoot? asked the voice, as I stared my best cold-as-ice stare right back into the eyes of the Sheriff. Indeed, said the man, shoot that miserable son-of-a-bitch bastard, right over there, and right now. Where? asked the voice, alarmed at my tone. Right between the eyes, if I can, I answered right then. Bang, you be dead, said my darkening mind, 'Bang' said my eyes to that grinning man. At which point conscience lost the power of speech, and withdrew.

But I couldn't, of course. Dodie and 'Bodie', or whatever the hell that guy's name was, were doing their thang, holding me like I was a steer about to be branded. That was likely their day job. I suspected nothing more would happen here, though; that would all come later, back at the jail... This was the way to prosecute justice in civil society: not in plain view. No need to add to the discomfort of the good folk gathered here. Unless. And the thing that made think 'unless' was not just a far hope, the last desperate sound of my own dwindling optimism, swirling clockwise -or was it anti-clockwise?- down the damn drain, but actually a noise... a noise like a shot... Like a...

'Bang!'

A gunshot! One, then another, then a flurry of them, bangbangbangbangbang! Music to my ears, certainly, as the effect was immediate: all those around us broke backwards, in a frenzy of mass movement. Hamilton bolted upright, and unlatched his gun once again, shouting commands to his deputies, the one nearest him, those in charge of the Apache and then, turning round, barking out savagely to those still holding me: 'Keep a tight hold on him, but get the hell down!' And with that, he was down again too, suddenly. We all were, me thrown forward by the force of my holders, now diving down for cover. Only the Indian, and, I could just see as I fell, Ruby, remained unmoving, both already down in the dirt anyway. Was the Indian unconscious, or just playing so? Or was he dying? My holders were fiddling for their irons now, with only one hand either side as a grip on my arms. I knew I could break free if I struggled just a little, but, my mind was racing to process it all: any untoward action now might get me unstuck, see me riddled with holes, from any number of sources. I kept my face in the dirt, but turned toward Ruby; Ruby, who, I noticed with surprise, was not actually alone, but being tended to by some elderly lady, in the midst of this chaos. She was holding her head from behind and dabbing her forehead with her silk handkerchief, whispering words of comfort. There was hope for them yet.

The ring of people was fast breaking up, the ranks of the onlookers peeling back rightly, screams and shouts from every quarter, the respectable citizens of the town having seen quite enough, not wishing now to get shot, mothers protecting their children, men steering women away, hands forcing heads down here and there, the dust rising up as the shots kept on coming, and yet not a sign of who was doing it, and, thankfully, no bullets ripping through bodies as yet. Hamilton wasn't waiting to be left uncovered, swiftly rolling right, to the side of the street nearest him, pistol drawn, eyes peering out through the dust and grand commotion. The Indian's guards soon followed suite, leaving the Apache just where he was, prostrate, in the dirt. Not worth the bother now. The deputy who'd told Hamilton of the Indian's capture, the one who'd dispatched Ruby with such delicacy, was less circumspect, however, just looking after them now retreating as fast as they could from the scene. Was he perhaps deaf? It was like he didn't seem to get it, until he got it, so to speak. Standing there, hat in his hand (not sure why he'd taken it off), ignorant of the sounds of the guns at his back, looking all querulous at Hammy and Co. as they made for the wood of the sidewalk, he also seemed unsure what to do when the first bullet hit him. A dull thud as it crashed through his shoulder. Being as rotund as ole Dodie, maybe it took time for the nerves to register a hit. But the next one got him square in the back, and he flew forwards with the force of it, his body slamming rudely into the hard dirt, dead, dead, dead.

I was released in a flash, Dodie and Bodie up on their feet, guns out, but fleeing, willy-nilly, Dodie skirting left and then skirting right, Bodie doing the same but in the opposite orientation. It was a wonder they didn't crash into each other. 'I hope they survive' was my thought at that moment, still in shock from what I'd just seen: a man gunned down in the street right before us. I raised up my head just enough to take things in, but not provide a target. Be-hatted figures on horses was all I could see, dimly, through the clouds of dust and the still-fleeing bodies of the good townsfolk. The riders, being elevated, could no doubt shoot down at me easily, but I felt I was safe if I didn't move for the moment, as they'd likely have better things to shoot at. Here, there, and everywhere. Dodie and Bodie for starters! Oh, how it feels, the moral dilemma of wishing your fellow man well, and yet gladdened they were taking the fire off me, being zigzagging targets in what had become a shooting gallery.

Ruby, I had now just noticed, was animated, edging her way backward toward the woody porch area at the side of the street. The elderly lady had taken her leave. I had to get over to Ruby, but movement right now was not in my best interests. Dodie and Bodie were going places, left and right, Bodie toward where Hamilton had snuck, Dodie to the opposite side of the street, both with guns drawn, but more likely so as not to drop them than to fire them. But, of course, having their weapons drawn made them fair game for the shooters, whoever they were. If I had to choose, I hoped it'd be Bodie drawing fire first. Dodie at least had a heart, I could see, even if he had given it to the devil for money and position, the best status a poorly-dressed, uneducated man could get in a town like this. Bodie? Well, he'd just jumped in, grabbing my arm, all vicious and uncaring as he'd be about a bull on the plains. I was just meat. And, yet, alas, BANG, now Bodie was meat, too. A bevvy of bullets to the chest felled him and he fell like a sack of potatoes, or old dog-bones maybe, next to the body of the first-shot deputy. This persuaded Hamilton and his two associates to speed up their movements something shocking.

Dodie was next, I was sure of it, out in the open, and, sorry to say, in the best place to draw attention away from the place I was in. Yes, I confirmed, the riders with guns were turning Dodie's way to a man, meaning it was now or never for me. I had to crawl. Hey, ole T.S.! -it occurred to me then- I'm scuttling! I'm scuttling! More crab than a man, don't you know, old chap! And in that timbre of mind did I scuttle, belly-wise, if not quite across the floors of silent seas, then, next best thing, through the dust and the dirt of this extremely wild Wild West street, over to Ruby, now, only now, realizing I was fast approaching. I launched myself onto her, over her, next to her, grabbing her arm, and dragging her further onto the wooden porch, and away from the madness, however possible. We were now one, of one mind anyhow, keeping down, but now we'd made it up on the wooden walkway, eager to find the nearest door to a shop. Further down the wooden walkway, Hamilton & Co. were already disappearing inside the door to some shop. Only ole Dodie was caught, out in the glare, running in panic, the proverbial chicken with his head chopped off, not an easy target, but, it seemed from the audible laughs from the riders, entertaining as hell. Each took a potshot, some aiming to prolong the inevitable with shots to the ground near his feet, forcing him then to kick up his legs in what looked like a parody of dance. Ruby and I couldn't keep looking: we were too busy having found the entrance to a shop, then roughly forcing the door handle in panic. Instead of pushing, we now pulled at the handle, it gave and we scrambled inside. Just as we did, I caught a last sight of ole Dodie taking a hit on the head. Blood splattered out. A goner was he, falling down dead. Oh, T.S., if only *his* headpiece had been filled with straw! *Alas!*

'Are you OK?' I'd taken Ruby's head in my hands as we lay side by side on the chequered floor, the door now closed over, and was studying her face for an answer. 'I'm OK,' she answered, shaken but not stirred (cliché!), asking back: 'Just what are we going to do now?' That was dialogue enough. We got to our feet, kept our heads down, and moved further into the interior, away from the door and the window. A quick look around. We'd barged into a pharmacy, or, to get it period-right, big letters and all, an APOTHECARY! Proprietor *Mr P. Folejewski*, in elegant copperplate, 'Est. 1887, APhA Approved'. 'Out the back door!' I shot back. A wonderful place, my mind then said to me then. Deep brown polished wood fittings throughout, a universe of bottles of diverse size and shape. Tiers of them standing, aloof. Orderliness. Mr Folejewski keeps a fine shop! My eyes had started to wander, my attention, too, it seemed. 'Keep focused!' shouted Ruby, seeing that happen: the lure of the Old West, again catching my heart. 'Extract of Witch Hazel.' 'Tincture of Iodine.' My eyes couldn't stop, as I looked over Ruby's left shoulder. 'Rochelle Salts' in a dainty little glass vase. 'Refined Powdered Borax.' 'Quinine. 2 Grains.' 'Vichy Tablets.' Square-shouldered brown bottles and round-shouldered blues. Transparent ones embossed with 'New York' and, intriguingly, I thought, 'Warner's Safe Nervine', whatever that was. 'Oi!' shouted Ruby again, and she then, placing her hands on my shoulders, shook me with some force. This convinced me she was getting back her strength, and woke me up to the now. 'Right!' I had clicked. 'Back door. Now!'

We turned to the counter, and I had soon figured out where the lid was to enter, and had also sussed out the passage back through the shop. That no-one was there was a plus, or no-one yet anyhow. I made for the end of the counter, but something wasn't quite right with ole Rubes. She wasn't moving. 'Wait,' she instructed. A look like a suddenly glassed-over waterfall came over her face. Gingerly, she stepped back a few paces, toward the front window. 'Rubes,' I protested, 'that ain't really the best idea…' 'Yes,' but the Indian,' she said, in a small voice, as though half-unconvinced herself about what she was doing. I walked over to her, and out we both peered. A rider had dismounted and was walking around, looking gleeful and, it had to be said, dangerously crazy with it. His face was a mass of gnarly black hair, and he wielded two pistols in a manner you could only call ostentatious, or as my Ma would say, 'like he was cock of the walk'. Being inside this shop gave us the strength to believe we were invisible, for now, so we just kept on watching to see what he'd do. Now there was no-one left in the street, save the bodies of Dodie and Bodie, and the first deputy to get shot. And the Indian, still there, his body fallen forward and his arms all stretched out, his face in the dust. He couldn't be dead, could he? Or, just out for the count? Gnarly face-hair man took his time to get round to it, now and again shouting out words and phrases like, 'Hey, what we got here, then?' 'A real live Redman, I see!' His companions were still horsed, and there were four of them (Biblically resonant for those so inclined), apparently enjoying the show.

Had I forgotten about the ole Apache, in my panic to escape? Sure I had. Ruby had brought me back to what mattered as well. Saving my own skin with no regard for others just didn't seem right. And me, with the power I had, I could do plenty, I suppose.

Gnarly face-hair man then did something unexpected, he holstered his weapons, but, in one sudden flash, whipped out from behind a Bowie knife, the length of a child's arm. He was now positioned a tad closer to the Indian, but not yet within striking distance, so to speak. But it wouldn't take much. A stride or two. He could strike anytime.

I could strike anytime. I could conjure up some instrument of death, and plug him right now. I had done it before, eons ago, far, far away, even if they were only clocks. I'd fostered the killer-instinct, allowed the 'gift' to re-sculpt my clay into something not wholesome at all. Yes, I could do it, materialize a Sharps .50 caliber buffalo rifle and blow that joker away, but that'd be murder, killing a human, ending his life, even if it was to save another's... 'What are you waiting for?' whispered Ruby tensely, 'Can't you just... do your thing, Conjuring Cowboy?' I could, I suppose, and yet, somehow I couldn't, not just like that anyhow. To conjure or not to conjure, that is the question... 'OK, OK,' I threw out in a tone you might even call peeved, not quite knowing what it was I would do when I reached for the door, and pushed the damn thing open. 'No!' pleaded Ruby, 'you'll get us both killed!' But I wouldn't be told. That ole Man's-gotta-do-what-a-man's-gotta-do crap!

As I pushed the door open, it making a creaking sound it probably hadn't made before we'd forced it open moments before, I wasn't sure what I was feeling. It wasn't like I had a plan. Or a choice. It was more like I was being led, some force coursing through my limbs, animating me, one step taken followed by another step, with no sense of precisely why it was I had taken it. Maybe it was because it felt right, and maybe it wasn't just Ruby who'd put this into my head, the idea to do something. '100 Gelatine Coated Pills Dinner (Lady Webster)', announced the label on one navy-blue-glass bottle to the right of the door. Wonder what that does? Or them 'Lithia Tablets'? Good for what ails ye. My attention being all taken up with these little things had maybe been a deferral exercise, a way of dealing with the idea of cowardice, the panic that had inevitably gripped me on entering the store. I had known what was right, I just didn't want to admit it would be difficult. To survive. Or to kill. I couldn't just do that. Turn sniper, aim, pull the trigger. I'd kill me in the process. Or something in me. Or could I?

So, I pushed the door open, thankfully not being noticed, and let the force take me, following the sudden auto-suggestion that a light-hearted approach just might be in order. It was quite something to conjure up what I did then, because from one tiny point in open space just in front of me soon came a precipitous expansion both up and down, and around, if very thin with it. *Very strange!* But I grabbed it, halted its flow, then, remembering the time in childhood I'd seen a clown doing this at a circus, flicked it forward, but underhand, with some force. Before you could say 'Voilà!', which I didn't think necessary quite yet, a child's hoop, just like the one I'd encountered at the beginning of this mad adventure, rolled forward to just about the spot where the knife man was confronting the Indian. Being slightly elevated made it just that extra bit tricky, but it worked like a treat: got the attention of the man, and his friends, in a manner that could hardly be taken as threatening. Obediently, the hoop, the backwards motion now catching up with it, started to roll back the way it had come. Out of the corner of my mouth, I shushed Ruby, who was now pulling frantically at my sleeve for me to get back in the shop. I wanted the bad guys to see me, to see me unruffled and, yes, even bearing a smile. Where I was going with all this I wasn't quite sure, but it worked: gnarly face-hair Bowie-knife man, after an initial whoop of something like genuine wonder, turned his head round at me. And he smiled, too. 'Howdy!' I called, both of my hands raised, fingers splayed out, showing there was nothing for him to react to, yet. 'Howdy!' replied the man with the knife, which he then returned to its unseen scabbard, behind. The hoop fell ignored, partly against the wood porch. I thought I better act quick or he'd whip out his guns and cut me in two.

But I couldn't think straight. What next to conjure to keep this bloke entertained? Then, my memory racing round Poly's old rooms full of junk, I gave two fast clicks of my upturned fingers, and just like magic, for magic it was, two fine willow-patterned china plates appeared. I clutched at them, glanced at them, noting their blueness and, again, wondered what the hell I was at. Initial satisfaction soon dissolved into panic as I then realized these discs I was holding make awful good targets. I saw the gnarly face-hair man look all attentive, his body stiffening just enough to make me understand he'd thought of that, too. Which gave me the nod as to what I should do next. In one half-panicked flash, I tossed each of them sideways, far over left-wise, as far as I could. My opponent reverted to type and whipped out his pistols, snagging them both in a trice. The ceramic exploded: I would be next.

Forcing myself: 'Wonderful shooting!' I shouted, as gleeful as I could, considering the shattering violence of what had just happened, and that, inadvertently, I'd coaxed out his irons. I had to think quick. 'Silver!' I called out, employing my best salesman voice. 'You like silver, right?' And this time, my hands returned to their status mid-air, palms open and fingers up, I conjured up two Morgan silver dollars, straight out of Poly's cash register -despite what he'd told me about that. Boy, were they large, and beautifully glinting in the hot midday sun! I'd gotten gnarly hair man's attention for sure. As he looked on, I slowly and deliberately took the one in my right, and, inspecting its two faces, the Greek-looking lass on one side, and the scary-looking eagle on the other, made like I was biting it, in true Olympian fashion. He seemed to like that, me confirming its authenticity and all. With a nod of my head, I tossed it over in his general direction, hoping he wouldn't be of a mind to try out his gunmanship on it. It fell in the dust with a thud and a dull thud at that. I tossed the other one, too, not realizing I might have ruined the moment: throwing good money into the dirt.

I had to think quick, once again. 'You're not thirsty, are you?' I threw out. 'Bit,' answered he. 'How about some Rye?' I asked, and as I did so, out -from my suddenly-flicked wrist- flew a bottle of RYE, which I caught by the neck. Surprise once again lit up the man's face. Surprise, and a touch of that look men get when they enter a bar. This next part was tricky: two tumblers. One I could catch. The other fell with a thud and a clatter onto the wood at my feet. 'Oops!' I apologized, transferring the tumbler I'd caught to the hand holding the Rye, and then popping out another into the left. The man's face showed absolute surprise now, even astonishment, through all the hair. 'If you don't mind, then?' And I gestured that I'd want to approach, holding up my fare, to share a wee drink in the street. I kept my eye on the riders, too, glad that none of them were pointing anything my way. I made my demeanour as light and friendly as I could, which was a great deal, as I'd entered into my performance, my role, with gusto, stepping off the wooden walkway slowly, and delicately, the ole smile still doing its bit, telling them butter wouldn't melt in my mouth even on an oven-hot day like this. Slow, deliberate steps, over the hard dirt of the street, past the inert bodies of the two slain deputies. But I couldn't look down: my eyes locked onto my opposite number's eyes, smiling my damn smile. As I got close enough, a distance that allowed me to make out his poor, broken, yellowed teeth, obviously objects of serious neglect, I stopped still, brought the bottle neck to my mouth and, with my own slightly-better-cared-for choppers, unloosed the cork, then spat it out. I held the two tumblers by the base in my left, and then filled each, to the brim, with the bottle in my right, spilling a drop, too. He remained unspeaking all this time, clearly taking it all in, studying my every move, and, I could now just tell, when his eyes fell on the bottle itself, the beginning of a dribble of spit forming at the left side of his mouth. I extended my left, with the two tumblers, out to him, slow and easy. Before he could take it, I was relieved to see him return his two guns to his side holsters. It was coming close to the moment of truth.

'You some kind of magic man?' he then asked. 'I sure am,' I replied, smiling still, but, inside, getting eager to move to the next stage. 'I'm the Conjuring Cowboy. Maybe you done heard o' me?' Gnarly-hair man's head tipped to the side just a skosh, in the tradition of a dog who's heard something strange. I took that for a 'No.' 'Oh, yes, I perform at all the State Fairs, don't ya know?' Had I overplayed my hand? A cloud grew over his face. He's sussed me out, I am sure, was my first thought. The next thing, he'll unholster and fill me with holes. 'Even performed once with Buffalo Bill. Oh, yes, me and ole Bill go back a ways…' His zero reaction was getting me down: whatever did this guy do when he wasn't killing people and robbing banks? He struck me as the classic mountain man, as burly and rugged as he was dirty and ragged. His beard flowed from his jowls like a river of black wrack. What sort of life did he lead? He wasn't what you'd call tall, but he had bulk, and he had presence. Black weather-beaten hat. Weather-beaten face under that. His facial skin was blotchy and cratered, unhealthily greyish in tone. A body-length coat he probably wore all year round, material unknown, somewhere between cloth and bear fur. Then, round his fat waist I noted what looked like raggedy wigs… He noticed that I'd noticed, so I had to say something: 'Mighty fine collection you got there, mister!' 'Yes, Siree! Got me fourteen o' the finest scalps you ever did see. Just about to get number fifteen when you showed up…' 'Have a wee drink first,' I suggested then, swallowing my disgust, 'and I'll show you my stuff,' I suggested, all mock-serio-comic with it. 'Just name it,' I continued, 'and I can conjure it up, yes, Sirree!'

'Mister, don't rightly know what kind o' critter y'are…' and he paused, leaving me worried at best, '…but, it's Saturday, bit tired from all this funning,' said with a contemptuous look all around him at the mess he had created, the dead in the dust…'so, I suppose one li'l drink won't kill me!' Then he chuckled. It was summer again in the foresty hills of his face, the sun breaking in. The brooding in his eyes gone, no doubt at the sight of the RYE twinkling in the glasses in the hot afternoon sun.

He held out his hand, and picked the nearest of the two tumblers, filled near to the rim with the dark amber brew. *Oh, what gnarly hands you have, Grandda…* About to just knock it back, he seemed unaware of the custom of clicking glasses. 'Eh uh,' I piped up, 'let's at least say "Cheers", little ole custom back from where I hail from,' extending my glass to the rim of his, ever so gingerly, spilling a tad as I did, to give him the idea that that's what civilized drinking men do. 'Here's to the day that is in it,' I pronounced, and he looked at me funny, like he'd had have to practice that one, and wasn't it better to just down these glasses right here and now. So we did.

Heads back, both us, knocking it back down our gullets in one, as though we'd done this a hundred times before, brothers in arms, we both shouted out: 'YEE-HAAAA!' and we meant it: this RYE was top-dollar hooch! It was so strong it'd wake up a hibernating grizzly! Now I was assimilating Mountain Man's being. Time to act! So I did: releasing my grip in both hands, the tumbler and bottle slipped from the space between us as Mountain Man's face registered incipient shock. I could see his whole body shudder into action, the hand not holding the glass just beginning to draw back and move down. But I had that covered: with a focus ice-cold and precise, I extended my right out toward him and conjured up, in a perfect 'summon & grab' movement, out of nowhere, plucked by a magic I had no idea about from the wall of Poly's Pots & Pans, the best hand-gun I could think of for the purpose at hand, model Smith & Wesson, 3 single-action revolver 'effective instrument of death & destruction, or was that law & order?' if I'd remembered correctly. It flew snug into my right hand, which then pointed squarely at the considerable bulk of Broken-Teeth Gnarly-Face-Hair Man. The look of shock in his features was worth every moment of danger I'd danced through just to get here. It was now his turn to drop his tumbler. And down it did fall, much like his feeling, I happily mused. *If only I'd been let alone!*

Two things happened simultaneously: the Indian revived, moving as though to get up, I could see, and to the right, at the wooden walkway, a glass pane was shattered, and then, through it, the barrel of a rifle suddenly appeared.

BLAM!

Gnarly face-hair man's arms flew up savagely and his chest billowed out, not unlike the sheet in the barbers, and towards me. He'd been shot from behind! His eyes, in a moment of absolute horror, caught my own and I didn't think I could feel pity for him, but I could: no more trees, no more streams, no more bears, no more waking at dawn with the cold in your armpits, no more scratching your butt and then feeling good, no more rattlesnake stew, no more cutting up deer, no more thinking up how to get out of scrapes, no more fellowship, no more whiskey, no more memories of Mama, no more shooting up towns or killing at random, no more ole Jesus up on the hill, no more fancy tricks to behold in this heat and this dust, no more chance to strut around cock 'o the walk, *'cause, good people, I'm beastly dead!* And I was dead, too, if I didn't bucktail it outta there now. Ole Hammy had likely thought we were real pardners, indeed, drinking a toast to the havoc and mayhem, and I wasn't about to allow him to prove himself right. I half-fell backwards, but then caught myself and turned in mid-air, and drove down my feet like pistons into the earth, keeping hold of my gun, 'get the hell outta here!' flashing through my mind like a siren on a sinking ship.

I hoped Ruby'd think of something, and, then, seeing I could run round down the street just a bit and turn left into the alley, I knew I could double back to the pharmacy. Sorry, APOTHECARY! I was counting on the obliqueness of Hamilton's position to assure me I'd make it, but I sure knew he'd be out in a flash.

With an urgency I'd not experienced before (excepting just yesterday in the saloon, oh, and just a short while ago in the hotel...), I ran down the alley, and then up, past one shop until I had come to the back of the shop with all the damn tinctures and lotions. It was locked and I stood there, desperate, until with a creak, the backdoor banged open and

Ruby came out. We embraced with some force, me still awkwardly holding the S &W, and Ruby half-crying at me, what a fool I had been to get into such danger, and me saying yes, what a fool, what a scene, what a day, what a hell we'd be in if we didn't just scoot.

We both knew what that meant. We'd abandon the Indian, pray for his skin, but going back now would mean certain death. Of course, neither of us said this, we could deal with it later, so we ran, ran up the backstreet we were now on, hoping our speed was enough to save our own skins. At any minute now, Hamilton and his deputy might scoot right round here, too, and start firing. Or the remaining riders might cut in through some side street... So, there being no place else to hide, we kept running, holding onto each other's hand and kicking up dust.

There was shooting not far away, just on the main street, parallel to where we were now. Hamilton and his deputy must be attacking the rest of the Tyler gang, for surely this was the Tyler gang I'd heard about just yesterday. Despite what I thought of the sheriff, I hoped he'd prevail, as they were indeed a seriously nasty bunch of individuals. Shooting up this poor town and killing people like they were just animals, what sort of way was that to prosecute the exigencies of life? Chaos and misrule, only checked by the harsh backlash of Hamilton, a kind of necessary evil, it seemed. Or, was he just evil too, part of the machine that had stolen the land, the inevitable fate of the dispossessor, to live in a constant state of chaos and war? It was all above me, or below me, or just near me, near us, for it was fierce and it was bloody: you could hear pitiful screams, too. The usual pattern was a gunshot followed by a scream. Once, though, with no gunshot, a bloodcurdling scream suddenly went up. It was all chaos. No glory here, I concluded, no allure either... We had to get out.

So, we ran and we ran...

CHAPTER NINE

We were parallel to 'Main Street', if they called it that, so we'd have to sidle in to the left to regain it, and after the ground we had covered, we thought we must surely have gone far enough. No-one around, thankfully, all cowering inside their barriers against the world and its woe. (Where'd I heard that before?) We'd run past, say, seven or eight buildings by now, time surely to test the waters. So, at the next left-turning alley we took respective deep breaths and made our way in.

'I know this alley!' I exclaimed. Ruby looked quizzical. 'This here's the darn place I kitted myself out!' Ruby still wasn't getting it. 'When I arrived!' I added, as though that cleared things up. It did, kind of. 'Did you just say "darn"?' asked Ruby then. Now it was my turn to look quizzical. 'Darn? As in socks?' she enquired, mock-serious, but then she moved on: 'Look, just get us out of here, Buster!' 'Tex!' 'Buster! Tex! Buffalo Bill, if you like! No time for trips down memory lane!' She was right. We had to get out. We'd been facing each other, but now we turned round simultaneously, at the unmistakable *thump-thump* of some new commotion coming our way. We soon saw what it was. A huge body, and coming toward us! I couldn't know why but eyes do not lie: none other than the ole Apache, Creased-Face hisself, was barrelling toward us at a jump, a leap and a bound. How he'd escaped was beyond me, but then, noticing the giant Bowie knife in his hand, I had some idea. Right toward me he was coming, thundering the ground with his strides. On instinct I raised up the ole barrel of that weighty instrument of death and shouted out 'Stop!' but he didn't. Ruby screamed to my sorry whimper, me unsure what to do, no time to weigh up the decision to pull the trigger or not. I'd just have to allow instinct take over, even if it meant shooting him dead. Or, I could move. Or Ruby could move. And she did, grabbing me in a sudden body-rush, her arms clasping round me, pushing me sidewise, her momentum impossible for me to resist: together we fell right-wise, just out of the trajectory of the running man. Fell hard onto dirt, but with enough distance to recover if need be... And yet -Whoosh!- on ran the Injun, thundering past, knife still in hand, dripping blood, I could see, but unraised, his lean naked skin rippling with the great strides and the shock of each footfall. I could also see he'd picked up his headcloth, and held onto that dearly in his other hand. Must've been important to him, like a token of his identity, perhaps. I could dig that, memories of a different alley, and my own humble sartorial fare, floating back... On and on he kept going, fleet as a god oe'er grass in Arcady, as though we'd never been there; he'd just kept on barrelling down the alley, ignoring us both, the dust billowing up in his wake. On down the alley, into the backstreet, across it, in through two buildings... Away!

'It was like we weren't there!' I gasped to Ruby, who, ever the logical one, replied: 'well, we haven't been born yet, boyo! Not for a few decades yet!'

Our initial glee at seeing one thread tied up, so to speak, and our consciences salved in the process (we wished him the best), was replaced with the thought of what had made him do that. In tandem, still on the ground, and me now enjoying our impromptu embrace, we looked back to where we'd been headed, and from where the Indian had come, expecting anytime soon to see ole Hammy filling the space before us, rifle in hand. Jesus Christ! (Where was *that guy* when you needed him?)

'Let's get in there!' I said, the two of us now scrambling up to our feet in some haste. I pulled at Ruby's sleeve, and pointed over to the blacksmith's barn, still conveniently open. We ran in there in a flash, stepping out of the light and into the dark, the two of us covered in dust and our faces flushed with all our recent exertions. In our mutual sense of the madness of what had been happening and what might happen next, we exchanged a range of Anglo-Saxon-derived utterances and pronounced the name of the alleged Supreme Being in multifarious, and, it had to be said, liberatingly disrespectful, ways before we'd calmed down. We stayed close to the door, as we needed to keep our ears open to whatever sounds might announce the next stage in this comedy of life-and-near-violent-death. I noted the iron brazier into which I'd stuffed my crap twentieth century clothes just 24-hours previous, thankful for what I saw now, just a smoulder of heaped ash. I noted also the slated wooden wall on the opposite side of the alley, knowing it was likely where that little girl lived, the girl who'd seen me conjure up stuff and had then pointed me out in the street just today. She didn't deserve to live in a town like this.

We couldn't go on, I surmised, waiting like this, like fish in a bowl: my mind was assaulted with visions of Hammy flying past with a shotgun and pegging us, or one of the riders boring down on us, murder firmly imprinted on tiny brain. 'We gotta get out, Rubes, gotta get out.' She assented, for once, with my 'plan'. 'Now or never,' she added, and I

parried, 'With all due caution, my dear, all due caution…'
So we inched out, me in the lead, my gun in my hand, my
hat on my head, and my boots on the ground, both literally
and figuratively. I'd steer us out! Adventure pulsed through
my veins, adrenaline coursing like spikes of electricity
through every limb. Energized. Step by slow step, out from
the dark to the light once again…

I'd been here before, a long time ago, when time is
measured by what happens in between: so much, it was
hardly true. Of course, what was true or believable anymore
was anyone's guess: if this was reality it wasn't the one I'd
been used to before. It was heightened, then, some mad
hyper-reality I felt, every last movement checked and
processed by cerebral command, every last synaptic
exchange part of the pulse of the moment, every last
particle of dust in the heat of the air, turning in and out
from an invisible dull to a short, brilliant shine, examined
and catalogued, part of the giant picture before us, the Old
West once again, exhibiting herself once again, putting on
show all she had to allure the eye and the ear and the sense
that something might happen, anytime now, so be ready,
watch out, or you're deader than dead. The BANK over
there, again announcing TWENTY FIRST NATIONAL,
EST.1848, and then the DRY GOODS, VICTUALERS,
DENTIST and GROCERS running beside it. Now no-one
here, though. No be-hatted gents, or three-cornered hat-
wearing stogie-smoking men on old nags either. Just eerie
silence was all.

Not quite.

We were tucked in close to the corner, so we couldn't be
seen from down the street, Ruby's head above mine, and
mine now minus hat for the moment, an encumbrance I
didn't need. Inconspicuous, that had always been my hope
from the start. Where did it all go wrong? 'Look!' Ruby

instructed, and pointed down the street, back toward where the ruckus had been. I was already looking, though, down past the rows of deserted shops and whatnot, down through the town to the place we'd come from. It was Hamilton we saw. Alone, hat on head, pistol in hand, the sides of his long dark coat swaying as he walked this way, our way. Now *he* was cock o' the walk, he'd regained his old authoritative step, no doubt filled with more righteous anger than a preacher at Jamestown. (Killing does that. Believing in God does that.) He derived from that stock, no doubt, too. The ole Pilgrim Fathers and all. Grim, no mistakin'. Scottish Calvinist written into his soul, if he had one. Hard as they come, hell and high water, fire and brimstone, he was right in his element, wearing a badge which told him whatever he'd do was God's own work. He'd see evil crushed, a snake underfoot writhing. I knew his type back where I'd come from. I was scum to that type back there, and scum to this one right here. Some people run to appointments, but Hamilton strode, knowing with every breath he was right and he'd stamp out the devil wherever he was. Talking of which, thinking all this, and seeing him come, I found myself whispering 'Jesus, Jesus' as though that might help. I was the one he was looking for now after all. He hadn't seen us yet. Technically, I could just take him out, like a sniper…

Or… hold him up… Could I do that? How? Well, the reasoning went, very simple. That man's got a handgun. He's still kind of far away, but still striding this way. I don't have much time, cause the gap's closing soon, but - calculating- I'd have the jump…with a…

'Winchester '73!' I half-blurted out. Retreating then suddenly from under Rubes, and detaching myself from the corner position, I threw out my arms and called it right up, tossing the S & W to the dirt. And there, into the space before my extended right hand, fingers out, filling the air with its now-materializing wood-metal bulk, it came into being and thrust itself forward into the grip of the left and the catch of the right simultaneously. Nice catch! as they say (or they will). The next part required the same kind of boldness I'd shown exiting the apothecary, not long before. The adrenaline was flowing, the testosterone, too, I had to admit, so I made myself not hear ole Rubes, who whisper-shouted at me, and even slapped at me with her palms, like I was a steel-drum. Ole Hammy'd had similar treatment, but I subsumed the pain of each slap with the thought that he'd suffered this too, and this was nuthin' to bullets punching through my feeble flesh. Now or never, I jumped out of her circle and into the realm of the street, charged with a force I was powerless to stop.

I didn't have to go far. Just past the corner a tad, a precipitous but short run into the sun, my weapon raised as I did so, ignoring Ruby's pleas to return. Too late for that, but I had him on distance: 'STOP, HAMILTON,' I shouted out, projecting force through volume and tone as all the best small dogs do when confronted with dogs of superior size, 'or I'LL BLOW YOU AWAY!' Bravado is great if you have it, but it takes practice, I guess, or something else. I was scared out of my wits, but I'd be damned if I'd show that. My plan had worked: Hamilton had stopped in his tracks, and wasn't raising his gun. Was I dreaming? Or had my idea been correct? He could see I was holding a rifle on him, to his teeny-weeny short-barrelled pistol. I'd got the drop on him, but we couldn't remain quite like this. I walked a little further out, and towards him. 'OK!,' I barked out (appropriately, but putting as much manly gruffness in there as I could). 'Drop the gun NOW!' Now, Hamilton's idea of 'now' and mine weren't quite the same, but, probably having thought through his options (for which I gave him the courtesy of about ten very long and very tense seconds), he complied, not dropping it straight, but tossing it forward quite a ways. Clever, very, I thought. 'Now walk towards me.' Seemingly nonplussed by the situation, he did just as I'd asked, so I asked myself once again if I was dreaming this up, some parallel magic to the ole conjuring thing. But there he was, weaponless, striding toward me, lamb to the slaughter, as the Ma might also say. And, yet, once he had made it as far as the point where his pistol lay in the dust, he then stopped. Clever. Very. Again.

'You can't get away with this, Mister!' he hollered, but calmly enough, to my earlier tone of manic insistence. 'Someone'll hunt you down… *like a dog…*' (Touché!) 'Put your hands up, where I can see them, Sheriff Hamilton,' I heard myself say. I was making this up as I went. So far, so good. Ole Hammy complied, his hands reaching up slowly. It was then when I'd planned to say: 'Walk towards me,' but what was that they said about the best laid plans of mice and men…? In fact, come to think of it, what was it I said about being inconspicuous, now holding a Winchester '73 on the town's sheriff, and all? (Even if, to be exceedingly pedantic about it, it was actually the 1894 model…) The sun beating down on my hatless head was a factor I hadn't thought of… He looked all square-shouldered and solid as a tree, and I was beginning to get tired holding this beauty, heavy as it was, wondering just what to say next. And then two things happened I hadn't seen coming. First: a bead of stinging salt-sweat dropped into my left eye. And, second, just as it did my right saw a flash far behind where my terse interlocutor stood. A rifle, its long metal barrel caught by the sun!

In my panic, I loosed off a shot over Hamilton's head. I thought this might deter whoever was there in the background, too. 'Don't even think about!' I shouted to Hamilton. And yet I was blinking now, fighting the sting of the salt, and, once again, yes, I could see beyond him, the flash of metal once again. Straining to see more, I unloosed my trigger finger and wiped at my face, thereby upsetting the hold of the Winchester, the barrel moving up, the sun beating down, my stance faltering, confidence slipping away. Hamilton didn't move though. It was like he was waiting for something better, some opportunity he knew he would get soon enough. Then I saw the flash once again, as clear as the day: to the right at his back, a figure had emerged out from in under the shadows of the wooden walkway and was pointing his rifle or shotgun very clearly at Hamilton, too. He'd shoot within seconds unless I was to act now.

So, I swiftly turned my rifle right-wise and fired off three shots in fast succession, cocking the lever as fast as I possibly could. BLAMBLAMBLAM! It was the ole little dog theory again: in my fevered mind, I'd made a split-second decision to ward that guy off, if not quite fill him with holes, something telling me that wasn't quite me after all. That barking (what a racket the sounds of the shots made in my ears!) would do the trick nicely enough. And it did, my bullets pinging all round him, right at his feet, I could see him now turning and running away. And yet in this moment, ole Hammy had moved, sussing things out, and moved fast, like a spectre, diving down into the dust for his gun, swivelling round and firing off shots of his own to the retreating figure. None of them hit, but it was enough to make the figure throw up his arms in serious fright, tossing his weapon away in apparent abject panic, and flee in a cloud of dust. I'd raised up my rifle, and was now rubbing my eyes, hoping to use the few seconds of the diversion. But now Hamilton was swivelling back, still on the ground, raising his gun toward me.

We were back at loggerheads, ole Hammy and me, just like yesterday, facing off, and *now both of us had guns*: the realization that I'd have to fire now at his body shocked me like nothing so far. If I didn't think of something quick, it would be me sending rude metal projectiles hurtling his way and crashing into his flesh and bone. He'd flail back like a doll, blood spilling out from his wounds and into the sand and the dirt of the street, and I would have won, but become a murderer in the process... OR... before my mind's eye floated a sudden vision of boxes and trunks, or anything large and unwieldly but not heavy that might form a wall between us... That one room devoted to travel at Poly's, I now recalled. 'Travelling gear for the Gent and the Lady.' No frill dresses and business-like suits. Rugged or bedamned, but elegant. Purses and wallets for paper and coin. Binding cords and huge blank labels. Smoking utensils, pipes and silver-cigarette cases aplenty. Boaters and parasols. Lorgnettes and spectacles. Nautical spyglasses, too! I remember them! How travel broadens the mind! And then, in the centre of that vast treasury of a chamber, a mountain of boxes, cases and trunks, giant and small. It was from these I now picked with my mind and my magic, near-suicidally discarding the Winchester, and throwing my two hands out and toward the man in the dirt, fifty metres away who was aiming his gun. BLAM! out flew the huge 'Gladiator' trunk, with its 'fancy zinc cover' corners all 'double iron bound' and 'iron bumpers', only $8.50! Its suddenly materializing bulk made a welcome if hardly long-lasting barrier between Hammy and me. In fact, after the initial wow of its sudden appearance, it soon crashed to earth in an inglorious clatter, rolling over once or twice before it just sat there in the dirt, looking ever so slightly out of place. So, in quick succession, born of a growing panic, out flew: 'Crown Prince' all done in cowhide, an elegant but doughty piece of travelware, only $5.50, flying out on wings of magic and then rudely crashing into the 'Gladiator'. Well, with its corners all 'double iron-bound' and its sturdy 'full iron bottom', it was never going to make gentle contact with anything, travelling at speed. This was followed by the conjuring of 'No.1. Saratoga' right after that, with its beautifully convex top, the whole all done in gleaming pine, crisscrossed with black iron bands and patent bolt locks, now careering into the space beyond my out-stretched hand -Hammy-wards.

Hammy-wards, perhaps, but gravity soon getting the best of it, it slammed with force into the others, and tumbled on beyond a tad, too, the ole momentum thing coming into play. Then, with my hands raised up quite a bit, to add a little altitude, out flew 'Zinc Empress', a beautiful piece, 'Favored by ladies', a wonderful chequered design etched into the zinc cover, a fine example of craftmanship if ever there was one, shooting miraculously skyward for a few, brief seconds, before landing -BLAM!- beyond the heap already there, throwing up a ton of dust in the process. Then, in quick succession: *French Saratoga! Union Pacific!* And *Extra Fine Zinc Eugenie!* like huge tumbling dice. The latter exploding as Hamilton fired his gun in a quick succession of his own, and I knew I had only bought seconds. BLAST! Out then flew more of these damned trunks and boxes and suitcases and satchels (some lovely pieces in alligator hide!) in a huge torrent of accumulating high-end bric-a-brac. More and more junk flowed out, piling up rightly in the middle of the street, big bits and small, items of every size and shape clattering out and into each other, making a barrier of sorts between us, but one that needed constant feeding. 'YAAAAAHHHH!!!!' I screamed, as my fingers, splayed out and shaking, went from a tingle to a series of sharp shocks to a point where all I could feel was pain in my joints and my arms and hands, and even under my very nails. I had never unleashed such a load of material all at once. It was working as a barrier in that Hammy wouldn't want to waste too many more bullets not seeing his target. But I had to get out while I could, so I dived to the left, as another bullet ripped through the growing mountain of travel gear and whatnot piling up on the street.

BLAST! went Hamilton's gun, then again, and I could hear the lead ripping through the air as I ran, past the corner, now itself exploding in shards. Hamilton wouldn't let up! And the realization that he wouldn't let up now filled me with panic, which then affected my coordination, so it was hardly surprising when, dread moment, I tripped in my rush, and fell -and fell hard- into the dirt of the alleyway. Ruby was screaming at me to get up. But I'd fallen forward and put out my hands and arms to cushion the fall, and yet, after all my mad conjuring, my hands were now numb with the effort required to shoot all that junk out. And I was feeling desperately drained of all power. I doubted I could conjure up a single bean right now, never mind a sackful. I turned round in the dirt, and motioned for Ruby to help me get up. I'd have to recover soon, or we'd be soon done for, as ole Hamilton also knew how to run, I was sure. 'Get up, get up for God's sake, NOW!' Ruby shrieked at me, pulling at my waistcoat, but, it was

...too late!

Sprawling there on my back on the ground, Ruby screaming blue murder, and a feeling of fate creeping over my soul, I felt my heart fail almost literally as round came the corner the dark shape of Sheriff Hamilton, his gun in his right hand. His eyes were like burning coals in a very dark place, somewhere like hell, I imagined. Whether he knew it or not, he was the devil, not I. They could write that one on my tomb, I now saw. 'Killed by Sheriff Hamilton. He was the Devil, not I. God Rest In Peace.'

I'd lost the battle, the battle that required not only strength of nerve but a kill-instinct I just didn't have. I could summon up weapons all day, but the thought of using one to shoot down a man was, alas, not part of me. This doomed me, here, in this dog-shoot-dog world, this was my fate in the midst of the harsh and the loud and the hard-hearted killers who saw humans as obstacles to need. If only I'd not taken this 'gift' or this 'curse', if only I'd stayed in my safe little circle back home, if only I'd never answered that stupid ad. If only I'd never set eyes on ole Poly, old Paul E. Clarence Rhumboldt, Esquire. And, yet, if he were here... If Poly were here...

'Poly!' I said, almost quietly, knowing I'd only seconds before the big Scotsman attacked. My voice was weakened with fear, with defeat, with a terrible sadness, for me, and for Ruby, for all we had dreamed of. 'Poly,' I then said, in a tremulous *sotto voce*, 'you said if I needed you, just to...' Hamilton had now come to a dead stop. He was nothing but a giant silhouette, a cut-out of death above me... '...holler,' I finished. Hamilton's arms were by his side, but I'd noticed he was now slowly raising his right, the one with the gun. 'Holler,' I repeated, just to myself, and then, with the last of my breath: 'POLY!' I screamed.

'Fella!' said a voice behind Hammy. I could see nothing. In his own heightened state, Hamilton turned round to the more immediate threat posed by the voice at his back, his gun coming up in a flash, ready to fire. But in one blindingly matching flash, something then happened against all expectation. Hamilton's gun spat its round with a deafening sound, which -strangely, madly- thudded against what I guessed could only be metal. I was shuddered awake to whatever it was that was just happening, straining to see against the light. But whatever it was, it was pushing the giant silhouette back, now beginning to topple backwards, a dark disk of some sort smacking into Hamilton's head, with a dull, somewhat sickening thwack, dislodging his hat in the process, and then flying on. Other disc-like and bulbous projectiles were coming his way, making hard contact here, there and everywhere on the man, with thuds, thwacks and punishing thumps. Now the great structure of Hamilton's form was falling ever backwards, down towards the place where I lay. Anticipating the blow from the fall, I then shuddered back, crawling rapidly backwards, Ruby now pulling me, too, her hands having grabbed at my shoulders. Incredibly, Hamilton shot again as his body toppled backwards, in slo-mo, it seemed, but it was useless for him, as hard thing upon hard thing rained down upon him, things iron and black and round and heavy as hell, clanging ever more onto his now fallen, now sprawling form. Talking of forms, there was now one to behold beyond where Hamilton had been, and his arms were outstretched, as all sorts of junk kept flying from the space they enclosed, like a river it flowed, till I could now see it was pots and pans, and woks and griddles, and kettles and tins, piling up over where Hammy had gone down, now getting quite buried, moment by wonderful moment. 'Poly!' I screamed. Poly stuck his face forward and then raised a finger to his lips: 'Quiet', it meant. He wasn't quite done. Last came a shovel, which he caught with aplomb, and then raised over his beautiful bonce and whacked down onto the pile with the force of jackhammer. 'Ow!' came a pathetic voice from below. Once more, with feeling he raised it up higher, and then, SLAM! brought the flat of it down with a viciously beautiful whack onto the very irregular surface of metal vessels of every shape and size covering poor Sheriff Hamilton. 'Ow!' said the voice down below, weaker, more pathetic than ever, beneath our contempt.

'Quick!' whispered Poly, and frantically motioned to us to get up, and follow him out. So we did. Then we ran, the three of us, three amigos, down the damn street, and away.

****

I was always being surprised by Poly, and now was no exception, not merely keeping up with us whippersnappers, but at times outpacing us, looking over at us from time to time, and solicitous with it. We hardly looked very inspiring, having been dragged through a bush backwards and then some, so to speak. Inside, though, was all sweetness and light: snatched from the jaws of death, we were free, almost there, at the end of this madness and strife.

Past the quaint last few structures of this Old Western Town, going too fast to exchange words, the street began to morph from its raggedy dusted-up surface, scored and marked with bits of this and that, to a firmer, hard surface, an easier grip for our feet. On we did 'fly' -as I'd 'figuratively' put it to Poly that time- until we could see it: standing out quaintly itself, the tin sign with the shapes dangling underneath: Poly's shop!

And that's where we stopped, and spent a full minute catching our respective breaths, bending and panting and wheezing a bit, too.

'Lordy, that was fun!' exclaimed Poly, to which we assented with our own this and that words. 'You saved our skins, Poly! We were done for, for sure!' I threw in, unconsciously reverting to my accent of yore. I went on, exhorting the man, and how we'd been doomed had he not appeared when he did. While Poly replied with a few dismissive words, Ruby remained strangely quiet, until she then reached into the folds, below the waistline of her skirt, and, slowly, catching my eye as she did so, pulled out the Colt .45 I'd seen earlier. 'Ruby! You had that all along?' Her eyes answered that one, but she wasn't finished quite yet. From another fold, out she then pulled another, smaller pistol. I wasn't sure what make. Poly and I watched her do so with widening eyes. Then, for her *pièce de résistance*, she pulled up her skirt a tad higher than you'd think decent, and reached down to remove the tiniest little snub-nosed Derringer you ever did see from under a lace garter high up on her leg. 'Boy, she had you covered!' chipped in Poly. She certainly did! 'We won't need these back there…' said Ruby, which made me wonder if she knew we shouldn't say too much about what 'back there' was. But there wasn't much time for chat anyway, Poly was telling us, as he neatly dropped each of Ruby's dangerous hoard into this voluminous pocket and that (what mysteries reside in the pockets of Wizards!): 'Ole Ham 'n Eggs'll wake up right soon, sorer than a bear with a scratchy back, so we'd better say our goodbyes here and now.' A sense of urgency was beginning to replace the elation at having escaped with our lives. But, it then hit me, if we didn't have time, how could I explain everything to Poly about what had happened, and about Ruby and all. And, weren't there some questions I still wanted to ask? It pained me to think I had to squeeze in so much in so short a time, and I flubbed a tad, trying to say too many things at once, till he said flatly: 'Just introduce me!' 'Of course! What was I thinking?' I then straightened up, dusted myself down a tad, pulled a hand over the ragged hair on my head, and got all formal with it: 'This here is... the one and only Ruby...!' I cringed, not knowing her family name, and, on top of that, that line made me sound like some crap pro-magician introducing his bimbo on stage. But it was okay: Poly was entranced, I could see. He'd extended his hand before I'd delivered the intro, his eyes widened as he pronounced: 'Charmed, Missy, charmed...' To which Ruby surprised us both with the deftest, cutest curtsey you could ever hope to see. Had she gone all nineteenth century, too? Poly then looked at me, a mysterious smile forming over his lips, which then suddenly hardened into a bold, forthright stare: 'Boy, you take good care of this gal,' he said, and as he did, he put a firm, almost paternal, hand on my shoulder. Then, classic Poly, he uttered his famous 'Ha!' with a toss of the head, and thereby broke the spell.

'Time is upon us, ole friend,' he said. His glasses-framed eyes held my own, a querying glint in them, somehow. I made to go forward, embrace, not quite sure if that's what was best, and then, Poly's hand came up, his palm opened, waiting. Quizzical look on my face. Stern look on Poly's. Ruby's face poked in, examining both, interpreting: 'Buster, I think that means you need to give Poly something, can't you see that?' Something? Me? Give Poly? Some... And then it hit me! 'Of course!' Again, too: 'What was I thinking?' The dreaded return of my linguistic tendency to repeat myself! (It was even the same phrase!) There followed a fumbling in pockets, accompanied by an almost ostentatious stepping from one foot to the other, like an impromptu jig, all presided over by a look on my face that was not unlike that you might have if someone asks you a difficult question and as you're desperately trying to answer it you realize you've forgotten the damn question. 'Try that one,' spoke Poly, a deadpan look in his eyes as he pointed out my right-side front denims pocket. He threw in 'Tex!' as he did so, in a tone you might just call pointed. I did, and sure enough, just as he'd instructed me... just that very morning!... the wee leather pouch was safe there within. I slipped it out, passed it gingerly over to Poly. Gingerly, mind, as only now was it dawning on me: THIS WAS IT. The end of my magic.

Poly accepted the small leather case, opened it, pulled out the paper slip, and questioned me with his eyes. I answered with what you might characterize as a reluctant nod: slow, hardly convincing, but enough to be answer. I noted that Ruby's face was still close, and her eyes had been questioning me, too, so I turned to her, looked into her eyes, and said: 'It just has to be...' She confirmed with a nod of her own, minimal, but laced with acceptance and mutuality, if a shared sense of loss. Even though we'd never known a normal life together, we thought such a thing might be possible... Damn the boring bits if they came. Meanwhile, Poly had clicked his fingers, summoned up a tray of matches, lit one, applied the flame, gently, then WHOOSH! The paper was gone in a flash.

After a moment, I threw out: 'I hope this town recovers...' I felt like I'd messed it up terribly. 'If the Tyler gang's finished, the folks can look forward to peace,' he averred, and in a tone that suggested he didn't wish to discuss it further. 'But, there was also an Indian...' Ruby chipped in. 'What'll become of him?' 'Ah,' mused Poly, 'ole

Genitoa?' Now his look became, all of a sudden, faraway, as though he was looking out to some place beyond our ken, beyond mine certainly, not knowing how he felt about 'Injuns', and yet wondering how he knew his name... 'Ole Genitoa,' Poly said once again, '...that ole buzzard...' A hint of a smile entered his features. Seeing this, even if I didn't quite get what it meant, made me somehow immensely relieved. I should have predicted the subsequent 'Ha!'

'Look! You good people, best you be getting along!' Poly'd broken his reverie with a start, adding new urgency to the moment. 'Git!' So, we did. I rushed a big hug on the man, which he fought off, then Ruby had her turn, whispering 'Thanks for everything! You're our saviour!' Poly quipped back, cryptically: 'And you, Missy, are mine!' We all laughed at that, whatever the hell it meant, us all patting each other and flapping round as is the custom when close family members break up at the airport or the harbour, all full of emotion, dragging us this way and that. Meanwhile Poly turned round, removing the 'Gone Fishin'' sign, as he then just clicked his fingers and, magically, had unlocked the door to P.P.P.. (*So that's all I'd needed to do?! Just click my fingers?* I realized with something like shock.) A physical barrier would do the trick best, he had no doubt concluded, fumbling his way backward, hollering out: 'Be seeing ya!' and 'Don't be a stranger!' as he did so, sidling himself out of our reach and behind the glass door, only his head left peeking out, as he called finally: 'Have a great day, folks!' And then he was gone.

Ruby and I stood there silent, unmoving. This is where it had all began, I couldn't help but reflect. I still felt the allure:

POLY'S POTS & PANS
GENERAL STORE

etched into the frosted glass in elegant capitals, the beautifully grained wood frame all around. Just beyond there it had all started, within that... hallowed space... with its soaps and its teas and its beans and its apples and its rings and its jewels and its cut-glass decanters and its whiskey and its grandfather clocks, or Regulator timepieces, its guns, and its pots & pans, too... I flicked out the fingers of my left hand, thinking apples. Nothing came out. I flicked out the right, thinking rings, just one for dear Ruby. But nothing came out.

'Don't be depressed, cowboy, we've got a truck load of stuff still back in the flat...' said Ruby, softly. 'Let's get outta town!' So, we did, my head down a little at first, then, after a few mins, much recovered, feeling happier about everything, hearing the clack of my boots on the cobbles -*oh what a sound!*- and walking beside the cutest gal this side o' the Missouri, how could I not?

CHAPTER TEN

Getting back to our flat meant jumping on a bus, the No.7, but neither of us had any -usable- money on us, so we walked. Which was okay, but a little tiring after a very long day and having to ignore the looks we were getting in our Wild Western get-ups. 'That was some party!', 'Shoot 'em up, cowboy!', 'Look, it's Buffalo Bill and Calamity Jane!' were just three of the -nicest- comments I can recall. We could hardly blame them, of course. We did, as anyone could imagine, stand out a bit. Most unnerving of all was a brief encounter with a policeman, who approached and asked if I knew anything about a disturbance at a bar a few weeks back. 'Moi?' I replied, 'Mais, non!' playing up the French side of my alter-ego, 'I don't even... *boire*... drink.' (The 'don't' pronounced 'dont', rhyming with 'font', and 'drink' came in two heavily-accented syllables with an accompanying gesture of my left hand motioning supping.) Ruby suppressed a giggle, and the policeman blanked me, but insisted he 'take down' my 'particulars'. I didn't like the sound of that, but, apart from feeding him a line, what can you do when you're back in the land of the ordinary?

There was a bit of that alright, the anti-climax of no longer having supernatural powers, but it didn't stop us from enjoying a bit of serious 'down time' (a *modern* Americanism?) together for the first time in yonks. Ruby and I were closer than ever now, and we blocked out the world of the ordinary with each other's company and with each other's bodies, too. Days passed and the only example of supernatural powers came via the telephone which we dialed up for deliveries of pizza and the occasional side-salad of beer. There was plenty of whiskey (potent hundred-year-old hooch) still lying around, and not only that: numerous pairs of cowboy boots, belt buckles, waistcoats, hats in profusion, gunbelts, handguns, rifles, huge glass jars filled with the teas of the world, sacks of dried beans, metal containers of every shape and size under the sun, knives, glassware, jewellery, stones both precious and semi-precious, timepieces, small and wearable and large and standing, soaps, skin-creams and lotions, towels and scrubbing brushes for the skin, hairbrushes, combs, toilet sets, apples and oranges in separate barrels, children's toys, children's dolls, skates, ladies' dresses, underwear too, over-coats and headwear, griddles and woks, kitchen utensils for helping you cook, or just getting food from the plate to your mouth, and then pots and pans, tins and cans, and vessels whose function I could no longer guess, and all of these items and more remained in our place like reminders of a world now long gone. And people now long dead, too.

There was a sadness, for want of a better word, as I thought about the loss of my powers, and the loss of that world where I'd felt so energized and alive. The Ireland I could spy from the window looked dour and bleak, and the more than occasional rain didn't help. I'd sometimes find myself, when Ruby wasn't looking, or when she was out, flinging my fingers out and concentrating on conjuring something up. 'Voilà!' I would shout, in my most hopeful tone. But nothing ever materialized in the space beyond the reach of my hands, left or right. I tried not to let that get me down too much, remembering the madness when it had seemed that damn-near everything would come out, and so much that I was a danger to myself and to Ruby. I had to learn to accept things as they were. Playing blues on the guitar helped. I even wrote a wee song.

Funnily enough, we got into watching old Westerns, this time, though, not for my image-training. We didn't have a television, so we would visit the local library and, sharing headphones, watch video tapes of John Wayne, Jimmy Stewart, Gary Cooper and Randolph Scott, and others, getting into all sorts of scrapes. I thought William Wyler's *The Westerner* was the best, and Ruby really liked *True Grit*. *One-Eyed Jacks* was also a fave for us both. Alan Ladd's *Whispering Smith* took me by surprise: in one scene the hero actually magics up a coin -pretends to, rather-, and the kid he gives it to is astonished. I had to re-wind and re-watch that one about five times. But we didn't talk that much about what we'd watched: it was too raw to know that we'd never be back. (Not completely accurate: we'd have impromptu mock gunfights out on the street just afterward -people thought we were acting like kids, we were- but then we'd lose energy and then be depressed, a bit.) Sometimes, we would go out on a sortie into town and have a coffee or a meal, or even enter the occasional pub, into Monahan's, say, to 'have a pint and set the world to rights' as the owner, a dacent man, often put it. Nothing excessive anyway. No whiskey. No uisce beatha... One time, we went to this big new supermarket that had just opened. It was enormous, like the inside of an aircraft hangar. We had to -Ruby did it- fill out some kind of form, for a trial, because it was an exclusive wholesaler's, and everything was price-reduced, but we ended up not signing up full-time. Even so, we had a look around.

The individual shelves were as long as most regular supermarkets, I thought, and stocked with the most amazing assortment of goods I'd ever seen (well, hardly, but in late 80s Ireland, yeah). Everything was generally big-sized, so that's what put us off, not yet being a family of six with a giant four-wheeled drive truck. But God in heaven, my eyes ate the stuff up. Tier after tier of giant-sized bags of crisps, in so many styles, some I'd never seen, like Garlic and Sea-Salt, or boxes of crackers for cheese, little illustrations on each of a few salt-encrusted yellow-brown slivers heaped with slices of Stilton or Cheddar, a wee classic-shaped glass of red wine in the soft-focus background, enticing, enticing… Pickles, not far from this section, subtle greens in the murk, cuts of mysterious vegetables, crammed into their small briny space. What was that about some vegetable actually transforming in the solution: a cucumber or something becoming a dill pickle? My mind would be beset with inquiries like this, as I took it all in. Next, in a large sunken refrigerated open display case, the cheeses themselves: individual cuts of blues and of hard-to-pronounce German types. Barrels of Manchego and Brie, one-eighth chunks of Wensleydale and Red Leicester, slices of Gouda and Roquefort, mini-cities of blocks of wrapped-up and labelled various types, the gold and silver paper wrapping sometimes glinting in the neon overhead.

Neon everywhere, the ceiling a patchwork of lights, pipes, tubes, cables and thickly-painted off-white surfaces. Crowds milling round, us being pushed around now and then, part of a flow of humanity, all of us pushing giant-sized trolleys and marvelling at Special Offers left, right and centre, and nonsensical muzak playing all the time. INTERIORS. All the fine fittings to fit out your house, and give it that special touch, even if the wood frames were all *faux*, or labelled, round the back, MADE IN CHINA. *Faux* retro-style clocks under glass, WELCOME mats, fake-stitched bouquet-of-flowers design or something abstract and modern. Light-fittings for every function: overhead room-lighting, book-reading, night-light, front-door auto-light, you name it. Mirrors, big and small: when I caught myself in a full length one, I remembered back to the huge length-wise one in Beeker's Barber's Shop. The difference made me shudder: no more cowboy gear, I was reduced to the very ordinary duds of late 20th C North of Ireland, and looking sheepish with it.

House alarm systems. Wallpaper rolls. Paint. Boxes of screws, and of nails, and of two-pronged pins, sheathed in soft plastic. Toilets and bathroom fittings, even full-sized baths and shower-curtains on rails. Visions of the perfect life. Beds. Furniture. Free standing chairs. Sofas and stools and little coffee tables, in glass and in wood, and a variety of styles to suit anyone. There would be these little spaces, where they had arranged sofas and low tables in conjunction and you could plunk yourself down and feel 'hey, this is my beautiful life!' Then, you'd stick your hand in your pocket and you could just buy your beautiful life, just like that. Of course, you'd need a fridge -they had them, too- and then you'd need to go back to the FOOD SECTION, and get a clatter of stuff and just cram it all in, and don't forget the bottles of wine and the six-packs of beer, which are 'just over there!' in friendly upbeat service tones. (I'm sure ole Elmer would fit right in here, I mused once. He'd be a sub-manager for sure.) So, it was perhaps serendipitous that we happened to wander back into that area of libations and comestibles, and then... the MEAT DEPARTMENT. (What was it with all the capital lettering? I mused. That still the vogue? Ah sure, ya can't kill ole CAPITALISM!) Anyway, as I was saying, we wandered next into the MEAT DEPARTMENT. Vacuum-packed chunks of unsliced pork-bacon, pigs feet on string, fillets of 'finest Australian beef', cuts of 'Prize Angus', salvers of whitish pig intestines and cellophaned trays of liver, and kidney, and tongue, under an 'ice-curtain' of flowing cold air/mist. Tenderloin steaks, lambchops, Silverside, and, behind all of this a battery of butchers, red-stained aprons on each, as they bent over some carnage, with long, dipping, super-sharp knives. I remembered the ole Apache, last time we saw him, with the Bowie knife dripping with blood in his hand as he escaped 'civilization'. Who was it said eating meat makes us more likely to kill? Well, by now we'd both had enough of this joint, and whatever we'd put in the trolley we just unloaded somewhere when no-one was looking, having caught sight of the patient hordes lining up in neat rows, ten trolleys deep at every PAY POINT.

We had to get out and we did, running away, literally, and, as though on cue, we went up to our sanctuary, up on the hill. Away from the 'atmospheric influence', just like Poly felt he had to do to escape the ravages of that terrible disease... Neither Ruby or I spoke much up there, just breathed in a lot and tried to forget all the noise and the madness of that dire place. Instead of magic, normal people used credit cards. And they could have whatever they wanted. No limitations. No magic. No bloody thanks.

Back in the flat, we'd occasionally step on sharp things in the dark. We could sell most of this junk, we decided, and put it all behind us. We still had a mint, but sooner or later, I'd have to get real, and 'buckle down' and go meet that guy with the elastic bands, the stackful of documents and his swivelling computer monitor. And there were loose ends, too, thinking back on the Wild West. *Where* had it been? *When* had it been? The failure to ascertain basic info like that bugged me. Big concept questions bugged, too: could we ever go back to the parallel world? I had no desire to try. It didn't feel right. We'd completed a circular journey there and escaped by the skin of our teeth. Anyway, there was probably some law of nature, or law of magic, which had now closed up the 'portal', if that was what it was. Maybe sometime... Another teaser was, thinking about the laws of nature: how was it that I could conjure stuff up endlessly, day after day? Surely that could result in the creation of duplicates of said items? If they were duplicates, what did that mean? And how much junk was it possible to call up, because whatever it was it was going to be in excess of what the shop had? So, how the hell had that worked? Or, was it taken as gospel that you are not supposed to overdo it? Well, from the look on Poly's face, it seemed the latter conclusion was right. It may have been magic, but only to be used sparingly, right? At that point, again, it seemed like the whole problem was not about magic or about physics, but about my appetite, which, if I wasn't careful, would kill me stone dead, superpowers or no superpowers. Of course. One must live simply. Like Caine. Inner strength, inner satiety, and all that. Why want and get everything? That way leads to...

And then there were other questions, like... just what the hell did the 'E' stand for in Poly's name? Paul E. Clarence Etcetera. He'd never said, and I'd never asked. *E Pluribus Unum*, by any chance? Just like Ruby and her friend and those weird things with the eggshells... Curiosity is great, but, perhaps I'd discovered, it is not boundless. The straight questions I could have asked Poly but didn't, because... well, because it would have damaged -messed with, the meaning of our communication. Just for that I would not ask... Or something like that... Anyway, all these unknowns niggled, but also tended to make the whole thing seem like a dream, like the one you wake up half-remembering but then have to witness disintegrating before your very half-opened eyes.

And then there were other things, like how we might have altered the future just by being there, interacting and all. Come to think of it, how did they report my magic? That'd be interesting to check on. Likely put it down to 'sleight of hand'... More to the point, what about that old chestnut of what it would have meant if I'd shot someone dead there?

Me: Well, you know it wasn't just me being wishy washy and all. [mid-afternoon, feeling like speaking about stuff with ole Rubes, as we lay on the bed after lunch, looking up at the -non-curlicued- ceiling] I could probably live with myself if I'd plugged Mountain Man, with his disgusting scalps and all.

Ruby: [mock encouraging tone] O, I know you could have, easily, you big man, you! Just BangBangBang, right? [mock-macho tone, gesturing using a pistol as she said so]

M: But, now that I think of it…

R: Yes? [flicking her eyelids ostentatiously]

M: Well… have you noticed anything strange in the papers recently, darlin'?

R: You mean like *good* news?

M: No, I mean like… [awkwardly gesturing]…like famous people suddenly not existing, or stuff like that?

R: [querulous look on her face]…No…

M: Thank God. [singing] *'…but I did not shoot no deputy…'*

R: Yeah, but would they have lived on if we'd not been there?

M: Aw, don't say that!

R: A butterfly flaps his wings and all that…

M: I know, but… you see…

R: Yes? [seeming to now take serious notice]

M: It was like the Prime Directive… *I* couldn't shoot anyone dead. It'd only screw up the future.

R: 'It *would* only screw up the future'. You've no excuse for overly casual grammar now, boyo. You did graduate from 'the best university in the country', according to you.

Me: [laughing, abashed] I beg your pardon. [adopting a mock-serio tone] It *would* only screw up the future.

R: I don't know about that guy, Mountain Man. His destiny was probably to get mauled by a grizzly. In a forest. During the rain. Nobody finds the body for years… Then, just the bones... Maybe Hamilton, though. If you'd plugged him, Jesus. You never know...

M: Indeed. Any jerks in America right now? Maybe they're descended from him.

R: *Any* jerks in America? How long have you got?

M: [laughing] Let's make a list! We could start with that jerk property developer in New York with the hair.

R: Oh, yeah, the guy with the ego and the quiff. [musing] Heard he's a fascist pig, too. Ah, but Hamilton's hair was all black...

M: Of course... Scots Calvinist, or Presbyterian, or whatever...

R: Ah, but, you know, maybe the Indian came back one day and got Hamilton [gesturing plunging a knife deep into the chest].

M: Now you're talking!

R: AND ANOTHER THING, BOYO! [precipitously changing the subject completely] Now we're together I think you need to tell me your proper name! It's getting ridiculous! [showing that this was indeed getting on her nerves]

M: Moi? It's... Buster... No, Tex.... No, Friz.... Ah, just call me 'Buffalo Bill'... Then again, no, he was a right evil git, killing all the Indians' beloved creatures...

R: Listen, BUSTER! [becoming almost seriously upset, turning her face to mine]. This is just crazy! You know my name, it's Ruby! R.U.B.Y. OK? Now, tell me *yours*. It's driving me up the wall!

M: [features acquiring a serious pall] Well, Rubes, you see...

R: [impatiently] Yes?

M: Well, my mother... she...

R: [insistent stare]

M: ...she kind of liked this name. It begins with... N.

R: Norbert?

M: No!

R: [thinking feverishly] Norman, Nelson, Navaho, Nicholas,

Nobby, Na… Ne… No…
M: Try Ni… [as rhymes with 'why']
R: Not… [looking suddenly shocked beyond belief]…
Nigel?!
M: [silence, answer enough]

At that point Ruby got up from the bed and started jumping around the room. She was shouting the name out with gusto, in a tone which changed from absolute surprise to deadening acceptance, as I remained watching her, my lower lip caught between my incisors, wondering how the hell she would take it.

R: [returning, her face close to mine now] Nigel! Ha ha! It's so funny! You're the best! Just the best! Nigel! Love it! You must be so middle-class! So *English!* Lah-di-dah! Lah-di-dah!
M: [eyes closing] You hate it, right? You can still call me 'Buster', you know! Or 'Tex'! I quite like that myself…
R: No, it's… you! It really is. I can call you 'Nige'! [pronounced 'naij']
M: Ha! Look, I really think 'Tex' has the edge.
R: OK, Nigel What?
M: That's a bit rich! I don't even know *yours*, come to think of it. *Your* family name.
R: Dedalus!
M: Now that *is* ridiculous! [laughing] C'mon!
R: Well, okay, but it's a bit of a mouthful…
M: That figures! Okay, just tell me the first letter, let me try and guess.
R: R.
M: I like it already! RR! I can take your name when we marry!
R: [looking mock-shocked] Okay, next comes a 'h'.
M: Thank God you didn't say 'aitch'. [Protestant pronunciation]
R: Don't worry, Convent of Mary, me.

M: Oh, very nice, we must say a Novena together sometime… Okay, so, we've got Rh… Mmmm…. Sounds kind of Welsh…

R: Not even close, Buster!

M: You see, 'Buster' comes natural!

R: U.

M: [beginning to look worried] Rhu…? Your family name starts with 'R.H.U.'?

R: Yeah, why? Is there something wrong with that?

M: Okay, let me guess… [voice now sounding tremulous], the next letter's not 'M' by any chance, is it?

R: Getting closer!

M: Yes, or no? [tone suddenly serious]

R: Yes! [now looking a little worried herself] Why?

M: Then a 'B'?

R: Yes…

M: And an 'O' and an 'L' and… a 'D' and… a 'T'?

R: Yes! [a look of surprise mixed with a trace of disappointment at having her name guessed for her] How could you guess?

M: Oh, Jesus, Ruby! [now looking pale] We gotta talk! I mean 'WE GOTTA TALK!'

That got Ruby's attention, right there. I shot up and off the bed. 'Ruby! Ruby!' I exclaimed over and over again. I was now dancing around, in a frenzy, no doubt looking a bit crazy to Rubes. I couldn't yet bring myself to say her family name, however. My mind was racing with the possible import of it all. So, I kept on dancing round the room, looking intently at everything, but actually looking *through* everything, so that I didn't see anything before me at all, occasioning the odd unpleasant surprise as I stepped on a nineteenth century cooking utensil or a ring or whatever. 'We have to get to a library, don't you see, don't you see?' But Ruby was now on her feet, too, following me, and occasionally stepping on stuff too, which added to the frantic aspect of the scene playing out. So, in between respective 'Ow!'s I'd say her first name out loud or blabber on about the need to visit the library, with Ruby shouting at me to explain -'What the hell's going on?'- until she reached out both hands and held me firmly by the shoulders, shaking me once in her insistence that I tell her the problem.

'Rhumboldt!' I half-screamed. I had never told her Poly's family name. I had always just referred to him as 'Poly'. Then, my mind on a different tack: 'Where does your family come from?' 'Ireland, of course!' half-screamed Ruby in response. 'But', me, exasperatingly, '*where before that?*' 'Tell me what you're upset about!' now screamed out Ruby, full throated and angry. So, I told her.

'Poly, Ruby. Poly was Rhumboldt, too.' Incipient shock on Ruby's face. 'Paul E. Clarence Rhumboldt. Esquire, if you want to add that on, too.' 'It's just a coincidence!' Ruby blared out. My eyes answered 'I don't think so.'

Silence. Then, in a suddenly markedly different frame of mind, Ruby said, quietly, with a faraway look in her eyes: 'Do you remember Poly's strange response when I'd said he was our saviour?' 'Remind me,' I answered. 'Well, I said "you're our saviour", right? and then he said: "And *you*, Missy, are *mine*."' We both dwelt on that for a few moments. 'What the hell did that mean, I always wondered,' added Ruby. Now, I was the one with the faraway look in my eyes, saying quietly: '"Only *you* passed muster..." he told me once.' I explained to Ruby the confusing way I'd apparently been accepted for the 'job' at P.P.P.. 'You mean you didn't ask for any clarification on that?' asked Ruby, betraying a modicum of frustration as she did. My eyes answered that one with a look you might find on a sad puppy in a cage, hoping someone might take pity on him. But at the back of my mind I was thinking of how much and how well Poly would always take care of his family...

After a moment or three to contemplate what all of this

meant, we turned to each other again, looking into each other's eyes, longingly, searchingly. 'We should get to the library, darlin', and...' 'Yes?' '...And then we can find out *everything*... The town's name, *and* the time. We know Hamilton, we know Genitoa. And not only that...' Ruby kept silent. 'We can research *you!*' I blurted out. 'You don't really think, do you...?' 'Ruby, I don't know anything, as Ole Poly once said. But in my mind I was seeing Lizzie. She'd survived. Her descendant was standing in front of me now: the one and only *Ruby Rhumboldt!*

I was shaking my head, as we broke up and got ourselves ready to leave the flat. Ruby was shaking her head, too. I somehow remembered doing something very similar with ole Poly once, too. Weird. The ideas floating through our minds were staggering, as was the excitement we now felt at the prospect before us of researching all this. I wasn't sure our local library would be up to it, but we could always go up to the city, and check the Central, too. And it wasn't like we had to worry about time: we had all the time in the world.

R: Wait [as we were just at the door], I can't find the key.
M: Over there, under the pillow, or cushion, or whatever that thing is...
R: [looking, finding nothing] No.
M: OK. Mmmm.... [a bit perturbed we couldn't find the key, feeling the clock ticking, each tick one more exasperating second of knowing what the hell was going on, and what we'd been through, *and why!*] Look over there...
R: Nah, can't see it there either... [extensive hoking about...] You didn't drop it down the drain again, did you?

M: [slightly ill-humouredly] *No!* [...more hoking about...]

M: [it now being about five minutes of us both searching through our messy flat] Darn!

R: You reverting to type?

M: Blast it!

R: That's like something my grandfather would say…

M: [eyes widening at the thought] American?

R: No! I don't know, maybe… Oh, can't you just wait?

M: We can't find the key anywhere, maybe we can just leave the damn door unlocked!

R: With all the junk we've got? And guns, too? Are you kidding?

M: [now getting truly exasperated] Look, where did you put the stupid bloody thing? You were the last one to use it!

R: Give me a break! We both came in at the same time last night! What do you want me to do, just conjure it up?

M: I goddamned wish you could do that!

R: *You're* supposed to be the magician, *not me!* [delivered in a decidedly pointed tone]

M: [flicking out my right arm and fingers, again and again, with some force, and not a little anger] I can't, see, I can't! I'm just a normal person, now! [tone clearly uncovering something under my skin, something buried, like a feeling of deep-seated disappointment at the loss of my powers…] Can't! Can't! Can't! No more bloody Conjuring Cowboy nonsense! [I had become increasingly angry as I said these words. I shocked myself with the revelation that I had been nursing such deep-seated negative feelings at all…]

R: Well, *I* can't do it either! We're just going to have to get used to living like a normal couple, and not relying on stupid damn magic to make it all funny and crazy and happy! [delivered in a tone which matched mine… no, it was even angrier!] You see, look, Buster, Tex, Nige, Friz, or whatever the hell it is you're called, I CAN'T DO IT EITHER: LOOK [then, Ruby flicked out her right arm and splayed out her fingers with a violence that betrayed that her frustration was every bit as deep as my own]

AND, YET, SOMETHING HAPPENED…

In a flash of blinding white light, what seemed to be some sort of object flew out from the space just beyond Ruby's beautifully manicured long fingernails. It flew out with great force and smashed into a framed picture on the wall (my rather lame charcoal sketch of 'Horsey & me in Monument Valley', if you want to know…), which then shattered, and fell, along with the unknown object, down onto the floor. 'Ruby!' I screamed.

Her hands went up to her face in something like horror.

After ten seconds of absolute silence, we broke out of our suspended animation, and moved, slowly, slowly, in tandem, to where the mysterious, suddenly-appearing object had fallen. We bent down in tandem, too. Amid the shards of the broken glass from the picture frame, there we beheld a metallic object, about the size and length of my forearm. People say when you encounter something you have never seen before you use your own terms of reference to describe it. In that way, I could imagine that what we were looking at had a handle, a barrel, and between these, like a link, the hint of a trigger. There were little tiny lights playing up and down the barrel, purpose unknown, but it certainly looked pretty. Ruby exchanged glances with me -surprise, wonder, curiosity: you wouldn't believe how eloquent eyebrows could be. Then, bravely, she slowly reached down her left hand and, after brushing away a glass shard or two, let her fingers close onto the svelte body of the thing ever so delicately. Bringing it up, we both studied it as she turned it slowly in her hand, until we noticed, simultaneously, the markings at the base of the handle. Three tiny markings, in a kind of *bas relief* on the surface, each the same shape, and that a weirdly futuristic font of… *the sixteenth letter of the English alphabet! Upper-case, too!* That drew a gasp from me, but Ruby…well, Ruby seemed to be warming to it. Like it was something she knew, or something she could enjoy getting to know. She held the mysterious thing by the 'handle', its 'barrel' pointing upward, her finger floating ever so delicately over the 'trigger', and, turning to me, and smiling her bestest-ever super-sexy Ruby smile, said: 'Buster, THIS is a different kind of key!'

'Jimmy-Jack Cracker to that, Rubes,' I replied. 'Jimmy-Jack Cracker to that!'

Ruby, Resoundingly, Responded: 'HA!'

THE END

SONG OF THE CONJURING COWBOY

I'M THE CONJURING COWBOY
OUT ON THE WESTERN PLAIN;
I CAN CONJURE UP A TON 'O STUFF
BUT MY HEART IS FULL OF PAIN.

POTS 'N PANS & BOTTLES O' RYE
FLY OUT FROM MY FINGERTIPS,
BUT I'D GIVE UP ALL MY POWERS
FOR A KISS FROM YOUR SWEET LIPS.

I'M THE CONJURING COWBOY
OUT ON THE WESTERN PLAIN;
I'LL NEVER BE A HAPPY MAN
'TIL I HOLD YOU ONCE AGAIN.

YEE-HAAA!!!